THE SONG OF
GENEVA CHANCE

KEITH DIXON

Semiologic Ltd

Keith Dixon was born in Yorkshire and grew up in the Midlands. He's been writing since he was thirteen years old in a number of different genres: thriller, espionage, science fiction, literary. He's the author of seven novels in the Sam Dyke Investigations series and two other non-crime works, as well as two collections of blog posts on the craft of writing. When he's not writing he enjoys reading, learning the guitar, watching movies and binge-inhaling great TV series. He's currently spending more time in France than is probably good for him.

THE SONG OF
GENEVA CHANCE

CHAPTER ONE

STEF MALYZS BIT off half a stick of Wrigley's Extra Peppermint chewing gum and offered the rest to the man in the passenger seat. Liam Fisher looked at the remaining half with disgust.

'You've got to be kidding.'

'Your loss,' Stef said, popping it in his mouth. He was a big man with a hard, dark face and sharp features—like an Italian actor, his ex-wife had said. When she was talking to him. Now he said to Liam, 'Stop looking at the house, it's suspicious.'

'It's one o'clock in the morning. Who's watching?'

Stef said, 'Is that bedroom light still on?'

'So you want me to look now?'

'Don't be a child.'

Stef knew there was only one reason he'd brought Liam along: Liam was even bigger than he was, and strong. A dim bulb behind those pale blue eyes, but at least he had muscles.

Liam turned his head to peer through the tall iron gates at the house beyond. 'It's still on—no, wait, it went off just as I was looking at it. Can we go?'

Stef shook his head. He knew he was acting like a dickhead but he didn't like being responsible for every single decision. It would have been nice to work with someone who knew what he was doing. Next job he'd use Brian. Brian was older and had been a book-keeper before realising it was just as easy to steal real stuff from people, instead of fiddling their books, so he had a bit more in the brains department. It seemed to Stef that everyone he knew used to have a good job at one time. What happened?

Now he said to Liam, 'Just think what's going on in there. The last person to go to bed has turned his light off, an hour after all the others. So maybe he's an insomniac or perhaps he's been watching TV late. Perhaps he's going to make himself a sandwich or have a drink. So we wait to see if anything else happens.'

'How long?'

'An hour, perhaps more.'

'Jesus! We've already been here two.'

'Sorry if I spoiled your social life. Crime can do that.'

Liam was strong but he fidgeted all the time, as though his thick arms and legs couldn't find rest. Now he shifted in the passenger seat and stared ahead as if trying to settle down for the long haul. But it wasn't long before he was glancing out of the side window, unable to help himself.

Ten minutes later the light in the house came on again and Stef had to resist the temptation to say, 'I told you so.' He started counting and got to a hundred and sixty-three before the light went off. Guy perhaps went for a piss.

After another forty-five minutes, he said: 'Okay, let's get the stuff out of the back. And be quiet.'

It was 2:21 a.m.

———

FIVE MINUTES LATER they'd gathered the gear together and walked across the road to the high brick wall that surrounded the house. They passed beneath the row of trees which Stef knew was going to hide them from nosey neighbours on the far side of the road, and Liam laid the first extendable aluminium ladder against the wall and gently eased up the second rack till it was level with the top of the wall. There was one yellow sodium streetlight forty yards away and the night sky was dark, the August moon concealed behind high cloud.

Stef said, 'I'll go first.'

Liam nodded, all business now, and stood to one side as Stef quietly went up the ladder and peered over the wall, which was half as tall again as he was. The big house was completely dark now, two cars parked on the gravel outside the garage, the corner of a white marquee tent visible on the garden to the rear. No animals roaming the grounds.

He turned back to Liam and reached down a hand, bringing up the canvas bag and dropping it over the wall into the flower bed on the other side. Then he lifted the second aluminium ladder and, manoeuvring it silently, lowered it so that its feet were planted next to the bag. He swung over the wall, pivoting on his backside, found the rungs of the second ladder and climbed down. They'd tied tea-towels around each step to muffle the sound of foot-treads but where each rack of steps met the other there was a distinctive metallic grating sound. Nothing to be done about that except take your time.

He hit the ground and a couple of seconds later Liam appeared above him. He sat on the wall while he picked up the ladder from the street, swung it over the wall, and let it down until Stef grabbed it and placed it next to the first one. Now there was nothing on the street to give their presence away.

So far, all good, he thought.

They paused a moment to see if there was any action in the house, then Stef set off across the lawn towards the building that was their objective, Liam loping along behind him. Their target was a single storey, flat-roofed extension to the back of the garage, with its door facing the main house. There were no windows. It was about ten paces long by five paces wide.

The door was made of white uPVC and had a keypad lock.

Liam said quietly, 'They must have some valuable shit in here.'

'We wouldn't be doing it otherwise.'

'You should have told me what it was. I don't know what I'm looking for.'

'You'll see soon enough.'

Stef was hunting in his pocket for his torch when Liam grabbed his arm. The house light was on again.

'Doesn't that bastard ever sleep?'

'Shut up. Keep still.'

They froze. Stef realised he felt insanely alive, every pore of his body tingling, his mind racing while his heart thudded solidly in his chest. This was one of the thrills of the job—the danger. It was why he kept returning to it. What else gave him this buzz?

The light went out and Stef heard Liam exhale softly. *Amateur.* He found the pen-torch in his pocket. He shone it on the keypad and after a moment pressed four of its numbers.

Liam said, 'How'd you know the sequence?'

'Doesn't matter. Stand back.'

Stef turned the knob and the door swung inward easily.

Before going in he stopped and turned to Liam. 'Just take two guitars. There's an electric Fender, deep maroon. And there's a Martin acoustic. Loosen the strings so they don't make a noise.'

'Guitars? What the fuck? How will I know which is what?'

'They've got names on them, at the top, where the strings are tied off. Use your torch. There won't be many to choose from. Carry one in each hand so they don't touch and make a noise.'

'You should've told me—'

'I'm telling you now.'

Liam was shaking his head. 'Fucking guitars. Really gonna make my fortune with these.' He thought of something. 'What'll you be getting?'

'A couple of bits and bobs. Don't take all night and don't turn the lights on.'

'Anything else?'

'Yes—try not to fall over the drum kit.'

BACK AT THE wall Stef unzipped and opened the canvas bag so it lay flat on the ground. He took two blankets from inside and wrapped each guitar, then placed them in the bag, fretboard to soundbox. He zipped up the bag and tested it for weight—not too bad.

Liam climbed the ladder and looked over the top, then straddled it while Stef handed him the other ladder. Once that was lowered on the far side, Stef took a length of nylon climbing rope from his pocket, doubled it, and threaded it through the handles of the bag, knotting it then handing the ends up to Liam. He took the weight gently and raised the bag, craning it over the wall, then shifted his position and lowered it to the other side. Stef wondered if he'd been too cautious—they could probably have just carried a guitar each over the ladders. But he was always cautious and the system had worked, hadn't it?

Stef looked down, dragged his shoe through the earth in the flower bed where the bag had lain to bring back its original texture, then climbed to the top of the wall and picked up the ladder behind him, lowering it into Liam's hands.

They crossed the road with the ladders first and laid them in the back of the Audi Estate. Then Stef went back for the bag of guitars, looked both ways up the street before he crossed on his way back, and placed the bag gently in the car. Apart from the wait, the whole thing had taken seventeen minutes.

Liam was grinning when Stef climbed into the driver's seat.

'Fucking guitars. A good job I can't tell anyone about this because they wouldn't bloody believe me.'

'You're in the big time now. No more robbing old ladies for you.'

Liam turned to him. 'When do we get paid?'

'Who said anything about getting paid?' Stef said. As Liam stared at him, he added, 'Shall I drop you off at home or is the bus-stop okay?'

CHAPTER TWO

STOREY KNEW THE man was going to talk to him before he'd said a word. He'd been agitated when he came in, grew more upset when he was told to take a seat, and after twenty minutes was on the verge of exploding. Police stations had a way of doing that to you, Storey thought: they slowed down time so you seemed to be travelling faster than the people who worked there.

The man was probably in his fifties, was small and thin, and wore a tan sports jacket and knitted tie even though the temperature outside was still in the seventies. He had red hair and the kind of pale skin that developed moles. It looked to Storey like he hadn't seen direct sunlight in thirty years.

Now here it was, the man turning to Storey, saying, 'This is pathetic, isn't it? How long've you been waiting?'

'Longer than you.'

'I know, which means I'll have to wait for them to finish with you before they get off their arses to talk to me.'

He paused for Storey to say something but nothing came. Eventually he asked, 'So why are you here?'

Storey hesitated, wondering whether he wanted to get into this, then decided it might pass the time and said, 'I caught a burglar in my house and brought him in. I'm waiting to make a statement.'

This set the man back, interrupted his train of thought. 'Really? Like, where was he? What was he doing?'

It was always the same when you talked about crooks and crime—people wanted the details. Storey already regretted giving the man bait, but he was as bored as the man was agitated.

'I was in my front room watching TV when I heard the back door open. A break in the adverts and I heard just that little snick when the catch has been turned.'

'Thing is,' the man said, 'you get to know the sounds in your own place, don't you? So did you, like, confront him?'

'No, I didn't know how many there were. I got up and listened at the kitchen door till I was sure it was just one person. My kitchen's not big. Like a wardrobe with a sink. He was opening the kitchen drawers one by one.'

The man nodding, 'You don't want to burst in if he's got a knife in his hand.'

'And if I went in I didn't want a fight in my kitchen, did I? So I sneaked out the front door and ran round the block to the back gate, which was open when it shouldn't be. He'd cut through a padlock chain and slid the bolt.'

'Wait—couldn't he have gone in to the rest of the house then, stolen your TV or something?'

'I left it playing so he'd think someone was still inside. There'd been a run of burglaries in the area just like this— they'd been breaking into pensioners' kitchens, stealing tools or microwaves or the tiny TVs people have nowadays. Then they legged it before anyone saw them. Minor stuff but a pain in the backside.'

'So what happened then?'

'I'm standing around like a spare part for ten minutes, waiting for him to come out with the goods, otherwise catching him in the house doesn't mean anything. He'd say he'd gone in the wrong house, looking for a friend, or he was confused and it was a mistake. Anyway, he came strolling through the gate with my microwave in his arms and I asked him what the hell he was doing with my microwave and he dropped the bloody thing and ran.'

The man was transfixed. 'I see it ... now there's a chase, with you like Tom Cruise running through the streets after the bad guy. And you caught him.'

Storey nodded, remembering how he'd run for fifteen minutes along the pavements behind the burglar, keeping him in sight until he'd stopped with his hands on his knees, panting and out of breath in the middle of the road. Storey was fit and had no problem catching up and using the youth's own belt to tie his arms behind his back, then returning with him in tow to the house, where the microwave lay shattered on the tarmac and being licked by a stray dog. The youth looked about sixteen but Storey had no sympathy for him. Burglary was one thing. Breaking into a house when the owner was watching TV was just stupid.

———

SO HE'D PHONED the police and they sent a car round and Storey followed in his and they all came to the station together. Over an hour ago. He'd been asked to wait and he knew the routine so he'd taken a seat and waited in silence until this talkative guy with the thinning red hair sat next to him.

Storey and the man were sitting on a bench in the entrance, near the desk sergeant, and now a bulky man wearing a thin blue windcheater came through the outside door, glanced in their direction, and stopped in front of them.

'Storey, you bugger. What are you doing here?'

'Evening, Morris,' Storey said, remembering the man who'd interviewed him a few weeks before. He was shrewd but brusque and was never sociable, so Storey kept it short. 'I'm reporting a crime. I think your men are chiselling it on tablets of stone. Can you get them to hurry up? There's a youth back there in cells and I'm waiting to give a statement.'

'Good to see you, Storey, but I'm not your messenger boy. Hope you're still keeping your nose clean.'

'I hope I can do you a favour too sometime.'

'Don't do me any favours, Storey. They just mean more work for all concerned, don't they? Now excuse me while I go for a pee.'

He turned and went into the back of the station.

The man next to him said, 'Who was that? How do you know him?'

'Long story. I did something that helped them out a couple of months ago and he was the one who wrote it all down. Now he thinks it was all his doing.'

'Wait a minute …'

Storey said nothing. He knew what was coming. He'd tried to keep to himself after the last business got him in the press again, but there was always someone who remembered. The things he saw on TV seemed to wash over him and leave no trace, but some people remembered everything.

The man said, 'He called you Storey. I remember that name. You're that man from the papers. I saw you in the Telegraph and on TV. Christ, you were all over the place for a week. The one who shot that Egyptian or whatever he was.'

'Syrian.'

'Then there was something else and it all kicked off again.'

'Human trafficking. The prevention of.'

The man was grinning now. 'And there was that boxer, what's his name, Doyle. He had a ruck with some blokes and their place burned down, I remember. Well I never expected to meet you here.'

'I never expected to be here.'

'I've met all sorts of people in my line of work, you know. Dylan. Robert Plant. George Michael, bless him. Nearly met President Bush once, but it was cancelled. Not sure I've ever met a real crime-fighter, though.'

Storey looked at the man again, thinking he hadn't seen any signs of delirium before now.

The man caught the look and winked. 'Frank Lamb. Thing is, I'm the manager of a group called Chance. You might have heard of them. They were famous once.'

Storey was about to reply when the desk sergeant called his name. 'You can go through now. Second door on the left. Don't keep them waiting.'

STOREY WAS LEAVING the station when he noticed Lamb had gone, presumably taken into another interview suite. He pushed through the glass doors and was hit by the heat of the warm August night. Ten o'clock and the sky still held a hint of blue. He went down the three steps and was heading towards the car park on the far side of Little Park Street when a voice said, 'Mr Storey, hold up. Wait a minute.'

Frank Lamb had been sitting on the low brick wall outside the station and now he stood up and walked towards him.

Storey said, 'Did they see you?'

'I didn't wait. I had a better idea. Can I buy you a drink?'

———

'THE THING IS,' Lamb said, his top lip wet with beer, 'the boys don't want me to report it. Personally I think they're crackers but I kind of understand it. Delicate time, wrong kind of publicity and so on. Thing is, if we want the insurance to pay up we need a police case number.'

Storey held up his hand. 'Start at the beginning.'

'Yes, sorry, getting ahead of myself. I mentioned the band I manage, Chance, didn't I?'

'Three brothers and a girl. I remember them. I might have had a CD once. They haven't been around for a while, have they?'

Lamb played hurt but Storey didn't believe it: he was acting The Manager with pride in his client. Lamb went on, 'It's a few years since their last hit, true. But they've been recording. They took some time off. Adam went and got married and then divorced. Johnny took a motorbike around Europe and Russia, fancied himself as Ewan McGregor. Anyway, they're back rehearsing again. First tour in nearly fifteen years is coming up.'

'So what can I do for you?'

Lamb glanced around the pub and leaned in, speaking more quietly. 'They had some stuff nicked last night. A couple of guitars. The burglars got into the studio and walked out with a Fender and a Martin. The Fender's signed by Clapton on the back—as a favour to Johnny—and the Martin's a collectible from the 1930s, worth quite a lot.'

'How much?'

Lamb sipped his beer. 'About twenty thousand dollars.'

Storey nodded to himself. 'Anything else taken?'

'We don't think so. We didn't find out till tonight. They were going in the studio to record—they've got their own studio next to the house—and the guitars were missing.'

'That must have pissed them off.'

'I thought they'd be angrier, to be honest. Especially Johnny—he can't stand his stuff being touched. As I said, they didn't even want me to report it to the police. But after I spoke to the insurance I had to come down to the station to report it.'

Storey thought about this for a moment, then said, 'So why didn't they want you to make a report in the first place?'

'They didn't want the hassle. They're in the middle of recording a new album and rehearsing for the tour. They didn't want police crawling all over the place and stories in the newspapers and then more journalists following up. Big story, etcetera. They're not ready yet. It did freak out Geneva, though. I think she took it the worst of all of them.'

Storey had a flashback to Geneva Chance. The youngest of the family, not yet twenty when they had their first hit. Long black hair, an oval face with translucent blue eyes. A sinuous voice that sometimes was light and upbeat but could also go into a deep Bluesy growl. He remembered he'd always liked seeing her on the television. She was perhaps a year or two younger than he was and when he was twenty he'd found her very attractive. He wondered what she looked like now.

This conversation was getting more interesting.

He said, 'So are they like The Monkees, all living in the same house? What's the set up?'

'It's complicated. Geneva and Johnny bought the land and built the house on it fifteen years ago. They'd all left London and I think these two were trying to get away from the others. Adam was getting married anyway, but divorced quickly and gave his ex the house in Notting Hill, so he turned up here on the doorstep one morning looking sorry for himself and they gave him a room. And then Tim came back too. Got fed up of living by himself, though he doesn't talk much as it happens. I think he felt left out, actually. And don't forget Bill, he lives with them too.'

'Who's that?'

'Bill Chance, their dad. Got his own separate place on the grounds.'

'So they're one big happy family.'

Now Lamb was looking away, not meeting Storey's eye. 'Don't quote me. They're a family so of course they row. Johnny's a … well, he's the youngest, except for Geneva. Nowadays they'd say he acts like he's entitled. Thing is, he can be a bully. But he's the one with the talent, wrote all their hit songs. He can just pull out a melody that works. To be honest he should have gone solo years ago, like Gary Barlow, cashed in.'

'Why didn't he?'

Lamb shrugged. Storey had the sense it was a sore topic. He said, 'So why are we having this conversation?'

Lamb became animated again and Storey saw the manager in him, the negotiator and persuader, the urgency in his eyes as he said, 'You can guess where I'm going with this, can't you?'

'Pretend I don't. Say it out loud.'

'Like I keep saying, the boys don't want me to report it, and from what I remember about you, you were in the police. So you've got some skills. Some contacts. Perhaps you could do a bit of digging for us, see if you can find anything out. Then we don't need a case number and I don't have to bother the insurers and everyone's happy.'

'You're crazy if you think I can do more than the professionals. I don't have any standing, any authority.' Wondering whether he could pull it off, though, be the detective. Could be fun.

'We'll pay. I'm sure I can get them to cough up a couple of thousand if they might get their instruments back.'

'I was never an actual detective.'

'So what? You know the ins and outs. You worked with guns, didn't you? Down in London.'

'I'm sort of retired.'

Lamb grinned. 'But you wouldn't turn down a couple of thousand. Why don't you come round to the house tomorrow?'

Storey had planned to stay in, clean his car, maybe paint the upstairs back bedroom.

He said, 'What's the address?'

CHAPTER THREE

As STOREY DROVE out of Coventry on the Kenilworth Road he went over what Lamb had told him about the Chance family.

He thought about the father, Bill Chance, a widower now and living in his own flat but still connected to his children by the width of a lawn. Whose choice was that? Were they being generous in looking after him, or was he so decrepit that he couldn't be allowed out on his own? He thought about his own father, a widower for twenty-five years, burying himself in projects around the house, and then the Internet when it came along. He never showed any interest in another woman after his wife died—in fact he didn't show much interest in anyone, male or female … He went inside himself and treated his small house like a fortress to protect from invasion. It was the house where Storey was now living and treating it in a similar fashion. He'd allowed a couple of women to live in it for a few weeks, rent free, but was glad he was back there now. It was the home he'd grown up in and, he supposed, the place he felt safest.

———

THEN HE WONDERED what it was like for the Chance brothers and the sister, Geneva, still living in one house as if they'd never grown up. Was it like an artistic commune with everyone high on drugs and wearing flowing robes and listening to sitar music? Or was it simply a business arrangement, saving money while running a commercial empire, selling merchandise all over the world from a small office in the attic?

He realised he had no idea what he was walking into, but Lamb had been persuasive and he couldn't hide the fact from himself that he was curious to meet the family.

Now he turned off into Beechwood Avenue, into one of the priciest areas in the city, and after a couple of further turns found the address Lamb had given him. A pair of tall iron gates was set into a high brick wall, with an intercom panel at head height. He climbed out of his Volvo but didn't get to speak into the panel because Frank Lamb was walking down the pathway towards him, waving.

As he got closer he said, 'I like a man who's on time. Let me press this button.'

The gates swung inwards and Storey got back in his car and drove in, pulling up behind two expensive-looking BMWs parked on gravel by a garage, both the 3 Series, Storey saw, one with tinted rear windows and a stripe down the side like the owner was making a point.

———

HE CLIMBED OUT and stood for a moment looking at the house and grounds. Lamb had told him it was built relatively recently, but it wasn't a modern design. It was stolid, red brick, with transom windows in the roof and a couple of traditional brick chimneys. Two steps led up to the wide front door with bay windows either side. There was even some ivy clinging to the side of the house and heading upwards towards the eaves. It could have been built a hundred years ago.

He wondered how much something that big would cost to build, with its multiple sloping roofs and three floors, plus the attic he imagined was up there somewhere. He knew there'd be a large kitchen and probably seven or eight bedrooms, perhaps a games room. He saw the white corner of a large tent behind the house and beyond that, tall oaks and sycamores that seemed to go back a couple of hundred yards.

He'd seen big houses before, though. They usually led to trouble.

Lamb was watching him, probably thinking Storey was admiring its size and the landscaping. Storey said, 'So how did the thieves get in? Climb the wall?'

'Why don't you come meet the band first? Then you can have a look around.'

Storey saw Lamb was anxious and remembered he'd said the boys didn't want any police involvement. Well he wasn't police, but maybe they wouldn't see it that way. Perhaps Lamb was worried he'd made a mistake by bringing him in, worried about what they'd say.

Ignoring Lamb, he walked towards the entrance and inspected the panel that opened the gate. There was a key pad and a button and an intercom grill. He presumed it could be opened by an electronic gadget attached to a car's sun-visor, or from within the house. He said, 'Any cameras?'

'One above the front and back doors but nothing showing the grounds or the gate. Didn't seem any point.'

Storey was walking on the lawn looking down at the earth of the flower beds, which were moist. A gardener must look after them, he thought. Pop stars didn't do gardening.

He stopped and pointed, 'There's your entry. See those oblong marks?' Lamb nodded. 'Ends of a ladder. Looks like two ladders in fact, though someone's had a go at erasing the marks. And look where the flowers are droopy here— trampled down.'

'I see it. I never thought to look before.'

'Okay, show me the studio.'

LAMB TOOK HIM back to the garage and walked down its length, to where another low building had been added to its rear. A single door was let into its side; there were no windows.

'They're inside,' Lamb said. 'Playing their little hearts out.'

Storey was examining the door and the keypad next to it. 'This where they got in?'

'It must be. There's no windows. But as you can see, the door wasn't damaged. It was like they had the code or something.'

Storey stood back. 'Okay, I've got a theory. I'll check it out. Do we go in?'

Lamb pressed four numbers on the keypad then turned the knob and pushed inwards. Stepping inside, Storey saw they were in a small room that was a kind of lobby. Directly opposite, in an interior wall, was a meshed window, through which he could see a control booth—computer screens, a large mixing desk, several banks of digital equipment and a man sitting looking straight ahead, through a larger window that looked into the studio itself.

Storey guessed that the door in the wall to their left led into the studio.

Lamb said, 'I'll introduce you to Pete,' and opened a door into the control booth. Inside there was an electric buzz in the air, as though a music track had just finished and the echo was still lingering. The walls and most of the floor space were filled with a number of flat electronic units showing flickering lights or connected by cables to yet more units. On the floor was an orange box about the size of a shoe-box and helpfully labelled 'Orange'.

The man at the control desk had long grey hair and wore a white tee-shirt over jeans. He was lean and tanned and was probably in his fifties. Two monitors were attached to the wall in front of him, above the window that looked into the studio. He was saying into a microphone, 'Let me do something with the top and bottom Shures on the toms. There's something not right.'

A voice came back over the booth speakers, 'Sort it fucking out, Pete. We don't want to spend all day playing the same fucking song.'

'Keep your hair on, Johnny Boy ... we've got strangers in paradise here.'

He turned to Lamb. 'This isn't a good time,' he said. 'But you know there's never a good time.'

'Ignore us,' Lamb said. 'When will they take a break?'

'Whenever I tell them to.'

'Bring them out, then. Go fix the drums. I want them to meet Mr Storey.'

At that Pete seemed to remember his manners and reached out a hand, which Storey shook. It was brown with nicotine stains. 'Pete Holt.'

'Paul Storey. Are they giving you grief in there?'

'No more than usual.'

Lamb said, 'Mr Storey's going to help us with the guitars. Track them down, I mean.'

Holt didn't seem impressed. 'Good luck with that. They're probably in the States by now, hanging on some collector's wall.'

'I agree,' Storey said. 'But no harm in looking, eh?'

'Knock yourself out.'

Later Storey would think back to when he saw the band for the first time, through the large studio window—all of them standing with their instruments, except Tim, the drummer, who sat behind his kit in the far corner. Geneva Chance was carrying an acoustic guitar, which surprised him; he hadn't known she'd played an instrument. She looked different in the glare of the fluorescents, but not because of the change from the concert lighting he'd seen her in before: these days her signature shoulder-length hair was chopped so it hung just below her ears. It suited her, made her eyes look bigger and was probably more in keeping with a woman her age. She stood with her weight on one leg, staring at them through the window and looking bored.

Johnny and Adam, like her, were still slim and still wore their hair long. Storey realised they were probably about the same age as he was, with Johnny maybe a year younger, mid-thirties. Funny, he'd expected them to look older and here they were, his contemporaries.

LAMB SAID, 'LET me take you in while they're not playing. Were you going to do something with the drums, Pete?'

'No, but that's what I'm telling them. Johnny likes to fiddle with stuff even when it makes no difference. Go through, I'll come out in a second.'

Storey followed Lamb out of the control booth and through the other door into the studio itself. The floor was littered with cables and monitors and music stands and the walls were hung with large baffles that looked like oblong rugs mounted on picture frames. Sound-proofing, he thought. Getting rid of echoes. With all the other sound-proofing they would have built in, it meant that once the burglars were inside they wouldn't have been heard by anyone in the house.

Johnny Chance had been talking to Adam and now he noticed Storey, saying to Lamb, 'Who's this? Not a fucking journo, I hope.'

Lamb said, 'Boys and girls, this is Paul Storey. I met him last night and he's going to help us with our little problem. He's well-known in Coventry for being a ... what would you call it, Paul? Crime-fighter?'

'Odd-job man,' Storey said, looking at the three men and Geneva Chance, who didn't look at him directly, though he'd sensed her watching him as he came in. The men were as he remembered them from the half a dozen times he'd seen them on TV—their family resemblance was carried in a fine chiselled nose, full lips and deep-set, pale eyes. A good-looking family. Tim, the drummer, was a little coarser and his eyes were flat and untrusting but the older brother, Adam, was classically handsome, tall and well-made and with a pleasant smile lurking in his lips and eyes.

Johnny, the youngest of the brothers, seemed to Storey to have a rage in him. His hair was wavy and long and was high-lighted with blond streaks, while his expression seemed cold and unfriendly. He stared at Storey and although he was the closest, he didn't offer to shake hands, instead running his fingers up and down the fretboard of his Stratocaster, making a jittery, screeching noise. He said, 'Did Larry tell you we're not bothered about the guitars? We've got tracks to cut and we can't be pissing about with police and journalists and hangers-on.'

'That's a coincidence—neither can I,' Storey said. He wondered who Larry was, then realised it was probably a nickname for Frank Lamb.

Johnny was glancing at Adam and Tim, his left hand now quiet on the guitar, saying, 'You think you can do anything? Like, find them?'

'Probably not. But I've been promised a couple of thousand pounds so the least I can do is go through the motions, make it look good. Do you reckon that's a workable plan?'

Johnny was looking at him closely now, assessing. He said, 'You don't give a shit, do you? You don't care whether you do this or not.'

'Johnny ...' Adam said, stepping forward.

'That's all right,' Storey said. 'He's right. I'm doing it because I thought it would be nice to see how a bunch of rich has-beens while away their time, now they've made enough money not to have to worry about their future. It was either this or find work with a professional footballer.'

Now Geneva Chance looked up at him, and he saw again the electric blue eyes he remembered from fifteen years before, the same full lips and high cheekbones, but now looking at him and not into some vague mid-distance where the audience stood, rapt. She said, 'Mr Storey, it's not true we don't want the instruments returned. Of course they're worth a lot of money but there's more to it than that. They're like memories. They bring back that whole time, that period when we were making music millions of people liked. I hope you understand that.'

Storey hesitated. 'Of course.' He liked the way she'd called him 'Mr Storey' and her voice was low and calming, and carried an air of vulnerability. He said, 'I'll do what I can. Though I have to tell you I'm not with the police any more and I don't have any official standing, so I'm going to rely on favours and guesswork. I might have to talk to you all separately to see if you know anything you don't think you know.'

Johnny said, 'Ah, police talk. Get your excuses in early in case you can't catch them. Can we get on with it, now? Have you finished with those mikes, Pete?'

Pete Holt had been adjusting a couple of microphones on stands above and below one of Tim's drums. He tightened up a knob, saying, 'Just there. Let's all get the hell out of Dodge, shall we, so we can carry on?'

STOREY AND LAMB stayed in the control booth for a while, watching the band start a song, play it for a minute, then stop while Johnny complained about something. Storey noticed that when Geneva was singing she closed her eyes, as if shutting out the world completely.

Lamb leaned over. 'They wanted a live feel for the album. Johnny used to moan about the clean production on the old songs, he wanted something a bit grungier, looser.'

'They sound all right to me.'

'Wait till you hear the finished versions. They'll be unrecognisable after Pete's tidied them up.'

Pete was staring through the glass into the studio. He said, 'So long as Johnny doesn't put his fingers in the mix. That boy can never let anything go.'

Storey said to Lamb, 'Can I see you outside?'

Lamb ushered him out, saying, 'Come into the house. You may as well. I'll put some coffee on.'

He was relaxing, Storey thought, now his *bona fides* had been established and his position made clear. He was even walking more confidently, striding towards the front door of the house, his thin shoulders bony in his checked jacket.

Storey caught him by the elbow and he turned. 'I'll come back tomorrow. If I'm right, this could be more complicated than you want to deal with.'

'Why? What do you mean?'

Storey nodded towards the studio, an oblong white concrete box. 'This was a set up. Someone fixed it so the thieves could get in. It's what we in the detective trade call an inside job.'

CHAPTER FOUR

So BREAK IT down: Liam was unhappy because he thought he'd been promised money.

But Stef knew there was never any money on the table and he was certain he never said so. Perhaps he said there'd be a good pay day. But he meant 'eventually'. He wouldn't make a promise he knew he couldn't keep.

Liam wasn't hearing that. He was hearing there was no money and he'd been depending on something: he had bills to pay too.

Stef knew that. He knew Liam was divorced, like he was, and had to pay maintenance. It was the first thing Liam had told him when they met by chance in The Spon Gate Wetherspoons and got drunk together. In five minutes Stef had Liam's whole life story to the age of twenty-three, including the face-saving marriage and subsequent divorce a year later, when the kid was six months old. That's what you get for having sex without looking at the consequences,

Stef thought. Just like Liam to go at it without a thought in his head.

Of course his own case was different. He'd been seeing Margaret for nearly five years before they had sex, and they got married a month later. It was only because he'd asked her to marry him that she agreed to have sex with him anyway. She was even more cautious than he was.

Perhaps that was what attracted him to her: the accountant's daughter who looked at all sides of a problem before committing herself. Perhaps he'd seen himself in that, seen a lifestyle he could buy into.

It was just a shame that the tool making company where he was head of the design office closed down. It'd been bought by an American company who thought the West Midlands was still an active player in manufacturing, and, to be fair, had been conned by the owners of the tool factory who were looking to offload it. And then the recession had come, the orders dried up, whatever work was left was outsourced to Romania and Stef had to sell his house because the mortgage was gouging him every month.

Two weeks after the sale, while they were living with his parents on a temporary basis, Margaret left him and life had been shit ever since.

From that time his story was no different to many others: he met a man in a pub who learned he was desperate for money and offered him a job. He'd told the man he'd run a design office — so the man asked could he work a computer and a scanner? Easy. Would he scan these notes and use Photoshop to make them look lifelike? Maybe. Don't worry, the man said, it won't come back to you. I've got a tame printer who's looking for a bit of money, his cancer's running wild and he wants to provide for his family before he pops his clogs ...

So Stef had scanned the ten pound notes on his home Mac and got the scans looking as lifelike as he could, then sent them to Simon, the printer, who made up the plates. And Stef was in the car with Simon when they were driving the plates to Simon's print works one Sunday afternoon, ready to print off the first batch, when they were stopped for a smashed brake-light by an observant copper, who then noticed the plates poking out from under a blanket on the back seat of Simon's Renault and said Hello, what's this then? and took them both to the station.

Two years in the slammer for the pair of them, though Simon didn't make it out the other end ...

So of course he was careful, looking at all the angles, thinking things through. He'd like to give up the thieving and burglary but it turned out he was good at it. Who knew? All that time living like a good citizen when he could have been earning more money for a couple of hours' work a week.

———

NOW LIAM CAME back from the kitchen with a can of Heineken popped open, swigging from it while his eyes looked at Stef as though he wanted to punch him. His right arm bent, the muscle filling the sleeve of his shirt as though it were blown up with helium.

He said, 'I let you get away with that the other night. I was stunned. Know what I mean? I didn't understand what you were saying to me so I thought I hadn't heard you right. Do you do that? You hear something you don't get and you start thinking you haven't heard it properly. Like my dad, when he started to go deaf. He'd ask me to repeat something and when I did he'd say, That's what I thought you said. You know, with surprise in his voice. As if he couldn't believe what I said first time because it sounded like I was talking rubbish.'

'And you weren't?'

Of course Liam didn't get that, just carried on: 'I ended up shouting at him to listen harder, which isn't fair, really, is it? Poor bugger couldn't help it. Broke an eardrum when he was younger. Someone punched him, I think.'

'So you've come around at nine o'clock on a Thursday night to tell me about your dad's hearing problems.'

'Don't be a moron, Stef.' Seeming more confident now, walking through Stef's apartment and sitting on his big chair, his legs apart, still looking directly into Stef's eyes. He was dressed sharply: Levis with a crease, green Lacoste polo shirt stretched tight across his chest, clean Adidas trainers. Always showing himself off to his best advantage, as if he might be called to an interview any second.

So perhaps he'd been thinking since the job, put together a plan of what to say now he'd had time to think about it. He said, 'It's my own fault for not asking more questions, isn't it? Should have found out more about the job instead of being surprised when we got there. Fucking guitars. That's because I trust you. So I know you've got the guitars stashed here somewhere and I've been thinking — it's not safe, is it? If someone puts two and two together and you get fingered, the cops come calling, you've got the guitars tucked away under the bed ... see what I mean?'

'We're not selling them.'

'There you go,' Liam said, opening his palm to demonstrate, 'being negative. I know you think I'm stupid, you only want me because I'm big and I don't mind giving someone a thump when it's required … but I've got a couple of brain cells and I've been rubbing them together.'

Stef could have predicted this. Every dunce he ever worked with thought he was the sharpest tool in the box. The first idea that occurred to them was always the greatest idea anyone had dreamed up in the history of the world.

But he couldn't afford to piss Liam off. He knew too much. At least make a show of hearing him out. He said, 'So what's the great idea?'

Liam leaned forward and the armchair groaned. 'We don't try to sell them—we just get cash for them.'

'You'll have to explain that to me.'

'I'm not in a position to go into details yet, I've got some more research to do.'

Stef couldn't help himself. He said, 'How much did you make from thieving last year?'

Liam lowered his beer can. 'Dunno … maybe a couple of thousand. That big job up in Henley Green helped.'

Stef had heard about that. A family had been taken in for questioning by the police on suspicion of trading in stolen goods. When they were released and got home, everything had been nicked while they were out. A burglar's joke.

He said, 'I don't want to brag but I made over forty grand.'

'Fuck me.'

'That's because I think things through. I don't mess about once I've started something. Just stick to the plan.'

Now Liam seemed deflated. He belched, then looked around at Stef's apartment—the big television, the bookcase with books that had actually been read, the nice lamp on a table behind the sofa. Couple of oil paintings of landscapes on the wall. He'd kitted the place out nicely but Liam seemed to take it as a rebuff.

'It's all right for you,' Liam said. 'I can't afford to wait for the cash, as well you know. My kid's mum is screaming blue murder for her money. She'll have the bailiffs on me. When were you thinking of selling the guitars anyway?'

This was the tricky part. 'I can't say. You're gonna have to be patient. A few weeks, after things have died down.'

'Are they worth something, those guitars? They were nice and everything but how much will they fetch?'

Stef cleared his throat. 'Perhaps a couple of thousand.'

'Is that all? Fuck sake. All that bother with ladders and a special bag … I'd a thought they'd be worth more than that.'

'Little and often,' Stef said, watching to see whether Liam believed him. 'You don't go for the forty thousand in one big hit. Just play safe, plan it out. They might not even have claimed insurance yet, so we don't want to put them out there on the market.'

Liam perked up. 'That's another question. Who's "they"? It was a big house and all—is it some kid and his mates, got dad to make a studio for them in the garden? Looked like some serious gear in there but I don't know shit about all that, do I?'

Stef had found that if you didn't say too much to dumb people they normally talked their own way into believing what you told them. Liam was a prime example. He appeared confident from time to time but deep down had a low opinion of himself. Stef thought he should feel sorry for him, really, but it was probably best just now to palm Liam off with a few white lies and keep his own feelings out of it.

He didn't need more information than was necessary, did he?

―――――

NOW LIAM stood up, crushing his beer can and handing it to Stef as he walked by. He stopped at the door and said, 'I know you think you're cleverer than me, and you probably are. But all this is bullshit, the fancy bookcase and oil paintings. Okay you've earned more money than me, but that's not always going to be the case.'

'What are you trying to tell me, Liam?'

The other man shrugged his shoulders as though he'd lost interest. 'I don't know. But there's something not right here. I'm going to do my research anyway and see what's what.'

'Those guitars aren't going anywhere. Get that thought out of your head.'

'Or what? You'll report me to the police?'

'Now you *are* being stupid.'

'Well, I wouldn't want to disappoint you. See, I don't think you're careful or cautious or whatever the hell you want to call it. I think you're scared. And I don't like that. I don't want you making decisions when you're scared. That fucks things up.'

He closed the apartment door behind him. Stef watched the space where the big man had stood. Then he realised that he did, in fact, see himself as both different from and better than Liam. Well so what? It was true, wasn't it?

Didn't he know what was going on, whereas Liam didn't?

CHAPTER FIVE

LAMB HAD GIVEN him a gadget to put on his sun-visor, so as he approached the iron gates Storey pressed a button and they slowly began to open.

The two BMWs that had been parked behind the garage the day before were gone and he could see activity at the back of the house, where the marquee tent was being dismantled. A large trailer attached to the back of a van stood on the grass and he presumed the marquee and its fixings would eventually be folded up and stored in it.

The approach to the house was up a few steps and after he rang the bell and waited a while, Adam Chance opened the door. He looked as though he'd been exercising, a sheen of sweat glistening on his forehead and damp patches forming under the arms of his white tee-shirt. He had a towel in one hand which he was using to wipe his brow and the hollow under his throat. Storey was alert enough to see that the expression on Adam's face was one of annoyance until he remembered where he was and relaxed, smiling and opening the door further.

Now Storey noticed the other man's physique—broad in the chest and with corded muscles from his neck to his shoulders. Not your typical rock star. He couldn't see him lying on a bathroom floor with a spoonful of cocaine congealing in his nose. Or some woman in a short skirt screaming down a phone saying this creep had tried to rape her … No, he probably saw himself as the grown up—Johnny was the tearaway, but creative, and Tim—Tempo, the drummer—was what? Middle of the road? Boring?

Now Adam turned back inside, saying over his shoulder, 'I'm not going to give you the tour, you don't mind.' Turning the boyish grin on him again, the one that made you complicit, part of his gang. 'Larry's out the back, watching them take the tent down. It's the most exercise he's had in a year.'

They walked straight through the house over a tiled floor and into a kitchen full of black granite and dark wood, then Adam pointed to a door that gave on to the garden. 'He's out there.'

'Can I ask you something?'

'That's what detectives do, isn't it? You going to be rude about us again, like yesterday? What was it you called us, rich has-beens? If I had any feelings that would hurt, man.'

'Why did they only take two guitars? And why those two?'

Adam crinkled his brow, his puzzled look. 'Hey, that's not hard. They were the two most valuable guitars in the studio. Anyone who knew anything about us knew Johnny owned them. There was even a piece in Guitarist magazine with him talking about the Martin.'

'So that's what I don't understand—they're two valuable guitars but no one thinks to bring them indoors when you've finished for the day. Lock them up in a big safe or something.'

Adam was grinning again. 'Sorry, man. You don't get how we live around here, do you? Look around. Yeah, they're valuable but it's only money. And there's plenty of cash for buying toys.'

'Geneva said there was more to it than that. Memories, she said.'

The other man looked at the black and white tiles on the floor and shook his head. 'That's Geneva. She's got a different take on things.' He paused and Storey saw a look of genuine curiosity light up in the back of his eyes. He rolled his shoulders as if ready for a fight, as if he'd suddenly been woken up. He said, 'I'm beginning to see what you are. You're a devil dog, aren't you? You don't forget anything and you don't take any shit. I had a dog like that once. Bolshy little terrier. Shame it didn't last long.'

'What happened to it?'

'Had to have it put down. Kept biting my hand, the one that was feeding it.'

He grinned again, then left.

———

OUTSIDE, ON A lawn that could have fitted a football pitch, half a dozen men were taking down the marquee, strapping together the tubes that had supported it and rolling stretches of white canvas before stuffing everything into long plastic bags that they tied shut. Another two men were taking down a lighting gantry piece by piece, laying it on the grass in neat piles.

He finally saw Lamb sitting on a white plastic garden chair, eating a sandwich and watching the crew at work. Storey walked over and pulled up another chair. Lamb glanced at him but didn't put down the sandwich.

'Look at these Poles go at it. They never stop.'

'What was the occasion?'

'Big party for Johnny's birthday. He does it every year. I'm sure the locals are sick to death of it but they turn up like drones every time, too frightened to piss him off by not coming.'

'Why would they be frightened?'

'Figure of speech. Thing is, if Johnny falls out with you it can hurt. He's still got some what-do-you-call it, cachet, so people come anyway. Footballers, businessmen, friends from when they were kids years ago.'

'How many people?'

'Couple of hundred. The boys and Geneva did a couple of the new songs from the album but mostly it was a DJ. I left at midnight like fucking Cinderella but I gather it went on till seven. You wouldn't believe I started as an accountant, would you? Or maybe you would. I was Bill's bookkeeper and when they started up he was the so-called manager and asked if I'd look after the money side. Who knew they'd get so big? So eventually I handed the finance over to a bigger accountancy firm and took over from Bill as their manager, seeing as they'd started to trust me by then.'

'They didn't trust you?'

'They didn't trust anybody. They'd already been let down by a couple of promoters by the time Johnny was seventeen. Big promises, no results. As it happened I knew a couple of people in the business in London, got them a couple of small gigs and a record deal came out of that. You should have seen them then. Pretty things. Geneva was barely sixteen when they started but she could bloody sing. Besides, the boys were all protective of her.'

'Where did their father fit in? Show-biz parent?'

Lamb glanced at him. 'Hardly. He liked meeting the famous people but I don't think he could be bothered with all the boring bits—the touring, even the TV appearances, in the end. I think the band knew that and they started moving him out. Getting him to stay at home, telling him not to talk to the press. Eventually he had enough and went to Spain for a few years.'

'I wouldn't blame him if he was pissed off. How did he feel about being side-lined?'

Lamb looked at him again. 'What's all this got to do with the guitars?'

'Nothing, so far as I know. Call it research. I think I'm supposed to ask questions. At least that's what Adam thinks.'

'You've been talking to Adam?'

'Just now.'

'Make a note of it. Adam barely talks to anyone. Unless it's himself, when he's looking in a mirror.'

'I noticed he looks after himself, doesn't he?'

Lamb had finished his sandwich and dusted his hands together, ignoring Storey's question. He said, 'Anyway, what are you doing here? I thought you'd be talking to contacts and tracking down leads or whatever the hell people like you are supposed to do.'

Storey shrugged. 'I thought you might like to know how the burglars got in. If you're not interested I'll go.'

'Course I'm interested. Let's see what we're getting for our money.'

LAMB WAS GETTING out of his chair, placing his sandwich wrapper on the seat behind him, when he stopped and said, 'Oh shit, don't look now. It's the old man.'

Storey followed the direction of his gaze and saw a tall man with slicked-back grey hair coming towards them from the far side of the garden. He wore a bright short-sleeved shirt and green shorts with big pockets, no socks but expensive-looking suede loafers. He skirted a pile of cables and loudspeakers and raised a hand. Storey could see a resemblance to his older son, Adam, in the shape of his head and his general build. For some reason he'd expected someone frailer but this man seemed strong.

As he came closer Storey noticed the sharpness in his eyes, which were still a piercing blue. They were Geneva's eyes. It shouldn't be a surprise that the whole family was built from this man's genes, he thought.

The man was slowing down now, smiling, saying, 'Damn it, Larry, I told you to let me know when Mr Storey here came back.' He stuck out his hand and Storey shook it. The man said, 'I know what you're thinking: how can a grotty old man like me have sired such a beautiful family? They are, aren't they? Even the boys. You can blame their mother for that, bless her heart. Straight out of Glasgow, she was, with the darkest hair and the whitest teeth and a sense of mischief that grabbed me by the balls.'

'Bill ...'

'I know, don't be maudlin. Don't break down and cry in front of strangers. Anyway, Mr Storey, I wanted to meet you because I'm a big fan. I read all the reports in the papers when you shot that bastard Syrian, then helped Bran Doyle beat those London gangsters. I admire someone who gets stuck in and doesn't mind getting his hands dirty.'

It seemed like genuine enthusiasm so Storey didn't argue with him. The way it was reported in the papers and on the television gave him a much more prominent role than he thought he had. But if Bill Chance, father of the famous band, wanted to believe he had special abilities he wasn't going to argue.

He said, 'When you're in those situations it doesn't seem like you have any choice.'

'Ah but you do, you do! You could sneak off with your tail between your legs, duck for cover or run for the hills. But you weren't made like that, were you? I knew Bran Doyle twenty years ago, just as the boys and Geneva were getting some attention. He came to a couple of gigs. Or rather I think that sexy wife of his brought him. If you worked for him you must have a hide of leather.'

'No comment.'

Chance laughed. 'I bet! I bet you've got some stories to tell.'

Now Lamb was heading away, telling Storey with his eyes that they should go. 'Thing is, Bill, we're just off for a meeting.'

'Then I'm inviting myself too. Anything I can do to help catch those swine who stole Johnny's guitars I count as a blessing.'

Lamb started to protest but Storey said, 'That's fine, come along. I was just going to show Mr Lamb something.'

'Excellent! I'm sixty-seven you know, but I'm not gaga yet. Still got all my marbles. Perhaps I can help.'

———

STOREY LED THE way back to the studio, feeling the sun on the back of his neck. This summer was getting tiresome.

He stopped at the door and waited until Chance and Lamb were standing next to him, peering down at the keypad. It was an old-fashioned unit with push-button numbers ranged in descending pairs towards a silver knob at the bottom.

He said, 'It's a well-known trick with these kinds of locks.' He took out the object he'd bought from Poundland earlier that day. It looked like a cheap purple pen with a round, bulbous end. He pulled this round cap off and showed the nib to the two men. It had a small white tip. 'This is an ultraviolet marker. You can write on a surface and it's not visible until you shine an ultraviolet light on it.'

'So where the hell do you get ultraviolet light from?'

'Easy,' Storey said. He put the bulbous cap back on the pen and pointed it at the studio door, then pressed a small button on its side. The end of the pen cast a pale purple light on the white door. 'You can't see anything yet, but wait.'

He shifted his position until he could direct the pen at the keypad, then switched it on again. The numbered push-buttons glowed pink, as though they'd been painted clumsily, perhaps in the dark.

'Bugger me,' Bill Chance said. 'What's that, then?'

'Someone's painted each of the numbers with an ultraviolet marker pen like this one. Can you see something else?'

The men craned in. Lamb said, 'Four of the numbers aren't glowing. Three, one, two, nine. Shit, those are the numbers of the combination.'

Storey switched off the pen. 'You paint the numbers with a marker that's invisible to the naked eye. After the keys have been pushed several times, by people entering the code, the marker wears off. Then if you use a UV light like this you can see the numbers that make up the code because all the other numbers are still painted, while the used ones have worn off.'

'Hold on, hold on,' Lamb was saying now. 'Those ones you just showed are the right numbers, but they're not in the right order. You don't press one, two, three, nine just because that's how they are on the keypad. It was Johnny's idea of a joke. It was supposed to be like the beginning of a song—not one, two, three, four, but a countdown: three, two, one … then nine, because he needed another number to make up the fourth. So how did the burglar get the right sequence?'

Storey said, 'Well that's the problem with this type of lock, why it's outdated. Because the sequence doesn't matter. We might think it does because that's how we learn the code combination, in a particular sequence. As you said, like a countdown in this case. But actually you can push the buttons in any order and they'll work. It's a primitive system and it's been replaced by more foolproof ones now.'

Lamb moved him to one side and pushed the buttons of the keyboard out of sequence—nine, three, one, two—and turned the knob. The door opened.

He turned back to Storey with dismay in his eyes. 'So anyone with one of those gadgets could get in at any time?'

'Cost me a quid this morning. There is a catch, though.'

'What's that?'

'After you've painted the numbers with ultraviolet, you've got to allow for around thirty presses for it to be worn away. That means the burglary wasn't a crime of opportunity. It was planned, and planned well.'

FRANK LAMB SEIZED Storey's arm and walked him away from the door and away from Bill Chance, who stared at the door for a moment then began rubbing at the keypad with his sleeve. Storey opened his mouth to stop him but it was too late. The evidence was gone.

Lamb said, 'What do you mean, it was planned?'

'Obviously someone put some time into it. Someone who had the opportunity to be here at some point and then was able to come back and take advantage of what he'd done.' He shook his arm from Lamb's grasp. 'I don't know why you're so surprised—you told me the guitars were valuable, so why wouldn't a burglar take his time? It's not exactly like the kid who broke into my kitchen on the off-chance and walked out with a microwave because it was the only thing not screwed down.'

Lamb ran a hand through his thinning red hair. He was wearing a blue Pringle pullover and cream chinos, and Storey thought he looked like he belonged on a golf course. Wherever he was, he seemed to be inappropriately dressed.

'It's just a shock,' Lamb said. 'You said yesterday it was an inside job but I didn't know what you meant. Now you seem to be saying someone here was involved. That doesn't make any sense, does it?'

'If you ever hear of a crime that makes sense,' Storey said, 'let me know. Criminals are the most irrational people you're likely to come across. Anyway, that's it from me. I can't do anything else for you now. You need to get the professionals in if you want to see those guitars again. Or to get a case number so you can claim back on the insurance.'

Lamb's attention came back to him. 'I'm going to pretend I didn't hear that. Thing is, you can't quit now. Especially having solved the first part of the puzzle. Why do you want to stop?'

'Because the next thing you'd have to do would be to dust the keypad for fingerprints, see if the burglar was stupid enough to use an uncovered finger to press the buttons, and find out if Helpful Dad over there has left any of them readable. I can't do that. Then you'd want to go and talk to anyone in the city who might fence off stolen goods. I don't know who that is—I haven't worked here, I don't know anyone.'

'Isn't there someone you could ask, someone you know like that big bloke who came into the station the other night?'

'If I asked him, the first thing he'd want to know would be what the hell I thought I was doing getting in the way of a police investigation, even if there wasn't one taking place at that time ... you can't reason with some people.'

Now Lamb was staring at the house as if he were trying to imagine who might have set up the theft, sorting through the possibilities in his mind. Storey wondered how well he really knew the Chance family. Lamb said, 'I'm very disappointed. I thought we had a relationship, I thought you liked the band. I thought you could see your way through to doing something, for a little consideration, of course.'

'Sorry.'

Lamb shook his head and without saying goodbye wandered off down the side of the house towards the rear garden, where the Poles were finishing packing the marquee tent into the back of the van and the trailer.

Storey walked to his car, asking himself whether he'd been too hasty. It did feel as if there were something unfinished in the air. But what he'd said to Lamb was true: he didn't know how he could start investigating without some basic knowledge. If he was going to begin knocking on doors, where would he start?

But was that it? Did he really feel unqualified to continue, or was there something deeper ... something connected to this family of pop stars? Apart from Bill Chance they'd all been distant, a little surly, at least the men ...

And as he was turning his thoughts to Geneva Chance, she appeared in front of him, walking along the path from the house, seeming both purposeful and ethereal at the same time. She was wearing blue jeans that accentuated her slim hips, and a loose blouse that was buttoned up to her neck. Her walk was long-legged but ungainly, as though her boots were too heavy.

She said, 'Can I talk to you?' and the expression in her eyes contained a plea.

'I was just leaving.'

'There's something you should know. Something I haven't told the others.'

'Good, I like gossip.'

'It's not gossip. As you probably know perfectly well.'

'Then I'm all ears.'

SHE WALKED HIM to his car and got in the passenger seat next to him. Storey felt a nudge of desire but concentrated on looking straight ahead, putting his key in the ignition and doing up his safety-belt. He didn't want to be distracted by her physical presence.

She settled herself into the seat, staring through the Volvo's windscreen at the garage door straight ahead. He wondered whether she was embarrassed by the physical proximity too.

She said, 'The guitars weren't the only thing stolen from the studio.'

She paused, perhaps expecting Storey to ask, What else? But she was going to tell him anyway so he kept quiet. Her right eyelid flickered. She said, 'I suppose Frank told you we'd been making this album and rehearsing and all that shit, didn't he?'

'He mentioned it.'

'But he probably didn't mention the fact we haven't made any new music in nearly fifteen years. He likes to put a brave face on it, pretend we're still doing well, just as successful as we were fifteen years ago. He didn't let slip that we've been idle, watching all these new bands coming up and just counting our royalties from the Best Of albums. He didn't say anything about us feeling terrified of going back into the studio because we didn't know if we could do it anymore, if Johnny's songs would still make people sit up and listen. Or stand up and dance. Or cry. Any of the things they used to do when we were good.'

'Miss Chance—'

'Oh call me Geneva. Everyone does. It's my name, isn't it? Well not mine, exactly, it's public property. Say the word "Geneva" and people have to think twice whether you're referring to the city in Switzerland or me.'

'What are you telling me?'

She sighed and lowered her head. Then she looked directly at him for the first time. 'Until the last four weeks we hadn't set foot in that studio in years. I mean we, as a band. Then Larry Lamb got us dates for this tour and we had to pull ourselves together.' She paused. 'But that doesn't mean I—me, personally—hadn't been in the studio. About a year ago I started having some ideas for songs and eventually I went in and started recording them. I didn't get Pete Holt involved—you know, the engineer. I just set a recorder going and went in the studio and played and sang. Then I downloaded the recordings on to a thumb drive and deleted it from everywhere else. Don't ask me why, but I didn't want anyone to know what I was doing.'

'Set me up with a statement like that and I've got to ask why, haven't I?'

'All right. Because I felt guilty. Johnny's the songwriter. He gives us all a credit on the songs, so we can all collect an equal split of the royalties, but he's always been proud of being the one who writes the songs we sing.'

'And something happened?'

'Yes. Most of the stuff I recorded I eventually deleted anyway. I'd write a song, play it a few times and then get sick of it and wipe it. But there was one song I recorded that seemed to stay with me. A very personal song. All the others had been about adolescent love and politics and crap like that ... but this one was different.'

'So you kept it.'

'I did. I deleted it off all the recording devices in the studio and kept it as a demo mp3 on my thumb drive. I didn't even put it on my iPod or Mac because I didn't want any of the others to catch sight of it by accident and wonder what it was.'

'What were you going to do with it, eventually?'

'I don't know. Who the fuck knows? Maybe I would have played it to the boys but I might have just kept it for myself. As a reminder.'

'Of what?'

She shook herself. 'Never mind. The point is, it's been stolen.'

'From the studio? With the guitars?'

'Yes. I don't know how a burglar would even know what it was. I'd gotten careless. Because I was listening to it in the studio more than in my room, I'd take it in there whenever I was going to write music. I'd listen to it to give me more inspiration. And to give me the belief I could do it again. It was just on a little black USB drive, you know the sort I mean?'

'Of course.'

'A couple of times I left it in there by accident, usually because it got late and I was tired and forgot to take it with me. But the next day it was always where I'd left it plugged in.'

'Until one day it wasn't.'

'Yes. And now I'm terrified the wrong people will hear it.'

CHAPTER SIX

LIAM LIKED THE fact that Stef was always stocked up with beer. You could go to his fridge and the bottom shelf would always have at least two six-packs—usually Heineken and Budweiser, but often something different, as if he was trying to expand his range.

Now he sat back in Stef's big chair, the one that faced the TV with its little black Philips sound-bar fixed to the wall beneath it, and wondered how it would go. Stef would be pissed off, count on it. One, Liam had broken into his flat. Two, he'd taken the guitars and got money for them, as he said he would. Both of those were bound to get on Stef's wrong side.

But Liam didn't care. It was done now. With the money he'd got he'd paid off the month he owed on his car and put something aside for his ex-wife the next time she got on his case. He'd also had enough to stash some in the account to pay for Jen's birthday trip to Spain. Those were the important facts. Never mind what Stef thought. Besides, he was big enough to look after himself, and wasn't coming here tonight a kind of apology? He was owning up, telling Stef what he'd done, being honest. That deserved some credit, he thought, so Stef should give him the benefit of the doubt. The teacher taught, or something like that.

True enough, he'd learned a lot from Stef. That trick with the ultraviolet marker was classic, though you had to have access to be able to paint the numbers in the first place. And what if the keypad was more sophisticated? One where you had to know the actual sequence of the numbers? It was a good trick but it had its limitations.

HE HEARD THE lift doors open in the corridor outside and a few seconds later the key was in the lock and then Stef came in, stopping dead when he saw Liam in his chair. He'd had a hair cut and was wearing clothes Liam hadn't seen before—a thin black zip-up jacket and a blue baseball cap with a Nike swoosh on the front.

'What's this?' Liam asked, acting friendly to show he wasn't a threat. 'You in disguise or something? Got another job lined up?'

'How did you get in?' Stef coming into the room now, looking around as though someone else might be there.

'I bumped the door, like you showed me. Watched a YouTube video to remind myself what to do. Easy with the right tools. You should get that lock changed.'

Stef stared at him, those hard eyes trying to look right through him, then he turned and went into the bedroom. He hadn't taken off his new jacket and cap.

Liam heard a noise from the bedroom and knew what was coming next. He took a swig from the can of Heineken and put it on the floor. Stef came back into the room, his face red.

'What have you done with them?'

'I told you I had a plan, didn't I? A way to get us some money.'

'You stupid bastard, you're going to fuck everything up.'

Liam stood, thinking he'd look better if he wasn't staring up from the seat. It made him feel as though he was being told off. Stef could do that to you.

Now Stef was pointing a finger at him, his eyes getting even darker. 'You've got to get those guitars back.'

'I can do that,' Liam said, then watched the surprise on Stef's face: wasn't expecting that, was he? 'But I'm not going to. Listen, I've got your cut here—' taking a wad of money from his back pocket '—I'm giving you five hundred quid, half of what I got. I reckon that's a fancy return on fifteen minutes' work.'

'Five hundred quid? So you got a thousand for a couple of items worth upwards of forty grand? Yeah, you didn't know that, did you? What did you think they were, Chinese knock-offs from Aldi?'

Liam felt his cheeks turning red but kept up his bluster. If that was true then he *had* fucked up. How was he supposed to know when Stef hadn't told him anything beforehand? But there was no way back now. 'If you're not happy we can go back before two weeks are up and get them returned.'

'Where? Where have you taken them?'

Liam had a sudden memory of the woman he'd spoken to, the one who'd given him the money after looking at the merchandise: long, raggedy black hair, probably dyed; olive skin; somewhere in her forties and looked like she'd lived a life. But she still had something … sexy about her. Her eyes were wide apart and her cheekbones were rounded and high. She wasn't difficult to look at.

He usually dealt with the other man—the one who was as big as he was and didn't say much, but said it with a sly smile, as if he knew what you were really up to. And if you caught him off-guard, when he didn't know you were looking at him, there was something scary about the way he stared at other people in the shop. Nasty piece of work.

He said, 'I'm not going to tell you. It's better if I deal with them, they know me.'

'Who are you talking about?' Stef's voice was quieter now, his anger dying down, Liam saw, trying to get him talking, being Mr Reasonable. He'd seen Stef do that before, turn on the hard eyes then back off as if he was giving concessions.

He said, 'Like I said, it's best if I deal with them. Look, this is my part of the job. My contacts said we could have them back if we wanted, after a cooling-off period, so to speak. I promised them it's a private deal and I keep my promises.'

'Yeah, like you promised not to bring up the subject of the guitars again. So you just nicked them instead.'

'I didn't say that, you're making stuff up now.'

Stef ran a hand through his hair and turned away. Liam knew he'd weathered the worst of the storm but it was still on a knife edge. Stef was unpredictable—you could never be sure what he'd do. He marketed himself as calm and rational, a professional, but Liam had heard stories about his wicked rages if things didn't go his way. It'd got worse since he came out of prison. They said that's why his wife had left him: nothing to do with the jail time … it was the anger she couldn't stand.

Liam said, knowing he was pushing it but feeling his power, the can of Heineken working on him a little, 'If you had a buyer at forty grand you should have told me. Who do you know who'd give you that kind of cash anyway?'

Now Stef was turning back to him and Liam braced himself, thinking this might get physical any second.

But Stef just said, 'You're not the only one can keep a secret. I can't tell you. Even if I could I wouldn't. You've shown yourself up here. The main point is, if you don't get them back, both you and me are truly fucked.'

That made Liam think again of the woman he'd dealt with, and the big man who worked for her, and he began to realise he'd put himself in the middle of something that was probably not going to end well.

CHAPTER SEVEN

THE NEXT MORNING, Saturday, Storey downloaded the last two Chance albums from Amazon. The later of the two, *Angry*, had been released in 2002, and as he listened to it Storey understood where the title had come from. He'd remembered the band as being rather sweet-natured, with nice harmonies from the brothers, melodies that you caught quickly, like a virus, and a compelling beat.

Angry, on the other hand, was the sound of a band arguing amongst themselves and scornful of their audience, with songs called 'Chiseller' and 'Spiked' and 'The End of the World', a dark sound that made it easy to understand why their popularity had fallen like a stone and probably explained why they hadn't released anything since then. At least the song he'd heard them recording the other day had a more upbeat and musical feel to it.

He turned over in his mind what Geneva Chance had said to him, the story about the missing song. Did he believe it? Maybe, maybe not. But why would she lie?

Would she invent a story just to keep him involved and on the case?

There was something in her honesty, her willingness to tell him about what the song meant to her, that had touched him. She wouldn't tell him about the song itself, its lyrics or intent, but he knew its importance to her was real.

The problem for him was knowing how to start an investigation. He'd got so far with the studio keypad, but now what?

THE PROBLEM WAS solved when she phoned him just before lunchtime. He hadn't given her his mobile number so she must have asked Frank 'Larry' Lamb for it. Showing some initiative.

But when she spoke her voice had the casualness that he'd noticed before, as if she were just passing the phone and decided to pick it up and dial. There was no urgency in her tone.

She said, 'I was wondering if you'd like to buy a girl a coffee in town.'

'Sure. Did you have a particular girl in mind?'

'You'd have to come and pick me up, though, because all the men of the house have gone out. And I don't drive.'

'I still haven't made a decision,' he said.

'You liar. You're intrigued, don't deny it.'

'I downloaded a couple of your albums this morning. To remind myself what you did.'

'What did you think?'

He paused. 'I'm no judge of pop music.'

'Johnny likes to think of it as commercial rock. Better for his street-cred.'

'Well it sounded to me more like Abba than Black Sabbath.'

She laughed. 'Good god, where have you dredged those up from?'

'They're the gold standard in their fields.'

'Well don't tell Johnny you compared him and his songs to Abba. He thought they were lightweight.'

'But I'm told they're great to dance to.'

'Says someone who looks like he's never danced in his life.'

He told her what time he'd be there and hung up, wondering whether she was flirting with him. He couldn't remember anything about her love-life ... he'd never followed gossip anyway, but he had the sense she'd always been a private person, and if the last fifteen years had seen Chance's career go downhill then she probably wouldn't have been of much interest to the gossip rags.

So then he told himself she definitely *wasn't* flirting with him because to think otherwise would be just too vain.

If flattering.

———

SHE WAS WAITING outside the house's iron gates and waved as he turned in a semi-circle and pulled up next to her. Today she wore a blue singlet and a flared skirt that rose above her knees as she climbed in and settled herself into the seat. She pulled the skirt down over her knees as he headed back towards the centre of Coventry. She smiled at him.

'I know it's pathetic I don't drive but we were in London when I came of age and we were driven everywhere. I just haven't bothered since.'

'It's okay. I'm used to it.'

'What do you mean?'

'I just finished working as a driver for a guy.' Wondering whether she knew the story, which had been all over the local news a few weeks ago, though she didn't strike him as someone who was interested in what went on in the world outside her head.

They drove in silence for a while, then he said, 'That story about the song—is it true?'

'I tell you something personal about myself, something I've not told anyone else, and you're accusing me of lying? What kind of detective are you?'

'An amateur one. And you didn't answer the question. That's one of the first things they teach us in interrogation school, you know, when you're a cop—if someone deflects, or answers a question with another question, they're probably lying. Or trying to come up with a reason they shouldn't answer you directly.'

'And when you've done as many interviews as I have, you learn not to trust that people are actually listening to what you say.'

'What do you mean?'

She sighed and he glanced at her. She was staring through the windscreen, her features set, a couple of lines showing at the creases of her eye and pulling down the corner of her mouth. But it was still a good profile, the features not yet growing larger or more defined as age caught up with her.

She said, 'There were times I did thirty interviews in a week, when we had an album coming out, or a hit single. Starting when I was seventeen. It didn't take long to find out people came to you with their own sets of prejudices.'

'They're just people like you and me. So what happened?'

'Oh, I don't want to go into it … it's boring. I'm not complaining, how can I? I've had a great life.' Saying this with a flat tone, like she didn't believe it and didn't know how it could be true. She added, 'Let's just say the words that came out of my mouth didn't always make it directly to the page. They went through some kind of bitchy translator, so I ended up sounding worse than I was. Or worse than I thought I was. I was seventeen for god's sake, so who knew what I thought? I knew things got twisted but in the end I couldn't stop myself—I enjoyed the attention, enjoyed being the pop-star. As for the rest, I was too young to care.'

Storey said, 'But not any more.'

Then he felt the heat of her eyes on him. 'You catch on quick for a plod.'

He said, 'Same thing happened to me. Down in London. It's kind of why I'm back here. I screwed up on something and quit, then came home.' He glanced at her, wondering whether to say more. But she was looking out of the passenger window and perhaps hadn't heard. He said, 'So why are *you* still here? You could be in a mansion in Hampstead. Or Esher. Somewhere more glam than off the Kenilworth Road.'

'Fuck that. When we made it big we had a place, me and Johnny, out in Hackney, before it got gentrified. But it was impossible to live there. Great for getting to TV gigs and clubbing, but crap for living your own life. Living in London's supposed to be anonymous, like no-one knows who you are or where you live. But that's rubbish. Maybe because we were really big for a couple of years, everyone knew us and thought they could touch us, shout at us, laugh at us. Really wears you down. So we came back here, took a breath and calmed down.' She paused, then said. 'Here I am again, Poor Me. Tell me to shut the fuck up, will you? I drive myself mad sometimes.'

Storey said nothing and concentrated on getting into the town centre on a Saturday afternoon. The modernist slab of glass that was the Friar House office complex on his right gave way to the more humble rows of estate agents and solicitors' offices in Greyfriars that he remembered from when he was a kid, and one of which he'd visited more recently to deal with his father's will.

He asked her if she had anywhere in particular she wanted to go and she said anywhere that sold coffee and a slice of carrot cake. 'I'm addicted to carrot cake,' she said. 'Rock star excess or what?'

THEY WOUND UP in a small Italian café in Smithford Way, opposite the tall glass doors of the public library. The place was full and the busy pedestrianised precinct outside reminded Storey of shopping trips into town when he was young, being dragged around the shops by his mother. He didn't remember much about her except her curly red hair and that she hated shopping, especially in the summer holidays when she had to take him along. He could still feel the tight grip of her hand on his wrist. His father had been involved in the rebuilding of the West Orchard Shopping Centre, behind where he sat now, working as an electrician as they fitted out the new shops in the mall. That must have been the late eighties, Jesus, nearly thirty years ago …

He nodded towards the library, saying, 'I'll tell you one of the few pop facts I know. That library used to be the Locarno, a dance hall.'

'I knew that. My dad told me. It might even have been where he met my mum. But carry on with your interesting pop fact.'

'Chuck Berry recorded "My Ding-a-Ling" there in 1972. His only number one hit in America.'

Geneva made her eyes wide and her mouth a circle, then said, 'Omigod, you're so clever. It's only the first thing any journo says to you, ever, whenever you mention Coventry and music.'

Storey sat back in his chair. 'I didn't say it was interesting. Just that I knew it.'

Now she grinned and patted his hand on the table. 'Never mind. Good effort. We had a few famous Coventry groups after that.'

'The Specials.'

'Of course. That's the second thing they say. Then there's Lieutenant Pigeon. King. All the greats. Oh, and The Selecter, who were okay.'

'We're both too young to remember them,' he said.

'But sadly we know the names, don't we?'

'What are we doing here?'

She smiled for almost the first time since he'd known her. 'I'm mingling with a member of the public. Why, what are you doing?'

'I haven't a clue.'

'Good, then everything's a surprise, isn't it? Have you finished your coffee? Right now, I want to shop.'

———

HE STOOD AND they edged through tables into the glare of the paved shopping precinct, a trend-setter in the sixties but now exactly the same as every other town centre in the country.

He was two yards behind Geneva when he saw someone—a man in his forties, perhaps—change direction and come to a sudden stop in front of her. He was wide and florid, with a round face that was split in a huge grin. He wore a short-sleeved red shirt and now he raised his arms as if to hug her.

'Wow, Geneva Chance! I never expected to see you here! How are you doing? I'm your biggest fan, since right back, when you started. I'm Ken Talbot, but you can call me Ken. I used to see you in the clubs around here, when you were practically a nipper—'

By now Storey had pushed himself between the man and Geneva. 'Thanks for saying hello but Miss Chance has an appointment.'

'That's okay,' the man said, glancing up at Storey with irritation but then shifting sideways so he could see past him. 'Can I at least have an autograph? I wish I had one of your albums with me, I've got them on vinyl as well as CD, you know. It would have been great if I had *Lucky Chance* with me, wouldn't it? Here … let me see, I've got my diary here, perhaps you could write something … ?'

Storey looked back at Geneva, who nodded. She suddenly seemed small and a little frightened.

The man handed her a small black book and a ballpoint pen. She found an empty page and scribbled quickly, then handed it back via Storey, who gave it to the man.

Storey said, 'If you've got what you want, we'll be going now.'

'Hey, no offence, I'm made up. Cheers, Geneva, hope you and the boys are doing well. Get that new album finished and I'll be first in the queue! Remember: Ken Talbot. I'll be in the front row of your next concert!'

She said, 'Thanks,' in a dull voice and the man turned away, raising a hand and waving as he went, his large backside wobbling a little as he walked.

Storey looked back at Geneva. She was staring at the ground and her face was pale. She looked up at him with tears in her eyes. She said, 'Take me home. I'm sick of the public now.'

WHEN THEY ARRIVED back at the house she'd recovered some of her equilibrium and said she wanted him to come inside.

They stood outside the house while she tried to persuade him, saying it wouldn't be long, just till she'd properly calmed down. However much he liked her, he didn't want to take on the burden of her problems. He'd been there before.

'You must be ready for another coffee,' she said. 'It's been at least twenty minutes since the last one.'

He finally gave up and and she walked him through to the kitchen. Bill Chance was standing at the sink, peeling potatoes.

'Hi, guys, where've you been? I thought we might go for a roast chicken with Lyonnaise potatoes tonight, what do you think?'

Geneva said, 'Whatever,' then turned to Storey. 'He thinks he's Rick Stein, always cooking up something fancy.'

'Aw, come on, Genny ... you know I like to cook. Besides, it pays my rent and saves you getting someone else in, doesn't it? None of my kids can cook.' This last sentence aimed over his shoulder at Storey, wondering what was going on because there was an undertone to this conversation, something deeper and more aggravated.

He said to Geneva, 'I'd better be going. Are you okay?'

Now her father was turning from the sink, shaking his hands dry before picking up a towel. 'What? What's happened?'

'A guy stopped and asked for an autograph, that's all. He was friendly enough but I think it took her by surprise.'

Geneva said, 'Don't talk for me. Don't explain me.'

Storey hesitated, considering which way the conversation could go. He said, 'You're right. I'll see you later.'

But now she surprised him by grabbing his arm. 'You haven't had your coffee. Don't go anywhere.'

He watched as she crossed to the counter and boiled a kettle, then put a teaspoon of instant coffee in it, asking if he wanted sugar. He shook his head and she brought it to him.

'Let's go in the front room.'

She turned him around and pushed him out. He let her steer him into a large room containing a sofa and chairs, a grand piano and several gold disks framed and hanging on the walls. The floor was wooden and shiny. An acoustic guitar leaned against the side of one of the chairs.

'Johnny's always got a guitar handy,' she said, as though she'd been watching him and seeing the room from his perspective.

'What's going on?' he asked.

'What do you mean? You said you wanted coffee. Don't you like it?'

'I don't think I had an opinion on the matter.'

They stared at each other across the room, Storey wondering how he'd got to this position so quickly with someone he barely knew—Geneva Chance had reached into him and pulled out a thread of sympathy of a kind he hadn't felt in a long time. Now they were connected and he wasn't sure why, or what it was she wanted from him. The incident with that fan—Ken Talbot?—had changed how she looked at him. He'd noticed it in the car on the way back, though he couldn't put a name to it. Perhaps he'd confirmed something for her and now she trusted him.

A bell sounded throughout the house, and looking out of the windows into the front garden he saw that the iron gates were swinging inwards. The black BMW he thought belonged to Johnny Chance crunched in and parked behind the garage. Storey had parked to one side under Geneva's instructions to prevent being boxed in.

She had been watching, too. She said, 'Okay, Little Hitler's back. You can go now, if you want.'

'Can't I finish my coffee?'

'He doesn't like finding strangers in the house when he's been out.'

'I'm bigger than him.'

'Maybe. But he outranks you.'

DRIVING HOME, STOREY thought back to how Geneva had reacted to her brother's arriving home. She'd called him Little Hitler but nonetheless seemed happy enough to see him. Was she one of those people who needed others around her all the time, so when her brother came back she didn't need Storey to talk to any more?

That didn't seem right. She wasn't a talkative person and besides, her father was right there in the house.

He also thought back to how she'd responded when she found her father in the kitchen. A coldness had come over her, hardening her features and turning her voice brittle. What was going on there?

Before he left her in the room, and before Johnny Chance had entered the house, Storey had asked her again about the stolen song. She wouldn't tell him any more about it except it was personal and she didn't want people to hear it until *she* wanted them to.

He remembered what Adam Chance, the eldest brother, had told him ... the guitars didn't mean much in terms of what they were worth, although in fact Lamb had said they were worth a lot. Geneva had said they had a sentimental value, but this was the least sentimental bunch of people he'd ever come across.

And besides, they hadn't even wanted to report the theft.

The idea came to him from nowhere ... what if the guitars weren't in fact the point of the burglary? What if the theft of the song was the real intention, and taking the guitars was just camouflage, a distraction?

Why would anyone want to steal the song? Because they liked it?

Or because they didn't ... perhaps it was a threat to someone. Someone like Johnny Chance, the group's chief songwriter. Someone who couldn't be found in possession of the song after the burglary because of the implications ...

Storey found himself shaking his head. Stupid idea. First, Geneva Chance could simply record it again, assuming she remembered it well enough. Second, if the song only existed on the stolen thumb drive, and somehow Johnny had found it, why wouldn't he just take it and throw it away? Or erase it and replace it?

There was no need for a massive charade involving contract burglars and stolen guitars to be used as a cover-up.

Then he started wondering what the burglars would do with the guitars if they weren't the primary reason for the burglary. Would they try to sell or fence them, just to get them off their hands, to get rid of the evidence? How would they do that?

He needed to talk to Jackie West.

CHAPTER EIGHT

KEN TALBOT SAVED and closed the Word document he was working on—it was no good, he couldn't get anything done tonight. So what if he had a deadline? Hadn't he met Geneva Chance in person that afternoon? Hadn't his timing been great?

God, she'd looked good, a skimpy blue top setting off her black hair and dazzling blue eyes, her figure still shapely even though she was thirty-five years and four months and, let's see, five days old ... She was still the same girl he'd fallen for eighteen years ago. He knew people changed—he only had to look in the mirror every morning to see that—but she'd just grown more into herself. She hadn't become cynical or jaded like other show-biz types. There was still a purity about her that appealed to him.

He tore off a Post-It note and placed it on the open page of the book he was translating, then closed it. It was a customer service manual for a Spanish company that was opening a chain of restaurants in the UK. They'd approached him after seeing his website and his list of French and Spanish clients and the recommendations they'd given him. This was a big job but he was nearly finished. Truth be told, he was tired of it, his head filled with the regulations the company used to manage everyone who worked in the franchises—how to make the paella, how long to cook the rice, what was the proportion of rice to water; or, if you were a manager, how to deal with customer complaints, what phrases to use, what your attitude should be—"These are customers, not the enemy!"—what kind of training to give the waiting staff and the chefs and the cleaners; what the bonus system was and how it worked; who was eligible to win and how to run the staff competitions; what criteria to use for employee of the month …

Talbot pushed back his chair and thought again about this afternoon's set-up … As usual, he'd sat in his car two hundred yards away from the Chance house, reading a book and listening to the radio at the same time. He recognised Johnny's flash BMW when the gates opened and it headed into town, followed a moment later by Adam's more sedate edition of the same car, with Tempo in the passenger seat. He knew Tempo's Mercedes was still being repaired, having been involved in a slight accident the previous week. Although he'd been given a courtesy replacement, a white version of the same Mercedes edition, he didn't seem to bother with it much, preferring to go out with one of his brothers instead.

That meant Geneva was in the house with her father.

And he knew she wouldn't stay there long: it was a nice day, a weekend, she was bound to do *some*thing, and when she did he'd decided this time he'd engineer a meeting. He'd been thinking about it for years, why not do it now? His only regret was he hadn't brought any merchandise with him—perhaps he'd get an autograph, or maybe a selfie ...

Sure enough, the gates opened again after lunch and she came out and stood waiting. So she wasn't going for a walk. Perhaps she'd called a taxi. Now she was looking at her phone but not texting, probably just reading something. Now glancing both ways down the street, seeming at one point to be looking directly at him in his little Fiat Punto. Perhaps wondering what such a low-rent car was doing in her world ...

And then the other guy turned up, Storey, wheeling his Volvo in a semi-circle to pick her up.

Did she smile a little when she saw the car? And did she then hide it, pulling her lips down so as not to appear too enthusiastic?

It was then he confirmed his decision: he knew who Paul Storey was, he'd read all the news coverage about him in the last few months and seen his picture on the local television news. But he wasn't going to be put off just because of another man's reputation.

So when Storey's car set off towards the centre of Coventry, Ken Talbot put down his Kindle and started his Punto. Today was do or die.

———

THE REST HAD been easy. He'd followed them into the car park just down from Primark, parked on the same level, and managed to pick them up as they walked into

Coventry's pedestrianised centre, Geneva not seeming particularly interested in window-shopping but leading Storey directly to a café where they had to sit inside, all the outdoor tables being busy.

So then he'd waited. He stood outside Smiths newsagent, parallel to them, facing the library, taking in the same view they would have, watching the same shoppers and pedestrians they would be watching as they walked past.

Biding his time.

And eventually, bingo. He saw her emerging through the shadowed door of the café, having to weave between the outside tables, and he set off on a diagonal path that would take him in front of her.

And at the last minute, with Storey still a couple of paces behind, he'd stopped dead in front of the glorious Geneva Chance and had his say.

Of course she was a little taken aback. He saw that in her eyes straight away. And that hulk Storey had put himself between them quickly and said something that Talbot didn't really hear.

But she'd *looked* at him. She'd said, 'Thanks' to him. She'd actually seen him and touched his diary and written in it.

In all the years he'd been watching her, during all of the concerts he'd seen when the band were touring, over fifteen years ago, she didn't know of his existence.

Now she did.

HE ROLLED HIS chair back to the computer desk and opened up the Windows Photos app. Then he found the photos he wanted and printed them out in high resolution on glossy photo paper.

There were half a dozen of Geneva Chance and Paul Storey walking through Coventry. They weren't all in proper focus because she'd moved so quickly and hadn't paused before heading directly to the café.

Nonetheless he cleared a little space on the corkboard above his computer and pinned them up neatly, two rows of three A4 photos, printed in landscape.

Then he stood up from his office chair and laid down on the sofa which ran along the opposite wall. Leaning back he sighed and took a tissue from the box on the corner of his desk.

CHAPTER NINE

HE'D LAST SEEN Jackie West two months ago, when she called him in to make a statement about the business with Bran Doyle, his previous employer. She'd been matter-of-fact and straightforward as she took his statement, but afterwards took him for a drink in a hotel bar where, she said, they wouldn't be seen by other cops who might draw the wrong conclusion. They had one drink then shook hands on the pavement outside and he hadn't seen her since, though he'd thought about her once or twice.

Sunday morning he called her on her mobile number and she agreed to meet him in the same bar that night, when she was off duty.

Now there she was, as usual earlier than him, sitting alone at a table against the wall, taking in the other customers, her pale eyes apparently open and friendly when he knew she could be cynical and tough as a feral dog when necessary.

And as usual Storey liked the way she looked without being able to commit to any real feelings for her. There was something in the way she held herself, the way she turned her eyes on you, that kept you at a distance. You always felt as though you were being measured and were coming up short.

When he compared her to Geneva Chance he realised it wasn't just the other woman's looks that attracted him — it was the vulnerability. He was wary of it, but it drew him in nonetheless. Jackie West didn't do vulnerable, even when she'd had a large gun held to her head by the Syrian arms dealer.

Now she was standing and offering her cheek to be kissed, which he did, and then they both sat down, Storey remembering again how petite she was, her legs slender, her face small and delicate. And he remembered her scent.

They exchanged pleasantries, talking about the heatwave that had lasted three weeks so far.

'So,' she said, 'I don't hear from you for two months then I get a call out of the blue. Am I going to like this conversation?'

'I wish you'd get straight to the point, stop all this pussyfooting around.'

'I've been here before, Storey. You forget. You get yourself caught up in stuff because you're too dim to say no to any invitation that comes your way. Do you really need money that badly?'

'Call me shallow.'

'No, it's not the money. It's the … what? The challenge? The dare? Playing with guns in London ruined you for the rest of us, didn't it? Now you get bored quickly and want to find something to bash your forehead against, so that it'll be nice when it stops.'

'I see you've moved to the psychological profiling unit, then. I had no idea.'

'Tell me I'm wrong,' she said. 'Prove you're on the straight and narrow. What are you doing now? Who are you working for? I presume you have a favour of some sort to ask. You usually do.'

Storey took a swig from his beer so she wouldn't see him grinning. He didn't want her to know she was right—he'd taken the job from Frank Lamb and the Chances because it was different and interesting and, he told himself, because he might be able to help. But there was no doubt the element of challenge, of solving the problem, helped make up his mind. When he told Lamb he was giving up the case he didn't believe it himself—he'd said it as a kind of defence mechanism against failure, as if saying it out loud meant he wouldn't be responsible for what happened later, should he not succeed.

———

NOW JACKIE WEST was leaning back against the faux-leather seat and sipping her red wine. He suddenly saw himself as she might see him—a spiky, difficult pest who in the space of six months had created an aura surrounding himself like a black hole, sucking in crooks, murderers and bad behaviour of all kinds. He imagined she dreaded every time he called or asked for a meeting, knowing there'd be something crooked bubbling under the surface and getting ready to break through.

In answer to her questions he told her who he was working for and how he'd been recruited by Frank Lamb to help find the thieves. He noticed she drew a sigh and then saw the knowledge settle in her eyes that she was going to tell him to back off, the Chances should report the thefts and then he should just let the whole thing go. Leave it to the professionals.

He didn't mention Geneva Chance's stolen song … it didn't seem relevant when there were a couple of specific objects—the guitars—to consider.

When he finished she was quiet for a few seconds before saying, 'So you're probably wondering who the burglars would fence them off to, the guitars.'

Chalk one up for her and for unpredictability. 'Well you are a surprise,' he said.

'I know. You expected me to tell you to steer clear, get them to report it, let the professionals take care of it and so on.'

He nodded, amused she knew how he thought. Or how he thought about her. Perhaps she knew him better than he wanted to admit.

'But that wouldn't work, would it?' she said. 'I'd be wasting my breath. Not once have you listened to anything I've said, so why should I bother? Other than throwing you in a cell and chucking away the key, I don't know what else to try.'

'You're pretty senior now, aren't you? You could mark my card. Get me in trouble for driving while looking at my watch or something. Make life difficult for me in general.'

'You and I both know that would just be a red rag to a pig-headed bull. Pardon my metaphor or simile or whatever the hell it is. The point is, it wouldn't work.'

'I always said you were a realist,' he said. 'So what do you think?'

'About what?'

'What would the burglars do with the stolen goods? Who are the likely fences, assuming they weren't stolen to order for a particular client, which I can't rule out.'

'For god's sake, Storey, that's the easy part.'

'It is?'

'You go to the places where people sell stuff for money. And you ask them politely if anyone's brought in a couple of nice guitars lately.'

'Why would they tell me?'

'You've said yourself the goods haven't been reported as stolen. Nothing's been mentioned in the papers or on the telly. So no one knows about the theft and no one who's likely to buy them will be asking tricky questions.'

'The burglars can't know that. They must be thinking the guitars will have been reported.'

'It doesn't hurt for you to try, does it?'

'Is it that easy?'

'It might be. It's the first thing we'd do. You don't know until you know.'

'Cop wisdom.'

'And if you think you're getting any more out of me, you'll have to revise your thinking.'

CHAPTER TEN

STEF DIDN'T UNDERSTAND why he hadn't seen Liam's arrogance before. It was like he'd kept it hidden while he was playing the part of student to Stef's teacher. Of course he'd been difficult to work with but at least he'd seemed willing to learn.

Now he'd got some money in his pocket another part of his personality was coming out, the one where he liked to show off, to prove to people he wasn't just a block of muscle but had a brain, too. A brain that could work things out ... so long as it was to his own advantage.

Stef wondered why he'd even agreed to come today. There'd been no contact between them for three days after the row on Thursday and then Liam phoned, all friendly, acting as if nothing had been said between them. And Stef thinking, maybe he could learn something, find out where Liam had taken the guitars, how he could retrieve them without holding a gun to Liam's head ...

So he agreed to the meet, acted reasonable as he usually did. Turned up at this big pub on the Keresley Road, looked like a slice of white wedding cake from the outside, and there was Liam sitting with his arm round this woman, Jen, must have been ten years older than him, somewhere in her thirties, anyway. Wiry permed brown hair and a scarlet gash of a mouth. Sitting next to him they looked like a couple of cartoon characters, Liam with his thick neck and shoulders and acne'd face—which Stef put down to steroids—Jen with her come-on eyes and raucous laugh …

And here he was, staring at the pair of them across the table trying not to react as if they were freaks.

Now Liam was saying, 'I didn't think you'd come at first, thinking you were still pissed off at me. Then I thought we had to let bygones be bygones, didn't we, if we were going to work together, like.'

'Why would he be pissed off at you?' Jen asked, looking up at Liam from under his arm. Adding, 'He seems like a nice man to me. What've you done to piss him off?'

'Nothing,' Liam said. 'Absolutely nothing. Earned him a bit of money, that's all.'

'Not enough,' Stef said, unable to help himself.

'Yeah yeah yeah, so you said. I admit that bothered me for a bit. But then I got to thinking, so what? Better to have the cash in hand than wait around for it, right? Who knows what's going to happen in the next week? The next twenty-four hours, come to that.'

Stef hoped Liam would stop talking. He felt his reasonableness being peeled away every time Liam spoke. There was a superiority in the way Liam was talking to him, as if he was now in charge and Stef was the student. If it carried on like this he knew his temper would come up, as it always did, no matter how reasonable he tried to be. It was only a matter of time.

Then Jen said, 'Did Liam tell you he's taking me away for me birthday?'

'No.'

'He says he's been putting money away from his job, as a surprise. We're going to Alicante for a weekend. A dirty weekend, he says, but that depends, doesn't it?'

She laughed one of her split-mouth and gravelly laughs, one of those that Stef already knew he'd like to knock sideways out of her, slap her across the face so she'd stop laughing and look at him with her mouth shut.

He said, 'What job's this then, Liam? I didn't know you'd found work. I didn't know they were taking people on again at McDonalds.'

He watched Liam shift himself on the pub's shiny plastic bench, still fidgeting, still full of nervous energy. Good, let him feel uncomfortable.

Liam said, 'You don't know everything about me, do you? I've been working for a couple of weeks now. Furniture delivery down at Ikea. Good pay.'

'And he gets to drive a fuck-off big blue lorry,' Jen said, digging Liam in the ribs. 'All them beds in the back, we'll have to try 'em out one day, eh? Have a bit of a party, get that lorry rockin'!'

Liam frowned and shifted again, moving his arm from her shoulders.

He said, 'Don't talk like that, Jen. Not here.'

'Why?' she said. 'You suddenly gone all prudish on me?'

'It's not that,' Stef said to her. 'It's that Liam likes his secrets. Likes to keep things to himself. Like sex and finances and guitars, things like that.'

Jen looked from one of them to the other, saying, 'Guitars? What's going on here? I thought you two was mates?'

'We are,' Stef said. 'And like mates we talk to each other, tell each other what we're doing, where we're going. What we're doing with our guitars. Stuff like that. Isn't that right, Liam?'

'Fuck off, Stef.'

'The thing is,' Stef continued, 'Liam doesn't like to give you all the information. You'll probably find that out one day, Jen. You'll think you know where you are with him and Poof!, it's all gone.'

'All right!' Liam said, slamming his drink on the table. Jen straightening up, frightened now, edging away from him.

Stef said, 'And the other thing you need to know, Jen, is that you can't actually trust this toe-rag. You think you've got a promise out of him and … well, he just ignores it. Does what he wants to do. So you end up not knowing where you stand.'

Stef was ready for it but he still didn't see it when it came. Liam swept out a hand and scooped his drink towards Stef's head. It was a heavy pint glass and Stef saw enough of it to turn his head but it still caught him on the side, just in front of his ear. Hurt like a bastard.

And then he was standing and Liam was standing, and Stef swung a fist, connecting with Liam's nose, and then he heard Jen beginning to scream and saw Liam slapping her in the face, telling her to fucking shut it, and then he came for him across the table, grabbing Stef around the throat with his massive hands and he knew he was swinging and connecting but nothing was stopping those hands or loosening their grip and it wasn't long before his vision began to blur and the sounds of the pub around him started to echo weirdly and he felt himself falling, though Liam's hands were still holding him up and it was true what they said, you started to see black … and then he didn't remember what happened next …

———

BUT NOW HE WAS upright again and walking and people were saying things to him he couldn't understand. And then he was being told to get inside, duck and mind your head. And the soft touch of someone's hand on his hair, pushing him down. And now he was in a car and he could hear himself talking to someone and he was glad he sounded calm but the car was moving somewhere, rocking back and forth gently, and shortly it was stopping again and he was being taken out and then he was in a room and someone was shining a light in his eyes and now he was walking down a corridor and suddenly his hearing returned, as if his ears had popped, and the world snapped sharply into focus and as the door clanged shut it all came back and he knew where he was.

And he sat on the blue plastic mattress in the cell and began to plan how he could remove Liam Fisher from his life.

CHAPTER ELEVEN

THE FIRST SHOP Storey went into was like an ordinary electronics store, except most of the goods were in glass cabinets on the walls—dozens of iPhones, iPads, tablets of various makes, Samsung phones with big screens, laptop computers, watches … he wandered around out of interest, seeing if there was anything he might like but also getting a sense of the place.

Guys wearing matching tee-shirts behind the counter. Storage space at the back of the shop and a couple of rather obvious cameras pointing into the spaces where customers were browsing.

As he watched, a man in his early twenties came in, took something from his pocket that might have been a phone and entered a negotiation with the man behind the counter. He also handed over some papers which the man looked at and took away, along with the phone. A couple of minutes later he came back and money changed hands and the young man left, folding the bills carefully.

Storey went to the counter and when the same assistant came over, said, 'Yeah, I'm looking for something particular. A guitar, acoustic.'

The man glanced at Storey but kept his eyes roving over the rest of the shop, a large space in which half a dozen men were idly flicking through racks of computer games or reading the descriptions of the goods in the cabinets. He said, 'Haven't got any in at the moment. Can do you a nice electric—see them down there? Next to the drum kit.'

Storey had seen them—two electric guitars, one a sunburst orange, the other white. Neither of them a Fender. He was looking for a deep maroon model with Eric Clapton's signature written on the back.

He shook his head, 'Never mind. So how does this work, if I wanted to bring something in to sell?'

'Have you?'

'I might have.'

The man looking at him squarely now, but deciding what the hell, saying, 'You bring something in, we test it, give you some money. You need to show us two pieces of ID and you go on our database and we verify the ID before you get anything. You have a month if you want to buy it back.'

'I can buy it back?'

'Pay an admin fee and it's yours. If you don't come back for it, we sell it.'

'So basically you hang on to something for a month and give me some money while you do it. Then if I change my mind I return the money you gave me, plus a bit extra.'

'You got it.'

'Do people come back, generally?'

The man was shaking his head. 'Not as a rule. They come here because they need the money, don't they?'

'I suppose so. You haven't got a Martin acoustic, then, or a maroon electric Fender?'

'Not this month, no. Can do you a nice line in harmonicas.'

Storey left, feeling in two minds about the place. It was clean and run professionally, from what he could see — unlike the old Exchange and Mart and second-hand shops he remembered from when he was young.

On the other hand it traded on people's distress, when they needed money and had no other way of getting it. That didn't sit particularly well with him, he realised. He remembered times when his father had been out of work, looking for a contract, and he remembered the stress it caused his mother. She wanted him to take a full-time job with the GEC or someone, get a salary every month. But he preferred his freedom, he said, so he could pick and choose.

The problems came when there was nowhere left to choose because all the jobs had gone.

He wondered if that had shortened his dad's life — the disappointment. Not living up to his own expectations. It was something Storey was beginning to understand.

———

THE NEXT TWO outlets he visited were variations of the first. One cut the redeem period to a fortnight and seemed more paranoid, with a big bald-headed guy walking around the floorspace looking over your shoulder when you took an interest in one of the items. The other seemed more like a pawn shop where you brought in your item and they gave you money immediately, without taking any details or offering any redeem period. Neither of them had any guitars at all when he asked.

The third was off the Foleshill Road, traditionally a place where Indians and Pakistanis had settled, and for proof there on the right was a large white temple that glistened in the sunshine. Then row after row of small terraced houses, then a line of shops, then more houses and perhaps a factory or a large retail store, a whole self-sufficient community with hairdressers and specialist grocers and dentists ... what Storey thought of as a typical Coventry development, a small world that need have nothing to do with the rest of the city.

He turned off the main road and found the next exchange: Odeta's Swap Shop. It was relatively downplayed, with plain black surrounds to the double-fronted display windows, the name in gold script over the door, a fold-out sandwich board on the pavement. He parked and crossed the road and looked in the windows — the usual collection of electronic gadgets, watches, jewellery and console games.

Inside, there were no customers but yet another big man behind the counter, this time with a drooping black moustache and spiked hair and a dark complexion, though not Asian. He wore a tee-shirt that was tight across his chest and read 'Odeta's Man' in gold script.

Storey began to wonder who Odeta was.

The man nodded at Storey and smiled, showing one gold tooth. Storey thought he was probably in his mid-thirties, though his eyes were hooded and had the jaded look of someone who'd seen everything there was to see.

'Can I help you?' the man said. 'Are you looking to buy or to sell?' He spoke with an accent Storey couldn't place. Something East European, he thought, not as heavy as Russian, not as obvious as German or Scandinavian.

He said, 'Who's Odeta?'

The man's expression didn't change except a sharpness came into his eyes.

'You see my tee-shirt and you want to know who owns me? Nobody owns me. Is not my idea.'

Definitely Eastern European, Czech or Yugoslav, somewhere around there.

'I was thinking of the name of the shop. I don't mind who owns you.' Smiling back at the man, telling him he's not serious.

The man standing up straight now, showing he had a good six inches on Storey. The smile had gone.

'So, you want buy something? What you looking for? Laptop computer? Watch? We have lots of things, you can go look.'

He nodded towards the walls which by now Storey recognised as having the standard glass cabinets to protect the various electronic goods inside.

He said, 'I'm looking for guitars. An electric Fender, preferably maroon. I like maroon.'

'What is maroon?'

'It's like purple.'

'Then why not call it purple? Why you have so many different words for things?'

'Where are you from? You've got an interesting accent.'

'Does it matter?'

'No, I'm just interested. The other guitar I'd be interested in would be an acoustic guitar … you know, you play it without plugging it into an amplifier. Brown. Called a Martin.'

'You play guitar? We have other guitars in window, I can fetch if you like. Very good. Very high quality.'

'I'm looking for a friend, not for me. So you haven't got anything like I want?'

The man relaxed, perhaps feeling the conversation was coming to an end, leaning on the counter again, now eye to eye with Storey. 'No, only guitars in window. You give me your phone number, I call you if anything comes in. Is something we do for good clients.'

'I'm not a client, am I?'

The man grinned again, showing the gold tooth. 'You will be if you buy guitar.'

Storey hadn't noticed the door behind the counter, beyond the racks of shelves containing what looked like cables, chargers, phone cases and other electronic paraphernalia. But now it opened and a woman stepped through, coming up behind the man. She was somewhere in her forties with straggly black hair that came down to her shoulders and she was perhaps attractive once, before a mixture of too much sun and what might have been stress took its toll on her features. Her eyes were dark and shadowed further by heavy make-up, and she wore lipstick so pale it was almost white. She wore a full-length black skirt and a loose black top. She reminded Storey of the gypsy who used to come to his mother's door selling pegs, though she was taller and more sensual.

She said to the man, 'Everything okay, Diamant?' Her accent was the same as his.

'Everything okay. This man is looking for guitars, but we don't have.'

'You showed him the one in the window?'

Storey said, 'It doesn't interest me, sorry. Not the right make. Are you Odeta?'

She raised her eyebrows. 'You are in my shop, yes. Is there something else you would like to see? A nice watch? Some jewellery for a lady?'

'No, it's two guitars I'm looking for.'

And there it was, the merest twitch of her eye towards Diamant, who didn't return it but stared directly at Storey, keeping his face amiable but unyielding.

Odeta said, 'We don't have many guitars. The one in the window is the first one we have for months, maybe a year. Not very musical around here. You leave a card or your phone number, we call you if something comes in.'

Storey reached for a pad of Post-It notes on the counter and wrote his mobile telephone number on it, and his name.

'And your address? If you want us to deliver.'

'That's okay, I'm happy to come here to see them.'

'Okay. Diamant, can you lock up? I want to close this afternoon.'

Storey waited for the man to lift the flap and come through the counter, then walked with him to the door.

'So, Diamant, where are you from, really?'

The man held the front door open for Storey and grinned his gold-toothed grin.

He said, 'Disneyland.'

CHAPTER TWELVE

NOT HAVING SEEN Stef while they were both locked up in the police station, Liam was surprised to get a call from him the next day, Monday.

'They let you out, then?' Stef said. 'They didn't charge you with being in possession of an illegal face?'

'They told me they had forty prior offences by you to deal with first. What do you want?'

'Someone I want you to meet. Come on over.'

'Can I bring Jen?'

'Now you're winding me up, aren't you? Just get your arse over here.'

He hung up and Liam stared at his phone's screen. He presumed Stef had been let out that morning, the same as him, the cops having taken a few details but saying no one had pressed charges. Keep your nose clean and don't do it again. He'd phoned Jen but got no reply—she was probably in one of her massive sulks. He shouldn't have hit her.

So he'd gone home and showered and changed and was now standing in his underwear in his bathroom. He caught his clouded reflection in the steamed bathroom mirror. He didn't need to see his face to know it would look confused.

THE FIRST THING Liam noticed when Stef opened his door was the big bruise on the side of Stef's head, just in front of his ear. It was yellow but turning purple already. Heavy things, beer mugs, he thought. And all those what do you call them, facets.

Stef said nothing but stepped back and Liam followed him into the room.

The energy was different from the last time he was there, and it seemed to be coming from a man sitting on Stef's sofa. He was not particularly big but seemed charged up, his mouth pursed, his eyes focused, almost staring. Perhaps in his late thirties.

The man said, 'So you're the arsehole who's got rid of the guitars.'

'Who are you?' He turned to Stef. 'Who's this, some junior fence you had lined up?'

'You talk to me, arsehole,' the man said, now standing. He was nine inches shorter and probably thirty pounds lighter than Liam, but there was something forceful in him, something that made you wary. He said, 'Stef's told me you've done something with the guitars but you won't tell him what. You've been and got money for them, which you're no doubt now pissing away.'

'Do I know you?'

The man turned away and walked to Stef, who looked as though he'd been enjoying the conversation so far. The man poked Stef in the chest with a finger.

'The deal was, you held on to the guitars. You said you could do that, said there'd be no problems. I don't know whether you were lying or whether you're as stupid as this sack of shit, but I need those guitars back. You don't know how valuable they are. In fact you have no fucking idea how valuable they are.'

Liam said, 'So this was a set-up? I sat in a fucking car for three hours to steal something that was set up to be stolen? Great fucking plan, Stef. Thanks for letting me know.'

'You didn't need to know,' Stef said. 'Your job was to hold the ladders steady and carry the guitars. Not to do any independent thinking.'

'So now,' the man said, turning back to Liam, 'your job is to get them back. In one piece. And keep them here, in this room if necessary, under fucking lock and key. If you don't, you won't get the rest of the money that's coming to you, understand?'

Liam stared at the man, realising he wasn't afraid after all, the guy was a squirt despite the big words. He stepped away and dropped into Stef's big chair. He said, 'So there's more money to come? Something else your man Stef didn't tell me. Well guess what, that's just doubled. Finders fee.'

He saw the rage in the man's eyes and was certain he knew him.

Stef said, 'Steady on, calm down, the pair of you. Let's be reasonable. Liam, how soon can you get the guitars back?'

Liam shrugged. 'Well that's a bit tricky now, isn't it?'

'In what way?'

'To get them back I'd have to return what I got paid, plus a commission for holding on to them. And most of that is gone, isn't it? Though I expect you've still got your half.' To the man, explaining: 'Not known for his extravagance, Stef. Despite these fancy pictures and all these books.'

The man said, 'How much will you need?'

Liam thinking quickly, saying, 'Fifteen hundred quid,' then eyeing Stef, urging him not to say they'd split a thousand between them.

Stef said nothing. Good—he knew which side his bread was buttered.

The man said, 'I'll get you a grand. You get the rest between you, right?'

'And then afterwards we get the rest of what we're owed.'

'You get the guitars back, sunshine, then we'll talk about fees.'

Liam grinned. 'I know you, don't I?'

The man answering quickly, 'I don't think so. I never forget an ugly face.'

'You're like on the tip of my tongue. Have you got a brother looks like you?'

The man glanced at Stef. 'You didn't say you'd be using a moron. I should halve the fee. In fact, you should pay *me* for having to deal with him.' Then back to Liam. 'Don't leave the country. And I want those guitars back by the end of this week. Can you manage that?'

'I can manage lots of things in a week. I know who you are, now.'

'Who's that, then?'

'You're some bloke who wants his guitars back and is willing to pay twice what he thought he was going to pay. Who's the moron now?'

Liam knew the man badly wanted to hit him. But instead he swallowed it, his cheeks red, his pale blue eyes staring down at Liam as if trying to burn him.

He said, 'I'll get you the money. A couple of days.'

'Stef's got my number. You've got his. It's magic.'

'You're not as clever as you think.'

'No? Then ask Stef what he did with the USB stick.'

The man turned and looked at Stef. 'What's he talking about? I thought you said it was safe.'

'It was,' Stef said. 'I put it through the soundhole of the Martin.'

The man closed his eyes and Liam knew he was on to something now.

'You stupid bastard,' the man said. He turned back to Liam. 'Is it still there?'

'Far as I know.'

'What does that mean? Didn't you take it out?'

'I don't remember. Depends on how important it is, doesn't it?'

The man turned away, grabbing Stef's arm and leading him towards the door. They stood for a moment talking while Liam watched, unable to hear.

And that's when he recognised him—when he couldn't hear the man's voice.

Finally Stef reached out and opened the door and the man left. Stef closed the door and wandered back into the centre of the room and sat on one of the couches.

He said, 'I never knew you had such a big mouth on you. It's going to get you in real trouble.'

'With him? I don't think so.'

'You're going somewhere you don't want to go, Liam.'

'You think I'm all muscles and no brain.'

'You have to admit, that's your reputation.'

Liam nodded. 'Well tell Mr Johnny Chance next time he calls I drive a hard bargain if he wants to see his fucking guitars again.'

CHAPTER THIRTEEN

DIAMANT DUSHKU WATCHED Odeta pour two whiskeys into chunky glasses and put the stopper back in the bottle. He admired the fact that she took after her husband, Toni, in drinking whenever she felt like it. None of that Muslim shit for them—he had friends who were Muslim but Diamant had never seen religion as useful for where he wanted to be in life. He knew Odeta felt the same way.

That's why he still worked for her, ten years after Toni was found one morning with his throat cut from ear to ear, his tongue pulled out through the slit. The theory was two bastard Kosovans had slipped into his bedroom and murdered him while he slept, paying him back for leaving Albania with 30 one-kilo bags of cocaine they considered rightfully theirs. Diamant had arrived the next morning and found Odeta in shock, having apparently spent the night in a separate room because Toni was drunk. She went to wake him up the next morning and found him with a sign round his neck, written in his blood and saying, 'Debt paid.'

She'd sold the house and converted the top floor of the shop into this apartment within three months.

Odeta turned and handed him a glass. 'You did the right thing in summoning me,' she said. 'I didn't like the look of this man Storey either. He wasn't a real customer.'

'He barely looked at the items and started asking questions too quickly. So I pressed the bell and you came.'

They spoke to each other in the *Gheg* dialect from the north of Albania, a dialect that was rarely written down and had no official status in Albania, where the *Tosk* dialect had been enforced by the Communist regime as the country's official written language over forty years before. Diamant liked the idea he and Odeta were preserving a part of his culture that was in danger of dying out, though Odeta in fact preferred to use English. It was what Toni wanted, she said: assimilation. Then you become invisible.

Now Odeta was sitting down, arranging her long black dress with its coloured embroidery, directing her dark-rimmed eyes towards his. It was true, Albanian women could be beautiful.

'Tell me about your research,' she said.

'There's nothing in the newspapers or the Internet about stolen guitars. So I researched the guitars. One of them is a Martin. It has a serial number and from the Internet you can find its date. It was made in 1938 and might be worth forty thousand dollars, according to a similar one that's for sale on eBay.'

Odeta didn't flinch but she took another sip of her whiskey.

'And were you able to find out who they belonged to?'

'Yes. The electric guitar has a signature on its back. It's by the English guitarist and drug addict Eric Clapton. I entered this into Google and it said this or a similar guitar was owned by Johnny Chance, a pop star who lives in Coventry.'

Diamant was gratified to see a small smile come to Odeta's lips.

'So somebody brings two guitars to our place of business and wants money for them. He doesn't know their value but he wants us to hold them for two weeks before we put them on sale. Meanwhile, neither the newspapers nor the television news report the theft. You discover that the guitars belong to a famous person but it's not the same person who brought them in. Is that correct?'

'The man Liam is known to me. He's brought me things before. I looked up a picture of Johnny Chance so I'll know him in future, if I meet him.'

'What do you think is happening here, Diamant?'

When Toni Morina had been killed, Odeta had removed herself from the world for six months' mourning. Once they had arrived in England she had a lot to be thankful for, Diamant knew, but now she had to rethink. She and Diamant had come with Toni overland, shipping out from the port of Vlorë in the south of Albania and crossing to Otranto on the heel of Italy, landing at night and wading ashore like immigrants, ten waterproof bags of drugs strapped to each of their chests.

And since Toni's murder she'd relied on Diamant to tell her the truth and to be her eyes and ears. She ran the business but she was a woman. That was disturbing for their contact in the south. While Ari Sallaku, the man they worked for in London, knew who she was, and liked the fact she'd taken over Toni's network, he didn't have to deal with her, which he was happy about. Diamant could act for her in every capacity because he was a man.

He said, 'I don't know what's happening, but I suspect that Johnny Chance is hiding his guitars. He has used this fool Liam to bring them here and hide them for two weeks, after which he'll retrieve them. Perhaps he's taking something from the insurance. Or perhaps he's hiding them from people who want to steal them.'

Odeta nodded. 'That is my thinking too. Everyone is lying to everyone else and perhaps there is only one person who knows the truth. And what about this man, Storey? Who is he?'

'Perhaps he's from the insurance, although he doesn't look as though he works in an office. He wasn't wearing a suit and tie and he didn't have a business card.'

'Perhaps he's a policeman. Perhaps the theft has been reported after all and they're trying to catch us performing an illegal act.'

Diamant was shaking his head now. 'He wasn't a policeman. He wasn't arrogant and he didn't know anything about us. He asked me about my accent. A policeman would have known about me and wouldn't have asked that question.'

'Then we don't know who this Mr Storey is.'

'No. I'll try to find out.'

———

AFTER THEY HAD finished their drinks, Diamant said, 'I have more useful information.'

'Ah, you've been saving the best for the last. You're turning into a leader, Diamant. Manipulating the conversation for more drama.'

There was a twinkle in her eye that disturbed him, but he said, 'When I learned that the guitars belonged to Johnny Chance, I remembered something. He's one of three brothers and a sister in this singing group. According to Wikipedia they were very successful in the years two thousand and two thousand and one. The three brothers are Adam, Tim, known as Tempo, and Johnny, who is the youngest of the brothers. He is a year older than their sister, called Geneva.'

'So what is your thinking here?'

'What I remembered is that the middle brother, Tim, is a client of ours.'

Now Odeta was leaning forward, allowing her blouse to fall open and show the top of her breasts. Diamant felt his mouth go dry. Odeta said, 'Now that is indeed very useful information. I congratulate you on your memory.'

'Thank you.'

'We must discuss a way to take advantage of this situation.'

At last, Diamant thought, now I can prove my real worth. He said, 'I've been working on a plan.'

CHAPTER FOURTEEN

STOREY FELT LIKE a real detective when he saw the man Diamant come out of Odeta's Swap Shop and walk to a dark blue Jaguar. When he'd left the shop he'd moved his own car and parked it around the corner, into a position where he could watch the front door. An hour later, Diamant came out, glanced both ways up the street, and climbed into the Jaguar.

Storey started up his Volvo and followed.

THEY HEADED SOUTH and then east, driving past the common on Mercer Avenue where he'd played football as a kid and heading towards the Jack Block—so called because when it was built in the 1960s as a housing development it had been constructed one floor at a time at ground level, then jacked up so the next floor could be built beneath it.

Diamant turned left at the post office on Coventry Street and then pulled up in front of a dismal terraced house with a faded blue front door. Storey drove past and turned at the next corner, then stopped. He took a can of Coke from the glove compartment and climbed out quickly, then leaned casually around the corner with the can to his mouth in time to see Diamant go up to the house and knock on the door. Storey saw that he was carrying a small bundle in his left hand.

After a moment another man with black hair and a small moustache came to the door, peered up and down the street, and let Diamant in.

———

FIFTEEN MINUTES LATER Diamant came out and drove off. He wasn't carrying the package any more.

Storey put his empty Coke can in his car and walked up to the house, thinking this was probably the worst dump of a street he'd seen in a long while—black bin-liners piled against a fence, cigarette butts, dog-shit and fast-food cartons strewn in the gutters. And the tell-tale signs of small plastic baggies abandoned everywhere, as though the users couldn't even wait to get home before hitting up.

Now he knocked on the door and waited. The same man opened it and stared at him, then stepped forward and looked either way up the street again, still vigilant.

Storey said, 'Gordon told me I could buy something from you. I should ask for Viktor.'

The man frowned, stepping back, saying, 'Who is Viktor?'

'I was told to ask for him. Viktor with a k.'

A voice called from further in the house, saying something Storey couldn't understand. The man facing him turned and shouted something back, then opened the door wider.

'Come in,' he said. 'We talk about Viktor.'

———

THE MAN LED him down a narrow hall and into a room that was made from knocking the front and the back rooms together. There was a threadbare carpet on the floor, a couple of chairs and a sofa, a big television on the wall over the gas fire. It was showing a football match with the sound turned down.

There was another man in the room, bigger than the one who'd opened the door. He was clean-shaven but had the same dark hair and large, liquid eyes. He sat in one of the chairs and looked up at Storey while the first man said something in a language Storey didn't recognise. Then the man turned to him and said, 'I told him you're looking for Viktor. We don't know Viktor.'

Storey said, 'A man called Gordon told me I should come here to buy something from you. Do you know what I mean?'

Now the second man was standing up, and just as Storey was starting to think it was getting crowded, a third man came in: black hair, black moustache, tattoo on his throat. Storey said, 'Are you Viktor?'

'Who is Viktor? There is no Viktor here. I am Jim, this is Jack and that is John.' He pointed to the other men in turn.

'A man called Gordon told me to ask for Viktor, and then I'd be able to buy something from you.'

'Buy what? We not sell anything here.'

Storey could tell from the man's voice that this was the one who'd called out imperiously when he was standing outside the front door. Perhaps he was the one in charge.

All three men were now standing around him, two of them his own height, one a couple of inches shorter. There are times, he told himself, when a little forethought would help.

He said, 'If you don't have anything to sell I might as well go. Gordon's going to be very disappointed.'

'No,' the third man said. 'You should stay. You can tell us about Viktor.'

Storey looked at each of them in turn. 'What's going on here, guys? I came looking for Viktor. I don't know him. Never met the guy. Can you tell me where he is?'

'What is it you want to buy?'

Storey grinned. 'You know. Something.'

'What is "something"?'

'Something I might like. Gordon said you were the people to come to. Well, Viktor. He'd look after me.'

'Does this person Viktor work for the police?'

'The police? How would I know? I shouldn't think so. Do you think he does? Perhaps we should ask him. Bring him in.'

The three men looked at each other and Storey waited for the first sign of movement so he could shift his weight, protect himself in some way.

Then the third man, the one he thought of as the boss, stepped back, taking an interest in the football match playing on the television behind Storey's head. He said, 'Take him to the door.' Then he added something in the same language used before and all three men laughed.

The one who brought him in took him to the front door. A flight of stairs led upstairs and at the bottom of the stairs, on a small table, was the packet that Diamant had brought. It was about six inches square and wrapped in silver foil, like a home-made sandwich. Storey doubted Diamant had driven all this way to deliver a chicken salad lunch.

The man opened the door and pushed Storey forward.

'We don't know Viktor and we don't know Gordon. Tell him he has the wrong address. Next time use Yellow Pages.'

He closed the door and Storey heard himself breathe out.

———

BACK IN HIS car he phoned Jackie West.

She said, 'This better be quick. I'm about to go into a meeting.'

He filled her in on his visit to Odeta's Swap Shop and told her he had a feeling the shop wasn't on the straight and narrow. He didn't mention following Diamant and his recent encounter with Jim, Jack and John. Or whatever their real names were.

She said, 'Odeta? That's Odeta Morina. Albanian woman. Came over, oh, fifteen years ago with her husband. He was murdered ten years ago in his sleep by assailants unknown.'

Storey asked, 'Is the business legitimate?' and heard her laugh at the other end of the line.

'Didn't you do any proper police work when you were down in London? Albanians practically run the cocaine business in the UK. Worse mafia than the Russians, though they're very big on being reliable, good business partners. Cross them, though, and watch out.'

'So is that what she's involved in? Drugs?'

'Not exactly my department but as far as I remember she's never been charged. I'm told the drugs come into London and then the bosses down there distribute via a network all over the UK. I suppose the thinking is that she took over her husband's part of the business when he was killed. Catching them red-handed is the thing, though, isn't it? Or finding a warehouse where they keep the stuff.' She paused. 'Why am I talking to you about drugs? Do you think she or her crew nicked your guitars?'

'Let's just say I'm of a suspicious nature. I'll keep digging.'

'I'm not having this conversation. But if you turn up face down in the Coventry Canal I'll never forgive you.'

'I'll try not to complain.'

———

HE DROVE AWAY slowly, trying to make the connections. Perhaps he was being too suspicious—perhaps the thieves had taken the guitars to Odeta and simply exchanged them for money. Maybe Odeta and Diamant were keeping them in storage for the grace period and didn't know their real value. Or, the Albanians were the actual thieves and had already got rid of them: why would they keep them if they knew their value?

But what about Geneva Chance's song? Was that still with the thieves? Did they know what they had? Or was it part of the deal with the guitars and was now in a collector's collection—a raw version of a rare song by the girl in the group who didn't write songs?

Then the question would be, who knew she'd even written it, never mind recorded it?

CHAPTER FIFTEEN

HE DROVE STRAIGHT to the Chance house, using his sunvisor unit to open the gates and park, as usual, to one side of the gravel in front of the double garage. He climbed out and stood for a moment looking at the large house, the tended lawns, the trees behind the house that seemed to open up almost to parkland beyond. There was no doubt, the Chance family had done well.

But still it was strange they all lived together. They were all grown men and women so you'd expect them to have developed separate lives, separate interests, families. But as far as he'd seen so far they hung out together, didn't have girlfriends, didn't have the usual roster of hangers-on, or a posse of deadbeats happy to bask in their fame and the delights that money could buy.

In fact they seemed insular, sad and unhappy with their lives.

Like you're some beacon of happiness, he told himself.

BILL CHANCE OPENED the door, smiling broadly when he saw Storey and standing back to let him in.

'It's the sleuth,' he said. 'Is that a word real people use, or just something I see in books? Come in, come in. I was just cleaning the kitchen. Can I get you a drink?'

Storey stepped inside. 'I wanted to talk to the boys. Any of them. Are they around?'

Chance's large, square head tilted as he mimed 'thinking'. 'I don't think Johnny's around and I haven't seen Adam. Genny's around somewhere. Here, follow me through.'

Storey let himself be taken through to the kitchen again, where Chance filled the kettle and set it going. He leaned back against the counter and folded his arms.

He said, 'I've done some reading about you. Larry Lamb said something and I looked it up. You're a bit of a hero, it seems. Are you married? How does your wife feel about all this?'

'No, not married.'

'So what do your mum and dad think? They must be proud.'

'I should go look for the boys.'

'Oh, wait, did I say a bad thing? Are your parents still alive? You're still young, so surely ...'

Storey hated talking about his family but felt if he didn't say something Chance would keep going into deeper and deeper unpalatable waters. He said, 'My mother died when I was twelve. My dad a few months ago.'

'Sorry to hear that,' Bill Chance said. 'And you were in London, weren't you, involved in some nasty business. You shot someone.'

'It was my job.'

Chance looked as though he was going to say something more but stopped himself at the last minute.

The kettle boiled and he made Storey an instant coffee without asking and then handed it over.

Storey sat on a stool at the breakfast bar, shiny and black and seeming as hard and angular as a slab of marble. He wondered why Bill Chance was immediately friendly and gossipy, wondering whether he was like some kind of pet that was kept indoors and rarely saw the outside world except when it came into the house. That would make you curious about people.

He said, 'When did you know the kids had talent? That they might be good enough to make a go of music?'

'It was Johnny,' Chance said. 'Adam was learning guitar, a couple of years older, and Johnny picked up one of his cast-offs and taught himself how to play. Then he started writing songs when he was eleven or twelve. So then the pair of them started doing duets at weddings and so on and suddenly Tim wanted to play, too. But he was too idle to learn the guitar so I bought him a second-hand drum kit and he thrashed the hell out of that.'

'Then Geneva came along.'

Chance grinned. 'The boys didn't want her to join in at first, but when they heard how she could sing all different kinds of song, and she was always on the note, they started letting her sing with them. She was about fifteen, I suppose.'

'Did they get it from you, the talent?'

He laughed. 'Not a bit, nor their mum, God rest her soul.'

'I understand she died young.'

'Younger than she should have done. Like yours, by the sound of it. If I'm honest I blame myself—having the four kids wore her out, and I wasn't at home as much as I should have been. She got a cancer and was too tired to fight it.'

His gaze had turned inward and his voice had gone quiet and Storey thought he was seeing something real in him for almost the first time.

He said, 'Were the kids good kids?'

'What do you mean?'

'No drugs, stuff like that?'

Chance stiffened. 'I never saw anything. I brought my kids up right. That's not to say they weren't all around us, the drugs. I saw a lot of people out of their heads, doing stupid stuff. But I must've got something right with them, they didn't go off the rails that way.'

'They were young, though—they must have been tempted. A lot of money, fame and fortune. Girls throwing themselves at the boys and so on.'

Chance raised his head and the smile reappeared. 'Okay, so Johnny was a bit wild at first, but when he realised how good he was he became really focused. He turned the wildness into a kind of perfectionism. You should see him in the studio.'

'I have. He seemed angry most of the time.'

'Ha! That's true. Nothing is ever good enough, right enough. We all fail Johnny every day.'

He fell silent and Storey saw a shadow in the older man's eyes. That was interesting, but he didn't want Chance to become maudlin. He said, 'How is he managing without his guitars?'

The question seemed to surprise Chance. 'I never even thought about it. There's loads of guitars around the place. It's the one thing Johnny was interested in, once he could afford it. He'll be irritated they're gone but he's got lots of others to play.'

'Are they all as valuable as those two?'

Chance shrugged. 'I stopped worrying about how much things cost twenty years ago, when the bank manager had a word with me and suggested we might like to start thinking about putting the money in some kind of account offshore. This place is paid for. The kids can buy cars and shiny things whenever they want. Money's not top of the list any more.'

'So what is? Why make another album and go on tour again?'

Chance was moving away from the work surface now, going to a cupboard and opening it and taking out two onions from a vegetable rack. The cupboard door slid closed quietly.

He said, 'I don't know what it's about. Johnny just being restless, I suppose. He tried making a solo album but it didn't work. He needed the other voices and his brothers to tell him when something needed changing. They haven't toured in nearly fifteen years, you know, so I suppose they wanted to see if they could still do it live. Problem is, they're in danger of being a tribute act to themselves, aren't they? Playing the golden oldies.'

'Hence the new album—something to sell. Or just an excuse to go on tour again.'

'Exactly.'

NOW GENEVA WAS coming into the kitchen, drinking from a glass. She saw Storey's glance and raised the glass in salute: 'Water. I know I'm a rock star and all but I don't drink till it's dark.'

'None of my business.'

'Maybe not. But you have a moralistic attitude around you, did you know? Like judge and jury rolled into one.'

'Sorry, maybe it's because I was a policeman for a long time. I can't help myself.'

She moved away. 'Yeah, well.'

She placed the empty glass in the sink and turned to him. 'So what can we do for you today?'

For some reason Storey found it difficult to talk to her with her father in the room. He had the impression she knew it but didn't want to move, so she just stared at him as if it were a dare. Then she said, 'Okay, come out here. I want to show you something.'

He followed her out of the kitchen and through the front door into the late afternoon heat and he realised they were heading for the studio. He saw that the old keypad still hadn't been replaced as she keyed in the code and turned the handle.

'Into the sacred cave of creativity,' she said, and walked them into the recording studio itself, closing the door behind her. Saying, 'Mind the cables. We're not insured for anyone but family. And Pete, I suppose.'

'What did you want to show me?'

She stopped and sat in a chair, looking up at him. There was a dark-wood acoustic guitar leaning against a loudspeaker which she leaned over and picked up, placing it across her lap. She took a capo from the end of the guitar and placed it across the strings.

She said, 'It's not exactly show. It's play.'

She began to strum a sequence of chords. Storey knew nothing about music but he realised she was varying the strumming pattern, picking and strumming some chords while just strumming others. It created an interesting rhythm.

Then she began to sing, her quiet but powerful voice filling the studio. Whenever he was confronted by musicians playing live, Storey always found himself enthralled and fascinated by the technique — how musicians could play their instruments without looking at what they were doing, how they fitted the words in time to the chords, how they played one kind of melody but sang a different one. It was almost like alchemy to him, something he knew he could never understand.

So it took him a while to pick up on the words and by the time he realised what he'd missed, she was playing the last chorus, finishing abruptly with a comical fast flourish, like the ending of a flamenco song.

Geneva said, 'That's it. What do you think?'

'The song that was stolen?' he asked. She nodded. He thought he should add something, so said, 'It's very melancholy.'

She gave a sort of defeated smile, as if his response was expected and typical. He felt as though he'd let her down. She'd probably expected more.

She said, 'What did you think of the lyrics?'

'To be honest I was too busy admiring the singing and playing to listen too closely.'

Now she was shaking her head. 'Yes the girl can play guitar too. That will be the first line of the reviews. Fuck sake, didn't you hear what I was singing about?'

And then Storey got it—there was one word that kept coming up in the lyrics.

She'd been singing about her father.

And she wasn't happy.

———

A VOICE FROM the door cut across them. 'What's going on here, then?'

Storey turned and Tim, the drummer, was walking towards them, Geneva still sitting on the spindly chair but now leaning her guitar against the loudspeaker again.

Tim said, 'What's this, private concert?'

Storey took his first good look at the middle brother, his hair longer than either Adam's or Johnny's, his skin more sallow and his eyes red-rimmed. He had the basic square jawline that all of the siblings had but in him the genetic line had taken a byroad, making him appear weaker than Adam and more dissolute than Johnny. And barely related to Geneva at all.

He came up close to Storey, saying, 'We don't usually allow foreigners in here. I suppose you get a pass because you're working for us but don't make it a habit.'

Geneva said, 'Tim ...'

'No, I get it, you've got a new plaything and you wanted to show off. Just don't embarrass yourself.'

'Don't talk to me like that.'

'Don't get on your high horse. You know I'm right. We're the only ones allowed in here, we don't want anyone ripping off our music, do we?'

Storey said, 'Do you know a shop called Odeta's Swap Shop? Run by an Albanian woman?'

Tim stared at him. 'I don't know any Albanians.'

'Are you certain about that? Because I'm equally sure you know lots of people—how can you be certain one of them isn't Albanian?'

'I'd know, wouldn't I? It would come up in conversation. They'd say, "Did you know I'm from Albania?" Then I'd know. I don't forget details like that. Hey, do you know what the rock star called his four daughters?'

'No.'

'Anna One, Anna Two, Anna Three, Anna Four ...'

'Very good. Are you feeling all right?'

'Why?'

'No reason. Just asking.'

Geneva said, 'Tim, you're acting a bit manic.'

'Well I would be, wouldn't I? I've come in here to practise and found you two in here, in my space. Can you just get the fuck out so I can beat the shit out of my drums?'

'Calm down, we'll go.'

'Good, leave me in peace.'

He walked to his drum kit in the corner and sat down hard on his stool, then looked around for his sticks.

Geneva said to Storey, 'We'd better go. He gets like this sometimes. They say drummers are weird and they're not kidding.'

'All that hitting things can't be good for you.'

'I know you think that's a joke but it's true.'

Storey glanced at her but her face gave nothing away. He led the way out of the studio, into the fading light, and behind them they heard Tim starting to thrash the drum kit loudly and without any discernible rhythm, as if he were getting something out of his system.

CHAPTER SIXTEEN

FOR THE SECOND time that day Storey waited for something to happen.

He sat in his car outside the Chance house, a hundred yards down the street, thinking about what he'd learned so far today.

It came in a jumble ... meeting Odeta Morina and her man Diamant, going into the house Diamant had visited to be confronted by Jim, Jack and John, presumably more Albanians and, from what Jackie had said, probably sellers of Odeta's merchandise; then the odd conversation with Bill Chance, who tried to appear jovial, a family man, but who seemed in fact to have a deep sadness at his core; and then listening to Geneva Chance's song—something to do with her father—and meeting Tim Chance in a highly strung-out frame of mind ... which in turn had made him ask whether Tim knew the Albanians ...

And somewhere in there was the theft of the guitars, which he believed had been set up to appear like a theft but wasn't really.

He told himself he definitely had a gift for getting involved with dysfunctional people. Perhaps it reflected something of his own personality. His friend in London, Millie, had often said he drew to himself the misfits and loners, the people who were interesting because they couldn't find a way to live normal lives. He'd been a cop, a firearms specialist, a pillar of the establishment, licensed to shoot citizens on a given command ... and yet the people he mixed with were outliers, non-conformists, inhabitants of the fringe.

Were they drawn to him, or was it rather that he was drawn to them?

When he thought about it, the split was there in his parents. His mother was sensible, traditional, a little fearful of the opinion of others. While his father was free-wheeling, argumentative, and willing to take a contrary view just to see where the conversation went. As a child Storey had watched the arguments go back and forth between them—his mother wanting to placate and keep her head below the parapet; his father complaining, arguing with local councillors, raising problems even with his employers, until it came to the point where he was no long employable and had to work as a sole contractor, beholden to no one.

Storey felt the same urges in himself: the need to fit in versus the desire to dig deeper and not give up until he discovered the truth.

Don't kid yourself, he thought, staring through his windscreen at the Chance's iron gate. *You're nothing special. You just don't like to lose.*

He knew some people thought differently about him because of what he'd done in the last few months. The maverick crime fighter, he'd been called. Frank Lamb's appreciation of him had suggested that opinion was still current in the city—but wasn't the end result of that regard just him sitting here looking at a brick wall?

He'd once walked Jackie West back to her place after they'd gone into town for a curry. Her street was dark, cars crammed nose to tail like metal sardines along the pavement, loud rap music coming from an open window and the sound of running feet somewhere ahead of them. He felt like he should hold on to her, but didn't. She'd looked at him sideways and said, 'What are you doing, Storey? You're living in your dad's old house. You haven't got a job and you don't seem bothered about getting one. God knows how you're living day to day. Where are you going?'

He'd fobbed her off with platitudes about considering his future and letting things settle down ... but he still thought about her question every now and then and still couldn't come up with a decent answer.

It saddened him he couldn't think more positively about himself and understand why people seemed to care. But no one knew what went on inside another person, did they?

IT WAS PAST eleven o'clock when the gate opened and a car he hadn't seen before drove out. It wasn't one of the BMWs but a white Mercedes, driven by Tim Chance. Storey realised it must have been parked in the garage when he'd visited the house.

The Mercedes headed towards the centre of town and Storey gave it a head start and then followed.

———

IN TOWN, THEY drove past the big blue box of IKEA and shortly after took a couple of quick turns before Tim pulled up outside what appeared to be a night club, judging by the two bulky men in matching black suits standing outside the door. Tim waited a moment then drove further and pulled on to the pavement, two wheels on and two wheels off.

He got out of the car and stood leaning against the door, smoking. Storey had pulled up behind a van, hidden from view. The night was still warm and Storey let down his driver's-side window. Immediately he could hear the music coming from the club: a beat-heavy drone that was nothing like the kind of music that the Chance family produced. The sign over the door read: 'Odeta's Night Club'.

Having seen one of the bouncers go inside the club, Storey guessed what was coming and after a couple of minutes the bouncer re-emerged with another man: Jim, the Albanian Storey thought was in charge when he'd followed Diamant to the house earlier in the day.

Jim crossed the road and shook Tim's hand, then they both climbed inside Tim's Mercedes. Storey thought it would be a quick transaction but it went on for almost fifteen minutes.

And then Diamant arrived, his Jaguar easing to a halt in front of the club.

Diamant climbed out of the driver's seat and at the same time Jim got out of the Mercedes. Before Tim could drive away, Diamant had opened the passenger door and taken Jim's place. Storey wished he was closer to hear what was going on but there was no way of approaching the car without being seen.

Whatever was being said, he didn't think it was good news for Tim Chance.

CHAPTER SEVENTEEN

ALTHOUGH HE WAS happy to be a supplier to their needs, the habits of drug users disgusted Diamant Dushku. They were people who had no discipline, no belief in themselves and no sense of where they wanted to be in life. They sacrificed their dignity for a moment's pleasure. How Western.

But their addiction was something he could use to his advantage. Like now, for example, when the man Tim Chance just wanted to drive away, to go home with his little package and satisfy his desire. That urgency made him vulnerable.

Diamant took in the man's dirty tee-shirt, the stained blue jeans, his unshaven face ... this was a man, clearly, with nothing left to live for. He would be easy to manipulate.

Diamant said, 'You know who I am?'

The man tried to be brave. 'I do and I don't care. Get out of my fucking car.'

'I understand. You want to go home and put that product in your nose. But I have some questions I would like to ask you first.'

'Questions? What que—' He looked down to where Diamant had clamped his large hand over his thigh, and was squeezing. 'Ow! What the fuck do you think you're doing?'

'Be quiet and listen to me, then answer my questions. Do you understand?'

Diamant saw Tim Chance's eyes withdraw and become fearful. Good. This was the correct attitude.

He said, 'Some items have come into my possession. They are items I believe belonged firstly to your family. Do you know what I mean?'

'How the hell can I know what you mean? What sort of items?'

Diamant relaxed his grip. 'Musical items. Instruments. Now do you know what I mean?'

Over the years he'd become expert at reading body language and now he saw Tim Chance's body shift, saw him take a quick breath and then lick his lips. His next words would be a lie.

Tim said, 'No, I don't know what you mean. What kind of instruments? And what makes you think they're ours?'

'One has the signature of the musician Eric Clapton on the back. It is an electric guitar. The other is worth a very great deal of money. Are you beginning to remember?'

So now Tim Chance had to change his attitude. He would not deny the truth, but neither would he admit it. To admit it would be to open a door he knew would take him into a dangerous place.

He said, 'What do you want?'

Perfect. They could now have a conversation.

Diamant said, 'We would like to have a discussion with you about what this means for us.'

'Who the hell is "us"? What kind of accent is it you people have, anyway?'

'I am from Albania, a small country a long way from here.'

'So Mr Albanian, I don't know what you think you're talking about but this business with the guitars is a big mistake.'

'I do not think so. They have come out of your possession and into my possession. Because of their value I'm sure you would like to have them returned. That is a possibility, but there is a lot to discuss before we arrive at that point.'

Diamant saw the man's eyes grow confused. His desire for his drug was beginning to overwhelm his ability to think coherently. Diamant had seen this before. He said, 'I will give you a period of time to think about this and talk to your family. I'm sure we can come to an arrangement that is satisfying to both of us.'

'Jesus Christ, you like talking in riddles, don't you? Just get the fuck out of my car.'

Diamant pressed down the door handle and pushed the door of the Mercedes open a little. It was a nice car, nicer than his own Jaguar. He said, 'You will notice that your package is a little heavier tonight than usual. It's my reward to you for this conversation. You see, this relationship can be good for both of us. Talk to your family and I will be in touch soon.'

He climbed out of the car and closed the door carefully. He thought Tim Chance would be watching him so he adopted a powerful walk as he went back towards the club, but then he heard Chance's car start up and drive away. Never mind. As he passed beneath it, he glanced up at the sign reading 'Odeta's Night Club' above the door. Perhaps the name of the place would have to change, depending on what happened in the next few days.

CHAPTER EIGHTEEN

AFTER CHANCE'S MERCEDES drove off, Storey hesitated only a moment before opening his car door and following Diamant towards the club. He knew it wasn't a good idea but he was running out of ideas, good or otherwise, and the notion of throwing Diamant off-balance appealed to him.

One of the men at the door thrust out a hand before he got there and he stopped.

He said, 'Tell Diamant Paul Storey's here to see him. I want to talk about guitars.'

The two men looked at each other, then the taller of the two said, 'Who's Diamant?'

'The man who just walked between you as if he owned the place. Don't you know his name?'

The same look passed between them again, then the tall one nodded to the other, who went through the swing doors and into the club.

Storey said to the man who'd stayed, 'What name do you call him?'

'Who?'

'Diamant.'

'I don't know who you're talking about.' Looking away now, as if the conversation was of no further interest to him.

Storey said, 'What about Jim?'

'Who's that?'

'The man who came out and got in the fancy Mercedes that parked over there. I think he was selling him some drugs, what do you think?'

'I think you should repeat that in a court of law and see where it gets you.'

Looking more closely at the man, Storey saw he was younger than he seemed, probably in his early twenties. His skin was smooth and his cheeks red and his broad back pushed out the shoulders of his jacket as if trying to tear it apart.

He said, 'You're not Albanian. What's your name?'

'Fuck off.'

'Well, Mr Off, I think you'd be advised to stay away from these jokers for a while.'

'What do you know about anything?'

'Not a lot. But you're too young to get your shit tied up in knots by this crowd. Go back to college. Work in Starbucks. Anything but this.'

The man had opened his mouth to say something when the doors behind them swung open and Diamant came out, his hands in his pockets, his yellow shirt open to the second button, his hair looking even wilder than it had when Storey met him that morning.

DIAMANT SAID, 'WALK away with me. Not everyone has to hear our business.'

Close up, Storey could sense the strength in the man, his certainty about himself and what he could do. He'd emigrated to the UK from Albania, learned English, was practically running a business … no doubt he deserved to feel confident.

Storey said, 'What's Jim's real name? I have a bet with someone it's not Jim.'

'You want me to say it's Viktor?'

Storey grinned. 'They told you about that, did they? Very interesting bunch of people, those three. They must lead terrible lives in that place. Having to rely on you to bring them sandwiches.'

Diamant frowned, then realised what Storey was talking about and laughed. 'Very good! Yes, I take them sandwiches to eat.'

'Every day? Twice a day? Do you take them so many they have to sell them on?'

'I don't know. How would I know? They're poor refugees from Albania, living off the British government until we can get them good jobs.'

'You and Odeta.'

'We give something back to our community. How can we not?'

'And you give them work here, at the club, where they can take sandwiches to poor people who drive up in Mercedes cars, looking for handouts.'

'This idea is boring now, Mr Storey. Why did you want to talk to me?'

'I wanted to know whether Viktor was inside. Gordon told me I should try here. What do you think, is he inside? Dancing? Having a drink? Buying something special from the bar, perhaps a sandwich or two?'

Now Diamant was shaking his head. 'I think you have the wrong idea about me. You think you can come and try to confuse me and I will say what you want to hear.'

'It must have been tough for you coming here from Albania—a country, by the way, I know nothing about.'

'You should go there. They would like you. Albanians are happy to meet people who tell them what to do.'

'How old were you when you arrived?'

Diamant frowned. 'I had my eighteenth birthday the day after I arrived. I was proud to be a man in a new country. Why do you ask?'

'I think it's a shame you've spent your whole adult life involved with a woman who's led you into a dark place.'

'You know nothing about Odeta and her life. You should not pass judgement.'

'Perhaps not. But I think you're the one passing judgement on her and you don't like what you see.'

They had been walking slowly down the street, the noise of the club fading behind them. Now Diamant stopped and turned to Storey square on, the muscles in his face working hard, as if he was trying not to spit in Storey's eye. 'Odeta and Toni rescued me, brought me from a place where you could trust no one to a country where I drive a Jaguar car and buy clothes whenever I want. You will never understand this because it has been given to you. You have not earned your right to be here, as I have. And as Odeta has.'

'I'm certain you've paid a price for your life here,' Storey said. 'But I don't think you know what it is.'

Diamant stared at him a moment longer, then turned back towards the club. He said, 'You should go to Albania. You can play your games with the police there and see if they laugh like I do. Or whether they throw you in jail because you make fun of them. What do you think? I can arrange a visit, if you would like.'

Storey followed him. 'It's an interesting idea, thanks. Maybe I will. It's been nice talking to you.'

Diamant stopped again and seized him by the arm and Storey winced—the man was strong.

'What is it you really want?' he asked. 'Why do you come here and play these games with me? Is it these guitars you say you're looking for?'

Storey shook his arm free. 'I like you, Diamant. You're very direct. I think you're going to find yourself in trouble one day because of your line of work and I think you're smarter than that. Be careful about the company you keep.'

He turned and walked back to his car, knowing that he hadn't dented the man's confidence and instead had probably made himself a target.

Then Diamant's voice came from behind him, saying, 'Kostas.'

Storey had reached his car and he looked back from the door. Diamant said, 'Jim's name is Kostas. Don't tell him I told you. He doesn't like it when others know who he is.'

Then he walked past the bouncers and into the club.

CHAPTER NINETEEN

BEFORE GOING HOME to his own flat, Diamant called at the shop, using his key and walking up the back stairs to Odeta's apartment. He knocked and she came to the door wearing a black negligee that was almost see-through. She was older than Diamant's taste but there was no denying she was still attractive. She was, he knew, only forty-four years of age and hadn't been with another man since Toni's death.

Perhaps she still had urges.

But how had she known he was coming here? How would she have known to prepare herself for him? Or was this just her usual evening wear in hot weather, and he was anticipating too much … ?

He realised he was confused and that his best tactic was to ignore her sexuality and remind himself he had intelligence to report. Accordingly he tried to ignore her languorous movement as she raised an arm against the door-jamb, pulling her right breast upwards and making it more prominent through the black nightgown. She still wore make-up and her hair was combed and was thick and lustrous. Her smile pulled her lips taut. Her eyes were moist.

He said, 'I have made contact with the Chance family.'

'Good, Diamant,' she said. 'Come in so we can talk about it.'

'It's not necessary.'

'I insist. Don't stand there, come in.'

She moved back into the room, swaying in a way Diamant couldn't ignore or take his eyes from.

She said, 'Drink? It's not too late, is it?'

'No ... no,' he said, and moved to his usual chair, one facing a long table containing several framed photographs of Odeta and Toni in younger days, a pair of wooden writing boxes, a large gold candlestick and her mobile telephone, plugged into the wall to recharge. A large gilt-framed mirror was fixed to the wall above the table, in which he could see the ornate chandelier Odeta had installed in the centre of the ceiling, and which he had to be careful of when he crossed the room because it hung so low.

She handed him his drink and sat facing him, crossing her legs. The negligee slid open and her top leg was revealed.

He looked away. This was a development he didn't want and hadn't expected.

She said, 'How did the meeting go with Chance? Was he still there when you arrived?'

'Yes, Kostas managed to keep him in the car until I arrived.'

'What's he like, this pop-star? Is he as good-looking as you?'

Diamant ignored this, saying, 'He's a drug addict. His eyes are frightened and his hair needs a wash. Little girls would not scream his name any more.'

Odeta nodded, sipping her drink. 'I looked at the group on YouTube. They have some old music films there. The music is empty but they had energy and the girl is very good-looking. She is perhaps the reason they were successful.'

'I told Tim Chance that I would contact him soon. When shall I do it and what shall I say?'

'This was your plan—what are your ideas?'

'My plan was just to make contact.'

'Do you think we should threaten them, promise to tell the world that their drummer is a drug addict? Do you think that is interesting to people these days?'

Diamant started to feel uncomfortable. There was something in her tone he didn't like, as if she were testing him.

He said, 'We could take some photographs of him with the drugs. The newspapers like photographs. The threat of telling the newspapers would increase the value of what we have to sell.'

He watched as Odeta turned her head away. It was as though the idea was distasteful to her, and Diamant suddenly felt stupid and a little weak for having suggested it. It wasn't the kind of thing Toni would have said.

Now Odeta reached down and pulled her negligee over her pale exposed leg. She said, 'When I took over Toni's business I knew there was a lot of resistance from Ari Sallaku in London. Toni had just begun to do well for him and Sallaku was angry that our security was so poor that two Kosovans could break into the house, leave me sleeping and slit his throat. I had to show I was strong enough to take over the organisation and keep providing him with profit. As you know, I went away for six months, leaving you in charge. You thought I was in mourning for my husband, and it's true I cried for a day afterwards. But the real reason I went away was to learn how to manage this system we have here. How to manage people. How to do the accounts. How to live a double life.'

'I didn't know that.'

'Of course you didn't. Nor did you know that in that period I brought Maltin Lami over to advise me.'

Diamant felt himself going cold. Lami was an associate of Lulzim Berisha, the biggest and most famous drug dealer in Albania. Lami was a hard man and a counsellor to Berisha. If Odeta had been working with him then Berisha would know all about their operation shortly afterwards.

And Berisha would surely have seen the operation as an opportunity for him to expand abroad … but Toni's murder was ten years ago and Sallaku was still their supplier and still their boss. There had been no contact or threat from Berisha. Diamant talked to Sallaku every month. He would have known if there was a problem, a challenge. Was Berisha just taking his time, waiting for the right moment to seize the supply-line from Sallaku and ruin their whole system?

Odeta saw his discomfort and said, 'Relax. Lami is an old friend of my father's. When he returned home he promised to say nothing to Berisha.'

'And you trusted him?'

'Of course. Have we had any problems from Berisha in ten years? Of course not.'

'But it was a risk. You should have told me.'

'I'm telling you now. And the reason I'm telling you this history is to explain what Lami said to me. He said it's never enough simply to *show* strength. You have to *be* strength. Everything you do, every dealing you have ... the other person must know you are dangerous. He must be afraid of you not because you've threatened him, but because he sees your strength and the danger you bring.'

Diamant realised she was talking again about the Chance family. He said, 'We have no idea how much money the Chance people have and whether it's worth dealing with them.'

Odeta stood up and Diamant knew that the meeting was ending. She said, 'I am a little disappointed in you, Diamant. I had hoped you would be able to bring this problem to a close.'

'It's only a question of time—'

'No, Lami also taught me you don't give the enemy time. They can use that time to make plans, to prepare themselves for you. To find ways around the offer you make.'

'I don't understand what you're going to say to them. If you're not going to blackmail them for money, as you suggest, what can they possibly do to make it worth your while to be involved with them?'

'This will be a little test for you, to work out what options I have and how best I can take advantage of the situation.'

'The man Storey was at the club tonight. I think he followed Tim Chance.'

'What did he want?'

'I think he's trying to scare me. He talks in riddles, trying to prove he knows more than he does.'

'And are you scared of him?'

Diamant laughed briefly. 'Of course not. You remember where we are from, what we have seen? What can this man do to scare us or stop us doing what we must?'

'I like your confidence. Toni liked it too. He said that was the quality in you he most admired, more than any bravery or cunning you showed.'

'Thank you.'

She took another sip of her drink to show she was going to change the subject, then she said, 'How is the project going? Is the house in Ryton ready yet?'

'Nearly. Kostas and his brothers are now going there four times a week. They drink in the pub. They buy drinks for other people. They've made some contacts. They must put in more furniture and then they can live there and we can begin. We have the telephone line already.'

'Good. You have told me that Sallaku is getting impatient. This is the first time he has used this system so it must operate well.'

Diamant agreed. The system of using boys from London to transport drugs to a house in the country was risky, but it was the system all the successful gangs were using now. They must make it work.

As if she were reading his mind, Odeta said, 'We will make it work, Diamant. Now tell me about these Chance people again. Will we succeed with them? Is our position strong enough?'

'They are musicians. They will crumple at the first sign of danger.'

'I hope you are right. Because I am going to ignore Maltin Lami's advice this one time. I am not going to demonstrate how dangerous I can be. I am not going to threaten them. I am going to be polite. I am going to be a businesswoman. I am going to make them an offer to do business. And they will know they cannot refuse.'

CHAPTER TWENTY

Tim, Tempo, Tim, Tempo, Tim, Tempo, ... who was he? What was he? Tim, Tempo. Man or drummerman? The question rattled around in his brain, back and forth, as he parked his car and trudged towards the house, seeing nothing.

Everything was such hard work these days.

Walking.

Eating.

Getting up in the morning and putting on his clothes.

His life was shit and he knew who to blame. Oh yes, *he* was going to get *his* any day now. When they were ready.

Soon.

He opened the front door and went upstairs to his room. In his bathroom he undid the package the man had given him and did what he had to do from the marble counter next to the bowl, taking the hit, throwing his head back as it went in, taking the dregs with a wet finger and running it over his gums ...

Tim, Tempo.

One of the Chance brothers, or just a man who played drums.

Not both.

———

A KNOCK ON the door and there was Johnny, staring at him with that pissed off and angry look, the one he used for everyone and everything these days.

Then they were sitting next to each other on the bed and fifteen minutes had passed. He remembered them passing while at the same time *not* remembering what was said.

All he knew was his brother was angry.

No change there. A fact of life.

A voice, his voice, said, 'I met a man who's got the guitars. Weird foreigner.'

Then tuning out … and tuning in again, hearing his brother saying, '… you tell him?'

'I didn't tell him.'

'I know you didn't tell him about the guitars. I asked you what you told him when he said he had them.'

'I didn't tell him about the guitars. You've got to listen to me: I didn't tell him about the guitars. He's got them. He told *me*. We've got to talk to him, tell him not to say anything, he can't let anyone know …'

He felt his brother's hand on his knee and looked down at it. There was something comforting about it being there. He felt himself starting to rev up, to see things more clearly, to see the plans behind the plans that people were working towards …

Now Johnny was asking about the man, where he came from, who he was. Tim, Tempo didn't know. He heard himself saying, 'I don't know. Outside a club. He's Albanian.'

'Jesus, you must be tired,' Johnny said. 'You're not usually this slow. That stuff is turning you inside out, Tempo. It's fucking you up.'

'I'm fucked up.'

'You got that right. Don't worry, we'll sort it out.'

Tim, Tempo felt his eyes welling up. 'I don't like what we're doing. It's not fair.'

'We talked about this, didn't we? It's fair. We worked together on the plan, didn't we? We thought it through and talked about it, remember?'

Now feeling angry, knowing Johnny was talking down to him, saying, 'Don't take me for granted. I'm high but I'm not stupid. I know what's going on.'

'Good. Tell me more about this Albanian. Who is he?'

'A man, a big man connected to the club.'

'What club's that?'

'A night club. Some woman's name.'

'Is it where you've been getting your stuff?'

'What if it is?'

'No problem. I just need to check it out. Find out more about this man, the Albanian.'

'I'm tired.'

'I thought you were. I said so, didn't I? You need to rest. When it's all over we can put it all behind us and you can get back to playing that kit. Making music. It's what we do best, isn't it?'

'The Albanian threatened me. Us.'

'Did he now? What did he say?'

'It's about the guitars.'

'I know, you told me. What about the guitars?'

'You're confusing me,' Tim, Tempo said, and heard the anger in his voice. Don't let him get to you. 'He's got them. He's going to have a conversation with us about them.'

Now Johnny stood up and walked back and forth between the two-seater sofa and his brother's bed, causing a large shadow to dance around the room. Tim, Tempo suddenly saw it all clearly, what the man had been saying and what he'd been implying. It was so clear, he wondered why he hadn't seen it before. He said, 'He's trying to frighten us. He's sending a message through me while hoping we'll be worried about what he knows. He's setting us up to be afraid when he turns up again.'

Johnny stopped pacing, said, 'Are you afraid?'

'No, why should I be? I haven't done anything wrong.'

'Yet.'

'I haven't done anything wrong and you can't tell me I have. Can you see what's wrong with this picture? There's no black and white. But we're as white as you can get. There'll be no discussion, no anger afterwards. Rules are rules and if you don't stick to them you deserve to be punished, one way or the other.' Then he remembered something else. He said, 'Geneva was talking to that man.'

'What man?'

'The one Larry brought in, to look for the guitars.'

'Where?'

'In the studio. They were talking.'

'What about?'

'I don't know … they stopped when I came in. I don't like him, that man. I don't like the way he looks at me. As if he knows better than me. I want to kill him.' Now he felt himself falling backwards on the bed, staring up at the smooth ceiling and then talking up at it. 'Two and two is four, an eye for an eye, two halves don't make a right.'

He knew Johnny was looking down at him now, probably wearing that same fuck-you face he always did.

Johnny said, 'Now you're getting it. It's all crazy. The whole world. Things don't add up, not even two and two.' He paused, then added, 'Never mind Storey. There's nothing he can do. And forget your Albanian. He's lying to you, there's no way he's got the guitars. He's playing you. Anyway, I've told my man to get them back.'

This was new information and he sat up. 'What do you mean "back"?'

'Nothing, forget it.'

'Did your man lose them?'

'Not really, don't worry about it. He knows what he's got to do if he wants to see any money.'

'It'll be all right, won't it?'

'Of course it will.' There was an uncertainty in Johnny's voice, though, and he heard it himself because he added, 'If anything goes wrong he knows what will happen. It's my own fault for getting someone else involved. You should always take care of things yourself, shouldn't you, rather than leave it to people you don't know.'

Tim, Tempo felt himself laughing—he knew Johnny would hate that, losing control. Giving power to someone else.

Johnny said, 'There's no need to tell anyone else about this, is there?'

'You mean Adam ... just say it. You don't have to treat me like a child. There's nothing to say, nothing to tell.'

'That's what I thought. Glad you've got the right idea.'

THERE WAS A knock on the door and Adam Chance opened it, remaining in the doorway and looking from one of his brothers to the other and back again. He wore a tee-shirt that showed off his muscular frame and he was wiping his hands on a towel.

He said, 'I heard voices. What's going on?'

Johnny said, 'Nothing. Stuff.'

Tim, Tempo watched his brothers as if he didn't know who they were. Did they know who *he* was? Which one was he, the man or the drummerman? Did they care?

He said, 'Geneva's been talking to that man.'

'What man, Storey? Forget him. He's a lightweight.'

'They were in the studio, talking. I heard her singing, too.'

'Singing what?' Johnny asked.

'I didn't recognise it. Not one of ours.'

Then he lost interest in the conversation. He stood up and walked past Adam and went downstairs. He could feel himself firing up now and knew he'd have to listen to something loud or go to the studio and play his drums, get the aggression and the tension out of his system. He opened the back door and stood in the warm air, breathing deeply.

It was coming soon, he could feel it.

What they'd been working towards was going to happen.

CHAPTER TWENTY-ONE

STOREY WATCHED THE breakfast news but he wasn't listening. He was still going over what he'd seen and heard the night before. Tim Chance meeting with an Albanian outside a night club and probably buying drugs, probably cocaine. Then his own conversation with Diamant in which he learned nothing except that the Albanian was canny enough not to give anything away.

Were the guitars important any more? Or was there something more serious going on? Drugs were serious, but closing down the drug trade in Coventry wasn't in his remit, and Jackie West would have every right to be pissed off at him if he got involved in trying to do it.

Which was going to make his conversation with her later on very interesting.

———

SHE MET HIM in a café near the central police station where they'd met before. She stood at the counter and waited for her latte to be made while looking around at the tables and the clientele. She was out of uniform and Storey thought most people who looked at her would think she was something in management … which in a way she was.

She carried her mug to his table and sat facing him. 'You certainly know how to treat a girl right. I'm just sorry I'm not wearing my tiara.'

'I don't think anyone would notice.' Storey was watching her closely, trying to gauge her mood, how much he could say.

She said, 'You mentioned drugs and Albanians and night clubs. Am I to arrange these words into a well-known saying? Or can you lay things out for me more clearly?'

'Come on, Jackie,' he said. 'Don't pretend to be an idiot. We've already talked about this and you know the connections better than I do.'

'Don't presume too much. Just because you prevented me being shot in the head doesn't give you a free pass forever.'

'I know that,' he said. 'I'm treating you as a professional, not a victim. I know full well I'm outside the law here, but you can at least meet me half way.'

She stirred a stick of sugar into her coffee and placed the wet spoon carefully on the table.

'All right. But you still haven't given me anything new. I've already told you what we suspect about the Albanians and drug trafficking. It's more than a suspicion, actually. But we can't take anything further until we have concrete evidence, which we've yet to find. The Albanians are tougher than the Italian and Russian Mafia combined. No one speaks. If they do they wake up looking at their head from the other side of the pillow.'

'So what *do* you have, if anything?'

'No, you tell me what you have first. Citizen Storey, doing his public duty, fighting crime.'

Storey looked away, exasperated. His father had told him sometimes you can't do right for doing wrong ... the bad deeds you do can cancel out the good ones so you begin to wonder whether it's worthwhile doing anything positive at all.

And now here he was, having been asked to do one thing—find a pair of missing guitars—and winding up in the midst of something else. The problem was, he didn't know what the something else was.

———

HE TOLD HER about following Tim Chance from his home to Odeta's Night Club, the same Odeta who owned the exchange shop off the Foleshill Road. Once at the club he'd seen Chance talking to two Albanians, one after the other, and then he himself had talked to the second man, called Diamant, who ran the exchange shop with Odeta Morina.

'Did you hear what was said between Chance and the Albanians?'

'No.'

'Diamant didn't tell you? Did you ask politely?'

'Not in so many words. He wanted to impress me with just how much he wasn't bothered by my questions or the fact I knew he was selling drugs.'

'How brazen they are,' Jackie said. 'Welcome to my world. Do you remember the good old days, when criminals were a bit more circumspect about getting caught?'

'Dinosaurs roamed the earth.'

'So before you ask the question, I asked around at the station and we haven't got anyone lined up on drug charges yet because … well, because. As I said before, lack of bloody evidence. Or at least enough to go on. We've put people in that club to scout around but all they've seen is a few individuals selling pills, low level stuff, nothing we could nail the club itself for. So I'm told. But there's a suspicion the Albanians might be setting up a county line. Everyone else is doing it, so why not them? They're just laying low at the moment.'

Storey knew county line networks, named after the single telephone line used as a contact point, often used children or young women as mules to transport drugs from a central point around the country. The telephone line would be the single point of contact for people trying to buy the drugs, which would then be delivered or collected elsewhere. As a result of the way they were set up, both drug- and people-trafficking crimes were involved.

He said, 'I read there's a big push to try to close them down.'

Jackie West said, 'If you could get anything for us it would be appreciated.'

'I thought you were going to read me the riot act for putting my nose in where it's not needed.'

She smiled wanly. 'Citizen activism. So long as you don't get your head blown off, have at it. Given your record you're getting a bit of slack.'

'Just don't start using a bat signal on low-lying clouds. I can't guarantee to see it.'

He liked the fact she was comfortable talking to him again. There'd been a time when it had been tense but she seemed more relaxed. He had a sudden realization. He said, 'Are you seeing someone, then?'

'Whoa, shift of direction there. What brought that on?'

'Man's intuition, a rarely used skill but I'm attuned to its nuances. I notice you didn't deny it.'

'I don't have to deny anything. You don't have any right to make any accusations.'

'Call it a friendly inquiry.'

She took a sip from her drink and he noticed she'd coloured slightly. She said, 'Just a couple of weeks. No one you know. Not even a copper.'

'Well good for you.'

She mumbled a thanks and he saw she wanted to move the conversation on, take the focus off her and back on to work. He'd always liked her professionalism though he recognised it might have been one of the factors that had come between them. Now he was no longer in the force, its rules, regulations and urgencies meant less to him but she was still constrained by them.

She said, 'Do you think there's a connection between these missing guitars and the Albanians? Or is Tim Chance just a drug-hound and it's a coincidence?'

'I don't know. I'm pretty sure the guitars weren't stolen by opportunistic thieves. The robbery was too easy and everyone's very casual about the potential loss of several thousand pounds' worth of instruments.'

'Everyone?'

'I think they all take their cue from the youngest brother, Johnny. If he's not overly worried they're not going to get distressed about it either. There's so much money sloshing around a minor theft doesn't seem to bother them.'

'They all live together in the one house? That's weird.'

'With dad in a separate cottage in the grounds. I suppose they look after each other. It's a bit like a strange cult.'

'Could the theft be an insurance scam?'

'They don't need the money, as far as I can tell.'

'You don't sound certain. You know as well as I do that most crime is about money or passion. I don't believe they can be passionate about a couple of guitars, especially if you say they're not worried about their loss. But maybe there are other money problems.'

Storey thought about this for a while and realised he only had the Chances' word for the fact they were still well-off. The expensive cars could have been bought a while ago, or be rentals. The house was paid for. They were gearing up for another tour and to release a new album after fifteen years ... perhaps money was in the mix somewhere after all.

He said, 'I'll have a word with Frank Lamb, the manager. He told me they didn't even want to report the guitars as missing. Which is odd if it's to scam their insurance company with a false claim. But he's the grown-up and he knew they couldn't process an insurance claim anyway without a case number, so he goes to the cop-shop to report the theft. Then at the last minute he meets me and changes his mind and asks me to help, perhaps because he's aware they wanted to keep it quiet, keep the press and police out of it while they're preparing for their tour.'

'Sounds like you're talking yourself out of it being an insurance scam.'

'Maybe there's something else ... if they didn't want the theft reported, maybe one of the brothers has sold them for quick cash. Perhaps it was Tim, getting hold of money to pay for his supply. Or to pay off a debt. Then again, if the guitars were owned by the business, as equipment on the books, then they couldn't be sold officially without tax being paid on the sale because they're an asset with value to the company—the band. So the Inland Revenue might find out they'd been sold and, I don't know, maybe the band's in danger of committing fraud or something … I'm getting over my head here. What do you think?'

'I think you should talk to this Frank Lamb character and see what he knows. If he's their manager he should know what's coming in, what's going out, and where the money is kept. That's his job, isn't it?'

'I had the impression his job was mostly to keep them happy. Not that it seemed to be working. They're a pretty serious bunch.'

'I'm sure you lighten their world.'

'Is there anything you can do, to help?'

'There might be, but I'm certainly not going to go all in if they don't even want to report a theft. We don't have the manpower to just sniff around in case there's something more serious going on. I know you saved my life and all, but I'm beginning to think you've had your money's worth out of that little adventure.'

'Ingratitude isn't an attractive quality.'

'Nor is using friendship to manipulate a police officer.'

———

FRANK LAMB SAID he could meet him at lunchtime and at five minutes to twelve Storey walked into the bar of the Jacobean Hotel, just off the Holyhead Road. He remembered it as the Brooklands Grange Hotel years ago, but it looked as if it had been refurbished and sent upmarket.

Lamb was waiting for him. 'Let's sit outside,' he said, and led him through the narrow dining room on to a wooden balcony overlooking a patch of lawn with trees beyond. He already had a pint of beer and asked whether Storey wanted anything. Storey said no. Lamb said, 'You don't mind the sun, do you? I spend so much time arguing with people in boardrooms it's nice to get outside.'

Storey said he didn't mind, and after a couple of pleasantries asked whether Lamb had ever seen the Chance brothers getting involved with drugs.

'Wow, you get right into it, don't you?' Lamb said. 'Thing is, first you'd have to define "involved". I'm sure they all had a taste when they were younger. You couldn't escape it, even in the dressing-rooms at Top of the Pops. You know how it is for kids with money and no self-control.'

'I can imagine. Was there anything more serious than just "experimenting"? That's what they always call it, don't they? Like experimenting with electricity or arsenic might be a good thing.' Storey watching Lamb closely now, ready for a prepared PR answer.

Lamb didn't answer straight away but returned Storey's gaze, took a sip of his drink, placed it carefully on a beer mat. Then he looked over the lawn.

'I'll pass over the fact that drugs would appear to have nothing to do with the guitars being stolen, which is your remit as I recall. Thing is, you wouldn't be asking me that question if you didn't already know something. What have you seen?'

Storey told him about following Tim Chance to a meeting with a probable drug supplier, then mentioned the connection between the night club and Odeta Morina's cash exchange store.

Lamb was shaking his head before Storey finished. 'Tim, Tim ... Jesus Christ, we went over this dozens of times.'

'It's not news, then?'

'I've lost count of the programs he's been in. He kicks it for a few months then he's back in there. Poor lad. Thing is, I think he's bored. He's not as musical as his brothers or Geneva so he doesn't write songs, doesn't have any friends in the business. Or out of it. So he spends a lot of time in his own head. It's the main reason they stopped touring so quickly all those years ago—they couldn't keep him straight. Wherever they went he found a supplier in five minutes flat and they spent the rest of the time before the gig trying to calm him down.'

'The family seem to pull together. You'd think living in the same house would drive them all nuts, being family.'

'Oh, yes, they look after each other. I've always thought it was because they started out so young, they only really had themselves to depend on. And of course their mum had died when they were all young, which didn't help.'

'Did you know her?'

Lamb glanced at him. 'A little. I met her a couple of times. Scottish girl, very pale skin. Had a nice laugh.' He finished his beer. 'Look, I've got to go. I'm on a plane this afternoon to L.A. You wouldn't believe it, but since the band announced a new tour we've had interest from all over the world. They were just going to do the UK but the

Yanks are interested, and Japan and Australia. Even had a tickle from China.'

'How long will you be gone?'

'Maybe a week. The boys have got my numbers and email if you need me.'

'Let me ask you this: do you think the guitars were really stolen?'

Lamb had half-risen from his seat. Now he sat down again.

'Why wouldn't I? That's what they told me. We looked all around the house to see if they'd been misplaced. Though I suppose that really doesn't mean anything. Thing is, if they wanted to deceive me for some reason they could have put them anywhere.'

Storey said, 'I told you on the first day I thought it was a set-up, not a real burglary. You didn't seem surprised.'

Lamb smiled. 'When you've seen the shit I've seen over the last twenty years, nothing surprises you.' He paused. 'We were in Kansas once, doing a big arena and using local people to do some of the humping, you know, local knowledge and everything. We turned up at the hotel before the gig and Adam says to this big biker-looking guy, Hey, could you get us some ice? The guy goes off and we go to our rooms. Ten minutes later the guy knocks on Adam's door and pushes it open and he's carrying one of those bloody ice-machines in his arms, wide as a fridge, he's got a big grin on his face, he drops it on the floor, says, Your wish is my command, then buggers off.'

'You should write a book.'

'Don't think I haven't thought about it.'

'Do the family need money? Might one of them have flogged the guitars for a bit of cash on the side?'

'You wouldn't believe the money that comes in,' Lamb said. 'You remember those reports all those years ago, when Elton John was burning through a quarter of a million each month? That's the kind of money we were talking about at their height. Five albums in four years, when album sales still meant something, before all this Spotify crap. Then the tours, the merchandise, all the Best Ofs and the re-released singles … even split four ways they don't have to work again.'

'Johnny could have kept the money for himself, as the writer.'

'He could have done. But he's loyal to the family, give him that. He made it so it was a four-way split, like Coldplay. And unlike Jagger and Richards, the selfish bastards.'

Storey wondered again whether he was wasting his time. How important were a couple of guitars in the great scheme of things? What would happen if he didn't find them? Nothing. What would happen if he did? He'd earn a couple of thousand pounds. Surely he could find something more useful to do with his time …

But then he remembered Geneva Chance. She seemed terrified that the song she'd written would get out and people would hear it. He didn't think it was fear of criticism of the song itself, as a piece of music — some critics had never been kind to the band's work. There was something more fundamental in the way she talked about it.

He said to Lamb, who had stood up to leave again, 'Do you think I'm ever going to find these guitars? Nobody seems to care whether I find them or not.'

Lamb shrugged. 'I'm not going to tell you your job, but maybe you need to understand how they think. I'm willing to consider the idea that the guitars weren't stolen—for whatever reason—and they were just having a laugh at our expense ... but really, why would they? Who benefits?'

———

AFTER LAMB HAD gone, Storey asked for a Perrier water and stayed at the table, enjoying the warmth and listening to the clatter of cutlery from inside the dining room.

He felt himself beginning to relax when his phone rang.

'Mr Storey? Bill Chance. Can you come here, please? I need to show you something.'

Storey agreed and broke the connection. Chance's voice had lost its usual confidence. He sounded worried.

So what now?

CHAPTER TWENTY-TWO

BILL CHANCE WAS waiting for him inside the gate. He was wearing khaki shorts and a multi-coloured short-sleeved shirt, as if he'd taken a break from a Caribbean holiday.

He looked grim and shook Storey's hand briskly, as though wanting to get the pleasantries over with as quickly as possible.

'Good of you to come, good of you to come,' he said, his bright blue eyes staring anxiously into Storey's.

'What's happened?'

'Best if I show you. Come this way.'

He led Storey through to the large lawn at the back of the house, edged with borders containing roses and other plants whose names Storey didn't know. It was eerily quiet, the traffic distant, the only sounds being birds and the occasional bee weaving a passage home.

Storey saw it before they arrived: on the side of the small cottage he assumed was Bill Chance's home, beneath a small side window, someone had daubed 'Go home, scum' in a vibrant red paint. Storey approached the wall and touched the paint—dry. Chance was standing back, looking on anxiously. Storey said, 'Do you know when it was done?'

'Some time over night. I didn't hear a thing. I sleep the sleep of angels, nothing disturbs me. Then early this morning Johnny was knocking on the door, asking what I'd done. Me! As if I was responsible.'

Storey looked more closely at the cottage and its surroundings: it was a small property constructed from weathered red brick, with a tiled roof and an oak lintel over the window and was probably Victorian. Perhaps it was built for a live-in gardener or groundsman, someone older, a widower, without abundant needs. Someone just like Bill Chance, a hundred and fifty years ago.

There was a ramshackle chimney poking out of the roof and, when he walked around the corner, he noticed a wood store filled to the top with freshly-cut logs. As for the cottage, it looked as though there was only space for one room downstairs and one up, though there was probably a bathroom upstairs as well. He'd seen cupboards that were bigger.

Lamb had told him Johnny and Geneva had built the main house, which was undeniably modern, but there must have been something on the plot before, something grand enough to include this cottage in its garden.

And now it was somewhere for Bill Chance to sit and watch television and sleep. He cooked and ate in the main house, with his children, then came back here for privacy. It was tiny but perhaps Bill was happy with the lack of responsibility and the simplicity.

He turned to Chance and said, 'You had anything like this before? Vandalism, that kind of thing?'

'No, nothing. I'm flummoxed.'

'Have you done anything to provoke it? Arguments with people? Rubbed anyone up the wrong way?'

Chance threw up his hands. 'Ever since the kids got famous there've been nutters—you know, people who write to you or send you stuff. But I don't respond now. I just chuck it away. We used to have a secretary who'd look after things but when the band stopped making new music it died down a bit and we got rid of her. We don't get much of anything these days. I send back form letters or emails when we do.'

Storey was still looking around the building. Where the walls touched the ground a row of paving slabs had been laid, perhaps as a way of preventing nature encroaching too closely. The far side of the cottage pushed into a copse of trees. A window in the back wall, on the first floor, presumably gave a view of the big house. A couple of terracotta pots containing geraniums stood on the paving slabs, softening their hard lines. Anyone coming close enough to paint on the wall next to the window would be standing on the slabs and not on earth or grass, so there were no footprints or strands of material hooked on brambles or rose bushes.

That would have made things too easy.

A VOICE BEHIND him said, 'So what do you think, Mr Ex-Policeman? Is it unemployed layabouts, pissed off by the fact we've got money and they haven't? Or annoyed gardeners, upset we won't give them any work because we've already got an Italian gardener who's taken their job?'

Turning, Storey saw the slender outline of Johnny Chance, still trying to cut a bandit figure in tight jeans, a denim shirt and a black leather waistcoat. Standing with his thumbs in his belt. Storey checked he wasn't wearing spurs on his boots.

'Your dad says you woke him up this morning. Walking the dog, were you?'

'You're sharp. You've noticed we don't have any dogs, though I've been thinking about it, keep the riff-raff away. Looks like I was too late, doesn't it? The barbarians have stormed the gates already.'

Bill Chance said, 'You talk to him, Johnny, you can explain it better than me.' He walked around the corner of the house and Storey heard the door close behind him.

He said to Johnny Chance, 'Did you see anything this morning? I mean, before you found this.'

Chance looked back towards the main house and the black electronically-operated gates, visible over the tops of the bushes surrounding the lawn.

'As it happens, I did,' he said. 'I woke up early with my guts feeling like shit, and I was standing by my bedroom window looking over the garden. Beautiful sunrise it was. And blow me down, as I was watching I saw a skinny figure running across the lawn towards the wall.'

'What was he wearing?'

Johnny Chance shrugged. 'Jeans, black pullover, scarf tied on his head like Axl Rose.'

'How did he get out? I take it the gates were shut and locked.'

'Of course, especially after the recent kerfuffle. But it didn't make any difference. There was a rope hanging over the wall. He ran up to it and started climbing, then side-saddled over the top and he was away. We might have to stick some glass pieces on the top of that wall. Put some more rips in the burglars' jeans.'

Storey was facing him now, seeing the faint air of irony in Chance's face, as if daring Storey to believe him.

Storey said, 'So what did you do then?'

'I started screaming and running around in my undies ... well no, I didn't. I got dressed and went outside, of course. It was barely getting light. I realised he'd run from the direction of here, Dad's house, so I thought I'd better check. When I got close I saw the writing and thought I should find out whether Dad was all right. Which he was, being spark out until I woke him up.'

'Have you reported it to the police?'

'What's the point? It's done. We'll never catch them. They're probably booking their tickets back to Bulgaria or Romania as we speak. Laughing up their sleeves.'

Storey gestured towards the writing. 'Why would Bulgarians or Romanians write something like this? What's your father done to deserve this kind of threat?'

Johnny glanced at the house then flicked his eyes towards Storey, hinting they should move away.

Storey followed him as Johnny walked back to the main house.

———

AS THEY WERE crossing the lawn, Johnny said, 'Don't you think it's weird we all live here together, in each other's pockets?'

'It's up to you. None of my business.'

'Well it is weird. It's a fucking nightmare. It was just Genny and me to begin with, then Adam split up with Angie and gave her his house and knocked on our door, so we gave him one of the bedrooms. Then Tim turned up looking like a wet weekend and he had another of the rooms.'

'I've been told none of you have to work again. Don't they want their own places, their own space? Don't you?'

'Shit, I'm not going to move. I was here first, with Genny. Neither of us has ever had what you'd call a long-term relationship and we've always lived in the same place together. Then Dad sold his house in Spain and lost a ton of money so we decided to give him that cottage, if he wanted it. At least we could keep him under observation, so to speak. Stop him leaking more money.'

'What do you think's happened to the guitars?'

Johnny stopped and looked at Storey, turning something over in his head, it seemed. He said, 'That's the question I should be asking you, isn't it? You're the expert costing us a couple of grand. What have you found out so far? Aren't you supposed to give us a report or something, so we know what we're getting for our money?'

'I can tell you what I've found so far.'

'Go on then.'

'Whoever got into the studio knew what he was doing.'

'Well, yeah ... he broke through an electronic lock.'

'That's not the point.'

'What is?'

'He knew the guitars were in there. As far as anyone knows they didn't try to break into the house—and look at it. If you were a burglar you'd take a chance, wouldn't you? You might think there's some expensive gear in the studio, but you'd also think there'd be something worth stealing in the house. And as you've come this far, you might as well see what else is on offer. Cash or jewellery, maybe.'

'So you're saying they came right to the studio because they knew what they were looking for?'

'Yes, and even then they took the two most valuable pieces in the studio. I've been in there. There are Apple computers lying around, tablets, expensive looking pieces of kit. You'd stick them in the haversack as well, wouldn't you?'

Johnny was shaking his head. 'I don't buy that … anyone who's done their research on me knows those two guitars were the two most valuable ones I had. And we both know there are people out there, people who hire crooks to steal things to order. Paintings, collectibles, whatever. I think you're barking up the wrong tree.'

'You asked for my opinion.'

Johnny continued walking to the house, talking over his shoulder. 'You're not a detective, though, are you? You're just a cop who quit because you shot someone you shouldn't have done, then you've got lucky with a couple of gigs up here.'

'So you want me to stop looking?'

Johnny stopped again and turned back, and Storey saw the hardness in his eyes. 'You don't understand a fucking thing, do you? We had a burglary and now we've had this graffiti or whatever you call it, calling my dad scum.'

'You think it's all tied in, part of the same thing?'

'You asked what my dad had done to deserve this. Well it might not have been Bulgarians or Romanians, but my dad made enemies in Spain. He shot his mouth off about us, about how rich he was and how much money we had. You know what southern Spain's like—riddled with gangsters who moved there with their gold chains and their blonde trophy wives. Well he pissed them off big-time. You've seen him all jolly and friendly but he's got a mean streak and he enjoyed lording it over the middle-aged wide boys because he thought his money was earned legally—not by him, mind you, but by us. Didn't matter. He enjoyed putting them in their place. When we had him back here he started having lots of hate mail, anonymous. Then that stopped and we thought it was all over, they'd forgotten him.'

'You think it's started up again.'

'First thing I thought of, when I knew the guitars had been nicked. Now there's been this writing on his house, I'm certain. I think they're threats. Someone's letting us know they're in town.'

'All the more reason to report the thefts and the graffiti to the police and sack me.'

'Do you think the police would believe us? And be better at protecting us than you, Mr Firearms Expert?'

'Those aren't the terms of our arrangement.'

'Maybe not. But I think someone's out to get him, and I don't mind admitting I'm scared.'

CHAPTER TWENTY-THREE

EVEN WHILE SHE was singing, Geneva Chance kept seeing pictures in her head of Paul Storey: stepping between her and that freaky-looking fan in the town centre; talking to her dad in the kitchen; standing in the living-room, looking out of the window with a slightly humorous expression on his face …

She liked the fact he'd made no attempt to come on to her, to ask for a date or make some leering comment about her looks. He seemed completely focused on doing the job he'd been hired to do, and somehow that made him more attractive. He'd made no reference to a wife or girlfriend but she found it hard to believe there was nobody at home for him … but then she knew she was considered attractive and there was nobody at home for her, either.

Perhaps that's how it was for some people.

Now she stopped singing and raised her eyes from the lyric sheet on the stand in front of her, sensing that something was wrong. Johnny was shaking his head at her. No one was playing.

She said, 'What?'

Johnny said, 'You're not with us, are you?'

'What do you mean?'

'You're singing by rote. There's nothing there.'

She stared at him, then said, 'Do it again,' and turned away. She could see Pete through the studio window and he nodded at her, bless him, and then Johnny counted them in again.

It'd been Johnny's idea to record as much live as possible, rather than add vocals and overdubs later. But she didn't like it. The responsibility was too much. When she sang alone, in a booth, she could make a mistake and they could stop and play the track again and no one was put out. When they were all playing together, everyone had to play the track again if she went wrong. It put her on edge and made her more likely to screw up.

They played two verses and two choruses of the song—one of Johnny's upbeat numbers about the wonders of being dumped by an angel who was too good for him—and then he brought it to a halt, spinning on his heel to look at Tim, who didn't return the look but stared into space instead, like a robot waiting to be switched on again.

'What the fuck?' Johnny said. 'You're speeding up, I can't get my breath.'

Tim said, 'Rock solid, me. Fix it in the mix if you're not happy.'

'"Fix it in the mix". That's your answer every fucking time, isn't it? Why don't you learn to play the bloody drums instead of waiting for other people to bail you out?'

Adam Chance stepped forward. 'Johnny, take it easy.'

'And you can fuck off, too. You keep playing G when it's supposed to be G7, don't you? What's the matter, all that testosterone damaged your hearing?'

They continued to argue and Geneva chose a spot on the far wall and stared at it, waiting for the argument to run its course. Johnny had always been difficult when recording but the pressure of time—having to meet delivery dates for each recording—had focused him when they were making their first albums. Now they were on their own timetable there was no pressure and Johnny could be as picky as he wanted and blame it on being a perfectionist.

An image of Paul Storey came into her mind again— this time arriving in his car and turning it lazily in a circle to pull up outside the gates to pick her up. His smile had been warm and genuine and he seemed interested in her as a person as they'd driven into town and then sat in the café, talking about Chuck Berry and The Specials and those other Coventry bands ...

Then she thought about the writing that had appeared on her father's cottage this morning. Where did that come from? Who was calling him scum, and why? Should she be worried—for herself, if not for him?

Now there was more noise behind her and she couldn't prevent herself turning. Tim had stood up from behind his drums and had come round to confront Johnny, and as she watched he snaked out a hand holding a drumstick and slapped Johnny on the side of his face. There was no obvious damage but Johnny was instantly enraged, lunging at Tim before Adam could step between them, their guitars swinging and clashing so that ringing feedback suddenly filled the studio.

Johnny and Tim had their hands around each other's throats, Adam between them trying to force them apart. Even Pete had stood up in the control room.

Geneva strode towards her brothers, pulled Johnny's shoulder back and slapped him hard. He drew back, shock on his face.

She said, 'Enough! One more word and I'm walking out and you can find another sister to sing your bloody songs.'

'He's a fucking coke head—' Johnny began.

'Come here.'

She lifted his guitar over his head and handed it to Adam, then seized Johnny by the arm and walked him outside, through the small lobby and into the afternoon sunshine, where the world seemed suddenly normal and calm.

She said, 'Do you want to finish this album?'

He said nothing.

She said, 'Do you?'

'He's a fucking drug taking zombie—'

'And you're a bully. Leave him alone. Find another way to get him to do it better. You know shouting at him doesn't work.'

'Nothing works.'

'Maybe. So just let's do the best we can. He's right—we can fix it in the mix if we have to.'

She recognised what he did next because he always did it, the little boy pleading for understanding: he drew a big sigh and looked at her from under his eye-brows, turning down the corners of his mouth. He said, 'We're never going to get this album right. The tour's going to be a fucking disaster.'

'You say that every time. And every time you're wrong.'

'That was fifteen years ago,' he said. 'It's a bit different this time.'

'Yeah, all the audience members will be dancing with their zimmer frames.'

He smiled. 'We'll need a line of ambulances at every gig, in case of heart-attacks.'

'And the women will be throwing their incontinence pads at you instead of their knickers.'

'Now you've gone too far,' he said.

But at least he was still smiling.

———

THEY WENT BACK inside the studio and found Adam and Tim chatting as though nothing had happened. Adam caught Geneva's eye and she nodded briefly. Johnny picked up his guitar from where Adam had laid it and took in several deep breaths.

He said, 'Okay, we've had our break. Let's nail this fucker.'

While he and Pete talked to each other over the intercom, Geneva took her place behind the stand microphone again.

There were only so many times she could call Johnny out like that, and she was probably near the end of her quota. She had to get serious about breaking away, moving house to begin with.

Johnny would hate it but she had a life of her own, didn't she?

She had to leave before she went mad.

CHAPTER TWENTY-FOUR

BILL CHANCE LIKED to be back for the ten o'clock news and then Newsnight immediately afterwards, though he didn't think it was as good since Paxman left. The interviewers were too soft for his liking. He preferred it when they asked tough questions and the politicians squirmed and couldn't give direct answers. Serve the bastards right.

Lock the door behind you, he'd thought as he walked from the main house, so he turned and slid the bolt on its chain. Nice chunky sound it made, very solid.

He'd never thought about his safety before but the writing on the outside wall this morning had shaken him, no question. He couldn't think who would have done it—who had he ever harmed? He just kept his head down, did a bit on the Internet, cooked for the kids most nights and watched television. He didn't like the idea of the kids going away on tour again, and without him, but if he was honest he couldn't have done it anyway—travelling hundreds of miles on a coach was exhausting, and even a nice hotel room at the end of it couldn't compensate.

He went upstairs and changed into his pyjamas. Still damn warm outside, even at this time of night.

He thought about Jess for the twentieth time today. She would have laughed at him wearing his pyjamas to watch television. He'd done it right from the very beginning, even when they were on their honeymoon, Jess saying, You trying to give me a hint or something? And him replying, More than a hint, girl—I'm ready for action! That became a catch-phrase between them—ready for action. They'd laughed about it even when she was lying in bed, the cancer roaring through her body ...

Downstairs again he made himself a cup of tea and then switched on the television, the nice Panasonic 50 inch job that was delivered last month. Nearly filled the wall opposite the sofa but who cared? He liked being sucked into the TV so he could forget everything outside, everything he wanted to forget, everything he'd done ...

———

HE WAS TEN minutes into the news when there was a knock on the door. He knew it could only be one of the kids but shouted 'Who is it?' through the door anyway.

'Dad, open up.'

Johnny. What did that bugger want now?

He opened the door and it was the two of them, Tim standing behind him, his hair a mess as usual.

He asked them in and they were all standing in the kitchen when he noticed something odd.

The boys were both wearing white jump suits, zipped up the front and with hoods over their heads.

'What the hell are you wearing? Is it a fancy dress or something? Don't tell me you're going out at this time of night ...'

'Dad, shut the fuck up for once in your life.'

'Hey, don't talk to me like—'

'Or what, what will you do? Beat me up? I don't think so.'

Okay, so that was the subject ... better to keep quiet, see where they take it. Breathe deeply, remember what that psychotherapist used to tell you, all those years ago: Don't let others anger you. Only you can anger you.

'All right,' he said. 'What do you want? I was just watching the news.'

Bill noticed Johnny glance at Tim and a nod passed between them. What the hell was going on?

Johnny said, 'There's something we need to show you upstairs.'

'What?'

'We'll show you,' Tim said, the first thing he'd said, always the quiet and weird one. 'We need to show you in the bathroom.'

'Christ, we won't all three get in! Have you seen the size of that room?'

'Okay, just follow me up,' Johnny said. He turned and went out of the kitchen and up the stairs, saying to Tim, 'Turn on the fucking light, will you?'

Tim flicked the switch and then all three of them were on the stairs, the boys' costumes rustling.

Bill said, 'Are those things made of paper? They won't last five minutes if you start sweating.'

The boys didn't reply, which he thought was odd. Johnny was ahead of him and Tim behind, like they were escorting him. He tried to think what they might show him upstairs but couldn't think of anything. Was it something to do with the writing on his wall this morning? Had they found something else?

At the top, Johnny went left and switched on the bathroom light. There was an Italian shower, without a shower tray and just a drain in the centre, a flush toilet and a sink bowl with a glass tray above it. He liked things simple.

Johnny went and peered in the shower, bending down to look at something on the floor.

Bill knew it wasn't dirty because he'd showered that morning, hadn't he? Everything drained away, even the bits of hair that were coming out more frequently now.

Johnny said, 'Look at this,' and stepped out, pointing down towards the plughole.

'What?'

'Have a look for yourself, I'm not going to tell you.'

Christ Almighty, he was missing the news properly now, he'd never catch up. Still, the boys didn't talk to him much these days so at least they were taking an interest, perhaps looking after him, taking care of the old man.

He sidled past Johnny, who said, 'Take your slippers off, you'll get it dirty.'

Bill frowned but slid his feet out of his slippers and stepped further into the shower space, bending down to see what was so important.

'See it?' Johnny said behind him.

'See what? I can't see anything, I'm in my own shadow. What am I looking for?'

Johnny's voice seemed to change as he said, 'Your conscience.'

And just as Bill Chance started to think, *What an odd thing to say,* he felt a sharp pain just beneath his ribs. What the hell?

He began to stand up straight but felt hands pushing him back inside and then another cold pain, this time higher up, under his armpit … that one really hurt.

He turned, frowning, towards his sons and placed his hands where he'd felt the pain. Looking down he saw blood coming between his fingers and dropping on to the floor.

He heard Tim saying, 'Mustn't get the place dirty, must we?' and then he was reaching over and turning on the shower and Bill Chance felt water on his head, which helped, because he was starting to feel a bit light-headed now and wanted to sit down.

But he knew if he sat down in the shower he'd get his pyjamas wet and it was so slippy he might not get up again. Whatever game the boys were playing wasn't funny now. They'd always had a strange sense of humour but this wasn't a joke.

He tried to say something about that, but realised the words weren't forming properly in his mouth, which had gone dry, ironic, really, him being in the shower and everything …

And then he wondered where Adam was.

He'd put a stop to this, make the pain go away, kick those boys' arses for them. He wondered if Adam knew what was going on, but he thought probably not.

He was the sensible one. The one who kept them in line.

And then he was sliding down the wall ... gently does it, don't hurt yourself at the bottom. Just stretch out.

And there *was* another voice. He thought so. He looked up but couldn't really see anything clearly. It must be the steam in the shower, everything going misty.

But he could make out a vague shape, and his heart sank.

He heard himself say, 'Not you, too.'

And then he couldn't say anything else.

Because he'd realised. He understood what they were doing, all of them here together. He knew it wasn't a joke and he knew Adam wasn't going to save him.

Nobody could, now.

———

KEN TALBOT HAD no idea why he was still there at twelve thirty in the morning.

Face it, he told himself, it's an obsession. You can't help it. Just one glimpse of her and that'll last for a few days.

Then you'll be back out here again, hoping for another fix. How sad can you get?

He estimated he was parked about eighty yards from the black gates of the entrance. From this angle he'd been able to see various lights going on and off upstairs in the house and he had the sense, with his window wound down, that there was something going on. The vague hint of voices. A door opening and closing. A car boot opening and closing.

And then, out of nowhere, the gates opened and Tim's white Mercedes rolled out, his courtesy car, with Tim driving and Johnny in the passenger seat. He saw their profiles briefly as they passed through a lighted section of the road.

So just Geneva and Adam were in the house now ...

But those boys were on an adventure. He saw it on their faces, however briefly. It might be fun to follow them.

AN HOUR LATER he slammed his door shut behind him, feeling his heart thumping in his chest, wiping sweat from the end of his nose. He'd parked a hundred yards from his place and run all the way home, looking behind him fearfully and trying not to trip over. He stood for a moment with his back to the door and caught his breath.

It couldn't be true. What he'd seen couldn't be real.

But he knew it was. He'd looked in the ditch himself and seen it.

The question was, what should he do now?

CHAPTER TWENTY-FIVE

IT HAD BEEN a while since Stef had been out to Liam's place, a small semi in one of the estates near the Airport Retail Park. The last time he'd been up there was to buy a laptop from PC World, November time, one of those Black Friday deals.

The first thing he thought when Liam's door swung open was he should have rung—he was trying to catch Liam off-balance, the same as Liam had done when he'd broken into Stef's flat. But now the door was open and he was staring at Jen, the woman he didn't like and who didn't like him. He knew for certain she didn't like him because of the way her mouth twisted when she recognised him, and given the fight in the pub and the fact Liam spent Sunday night in the cells he couldn't blame her. It crossed his mind she was probably questioned by the cops before being released to find her own way home: so no, she wouldn't have liked that. Who would?

And he saw in her eyes that the outrage hadn't died down in the three days since the fight. She thought she was going down the pub for a drink and a bit of flirting and wound up in the middle of a ruck with heavy objects flying around.

He said, 'I'm looking for Liam,' as though that might pacify her but knowing straight away there was no chance that was going to happen.

She said, 'You've got a bloody nerve coming around here. Have you seen his nose? You damn near broke it ... he looks worse than you, in case you're wondering.'

Stef thinking, Liam's not told her he's already seen me since the fight. Sensible.

He said, 'So he's not here, then.'

'Course he's bloody here. Where else is he going to go, looking like that? Ikea have been on the phone every five minutes asking when he's going back to work and now you come round looking like butter wouldn't melt in your mouth ...'

She shut the door and Stef wondered whether he'd been dismissed. No, he told himself, she's gone to get Liam. Won't let him in the house, even though it's not hers. Funny how some people take over others' lives like that, bossing them around, taking ownership of their property ...

The door opened again and Liam was filling the doorway in a white tee-shirt and black cargo pants, his face looking calm but determined, as though Jen had given him instructions how to behave and he was concentrating on remembering them. Jen was right—his nose had got worse, beginning to look like an old green potato.

Stef said, 'Can we at least walk somewhere she can't hear us?'

LIAM PULLED THE door shut behind him and Stef walked ahead down the path, through the gate, and waited for him to arrive. Early afternoon, no cars around, the sky a bright blue and Stef felt himself sweating in the heat. One of those days when everything stops and people stay indoors because it's too hot to do anything else.

He watched Liam pull a weed from his ragged front garden then throw it on a pile in the corner. Getting domesticated already.

Don't get used to it, mate.

Liam arrived and closed the gate behind him, saying now, 'What do you want? Johnny-boy been in touch?'

'Not yet. I wanted to hurry him up but thought I'd better arrange a date with you first.'

'Do you trust him? Seems to me like he'd swindle you on a deal as soon as look at you, just because he can.'

'He's got more to lose than we have. Rich pop star steals own guitars. Pays for their return. Doesn't look very clever, does it, if it gets in the papers?'

'Would you do that?'

'What—tell the papers?'

'Or threaten to,' Liam said. 'I've been thinking—there's lots of ways we could run this and come out with more money.'

'Assuming that's what we want.'

'Well isn't it? I thought that was the whole point of doing this. Fifty thousand a year, you said. Easy money. So why don't we work ourselves into this deal?'

They'd arrived at Stef's long Audi. The ladders they'd used to rob the Chance house were still in the back. Stef said, 'Get in the passenger side. Better if we're not seen on the street.'

Liam walked around the front of the car and climbed in; Stef got in behind the wheel.

Stef said, 'I think it would be bad news to rip off the Chances.'

'You scared of that little squirt?'

'You ever looked in his eyes? Black as tarmac. He might be little but I bet he doesn't fight fair. I was reading up on the Chances before I did the work for them—they were brought up pretty rough, over in Wood End. Street kids, all of them. Especially after their mother died. Then a couple of them took up the guitar and started playing locally instead of throwing stones at greenhouses. But that's still in them. I wouldn't like to go up against them in a fight.'

LIAM SEEMED TO be thinking about this and he asked a couple of questions about the Chance family upbringing which Stef couldn't answer. Then he said, 'How did you meet up with them anyway?'

Stef grinned. 'Remember that marquee in the back garden when we went over the fence?'

'Big white job?'

'That's the one. It's my brother's. His business. Employs a lot of Poles, people he knew when we were growing up, their cousins and friends who've come over later. They put up marquees for birthday parties and anniversaries and so on. Guess what he calls the company.'

'How the fuck should I know?'

'It's called "Tent Poles". Laughed himself sick when he came up with that.'

'So you're Polish?'

'A name like Malyzs, what did you think?'

'Never thought about it, never saw it written down.'

'Anyway, I help my big brother out from time to time, gives me a legitimate source of income for the tax man.'

'And what happened — Johnny Chance walks up to you when you're tying a rope and asks if you want to rob him?'

'Not far off. I'm more like a supervisor when we're working, so I was standing around checking it was going all right when he comes up and starts talking to me about the business, what sort of money it makes, is the work seasonal, all that guff. I could tell he was a wrong 'un pretty quick.'

'With your jail experience.'

'I suppose. So I let him ramble and sort of let him know I was open for external contracts, as it were. The Polish Mafia. He fell for it. I had no idea what he wanted, and it took him a while to pluck up his courage, but eventually he rang me with the plan and made it seem straightforward. He even gave me the code for the keypad on the studio door. I had no idea why he wanted me to steal the guitars but I didn't care. It's a job, isn't it?'

'So all that stuff with the ultraviolet pen and so on … that was for show?'

'It was better to do something like that than just give me the passcode … looks too dodgy if we waltz in because he's left it unlocked or because someone's given me the numbers. So he put the ultraviolet paint on and made sure the keypad got plenty of use so it would wear off on the right numbers in time. Fooled you.'

Liam was quiet now, staring through the windscreen at the dead street, bright in the sunshine. Then he said, 'You could have told me all this. I wouldn't have been such a dick if I'd known what was happening.'

'You're always a dick, Liam. That's why I chose you for the job.'

Liam turning his head quickly at that, but Stef was smiling, making light of it, all friends together now. He said, 'So the plan is, I'll get him to turn up tomorrow with the money to get the guitars back. He'd probably want to come with you to the place and watch you do it, but he can't risk being seen. People might put two and two together, especially if they've recognised the guitars. So you go get them and let us know and then we hand them over to him and get the commission. All right?'

'I don't trust him, that little prick. The names he called me.'

'Short man syndrome, they call it. Let it go. He's the client here. Just don't let your guard down.'

'What do you mean?'

'I think he enjoys taking risks. Don't tell him anything you don't want him to know.'

'I never liked them, Chance. The girl was all right but they all looked like pricks.'

'What were you, ten, twelve? What did you know?'

'I was pretty advanced when it came to sex. I fancied her. Did you come across her, when you were putting up the tent?'

'I saw her a couple of times,' Stef said, thinking. 'Going back and forth to the studio. She walks like she's got flat feet, kind of loping, you know? And she's cut her hair since they were famous. I'd still do her, though.'

'Me too.'

'What about Jen?'

'Fuck her.'

'And you're the one says he doesn't trust Johnny Chance.'

STEF GOT JOHNNY Chance on the fourth try.

He said, 'You're difficult to get hold of, especially as I thought this was urgent.'

'Never mind buttering me up, are you ready?'

'We were always ready. It's you we were waiting for. Have you got the money?'

'I will have by the time I see you,' Johnny said. 'When do you want to do it?'

'Tomorrow afternoon. My place again.' Stef hesitated. The tricky part. He was about to take a massive gamble. 'I might need a favour from you.'

Johnny Chance laughed.

'You've got to be fucking kidding me. When I've got these guitars back I don't want to hear from you again.'

'Well that's part of the favour.'

'What is?'

'Making sure you don't hear from us. Buying silence, you might say.'

There was a pause at the other end and Stef could almost hear Johnny thinking, wondering what this was about.

Then Johnny said, 'Is this, what … a shakedown? More money to keep your traps shut?'

'No, it's not. That's Liam's plan but not mine. Mine's a bit more serious. And it would help us both out.'

'You know me—always willing to extend a helping hand.'

'Wait till you hear what it is,' Stef said.

CHAPTER TWENTY-SIX

HAVING CONSIDERED IT overnight, Storey couldn't see any way of avoiding it: he had to talk to Tim Chance again about the Albanians, see if anything shook out this time when he confronted the drummer with what he knew.

The black electronic gates closed behind him and he climbed out of his Volvo. The first time in a week there'd been a cloud in the sky but it was still hot. Coming up to lunchtime and sweaty hot. That was good, he thought, if Tim was tense.

There was a new car in the drive behind the garage. It was another Mercedes but a black one. Did they have another visitor?

Before he reached the front door it opened and Geneva stood there in white shorts and a pale blouse. He thought she looked like a tennis player leaving home for the courts. She was slim and sporty.

He'd been looking forward to talking to her again but now he wondered whether he was here on a pretext—it wasn't Tim he wanted to see, it was her. He wanted to hear her voice talking to him, hear its rise and fall. He wanted to see the glint in her eyes when her head was turned just so and the whites were clear and moist against the serene blue of the irises ...

Christ, what was happening to him? He'd be writing poetry next.

By now she'd come down the steps, saying, 'You read my mind, I was going to call you.'

'Is Tim around?'

She glanced towards the garage and the black Mercedes, saying, 'Yes, he's back. They were fixing his old car after a smash. He went to fetch it this morning. And hello to you too.'

'Sorry, hello, I wasn't thinking.'

'He's in the studio—we're going in later. He's just practising before we start. Why do you want to talk to him? Do you think he's the great guitar thief?'

He turned to walk with her towards the studio. 'I wouldn't tell you even if I knew, would I?'

'No, you keep everything to yourself. You know everything about me and I know nothing about you, except your dad worked on the buildings in the city centre ... as what, electrician, was it? I'm hopeless at remembering what people tell me. My problem is I don't listen. I had this reputation of being shy and quiet because I never said much when we were interviewed. But that was all Johnny's fault—you couldn't shut him up. I was almost as talkative as him but my voice was too quiet for the microphones— my speaking voice, not singing, obviously.'

'Obviously.'

'But when other people are talking I can't concentrate on what they're saying for long. I get caught up in the rhythm of how they're talking, not what they're saying. I have to really focus.'

They'd arrived at the studio door and she suddenly reached out and put a hand on his forearm.

'Don't go without talking to me. I want some advice.'

Storey felt the lightness of her touch but it was electric. He forced himself to not look down at her hand.

He said, 'I'll only be fifteen minutes. Some things I want to clear up.'

'Poor old Tempo,' she said. 'You'll make him nervous just talking to him. He'll confess to anything.'

'You think?'

'I would,' she said, and walked off.

HE HEARD NOTHING until he opened the door to the studio, when Tim Chance's battering wall of percussion suddenly became audible.

He knew the drummer had seen him come in because he was facing the door and anyway Storey supposed the acoustics would have changed as soon as the door was pulled back. But Chance's head was down, his hair falling over his face, his hands flying left and right on an extended solo, his left hand moving between the two tom-toms in front and to his left, the right slashing at the cymbals, all the while his foot pounding the heavy bass in time with the music in his head.

Storey watched for a minute, then moved forward and stood directly in front of the drum kit, Tim Chance slowly raising his head, keeping up the rhythm, which was more regular now, less percussive, staring at Storey with a slow smile developing on his face, his hands working back and forth automatically.

Then he produced a brief drum roll and stopped, twirling the drumsticks and bringing them down hard one last time.

The room grew silent.

Storey said, 'Isn't it frustrating?'

'What?'

'Never being able to cut loose like that on the records. They're all songs, aren't they, verse and chorus. No fancy diddling.'

'What do you want?'

'I followed you the other night. When you went to that club.'

Tim Chance placed his drumsticks in a pocket attached to the side of his seat. He said, 'I didn't see you.'

'That's because I'm a trained professional. You talked to a couple of Albanians. What was that about? Apart from the drugs, of course.'

Chance looked at him as if trying not to show anything, Storey thought, not blinking, not swallowing, not glancing away ... just a straight-ahead stare while he thought of something to say.

Eventually he said, 'That's none of your business, is it? You were hired to find the guitars, not to monitor my behaviour.'

'Quite right,' Storey said, moving to sit on a Marshall loudspeaker. 'I absolutely don't care what you stick up your nose. But it's interesting that the last Albanian you talked to, Diamant, works in a cash exchange shop—the kind of place where your guitars might be locked up.'

'Really? So why haven't you done anything about it? Reported it to the police, for instance.'

'Frank Lamb led me to believe you weren't much interested in involving the police. Personally, I'm more interested in the Albanians. So's a police inspector friend of mine. What do you think? Is it coincidence you're buying drugs from someone who might be behind the theft of your guitars? Or is there more to it?'

'Like what? I don't know anything about the Albanians. I didn't even know they were Albanians. I thought they were Greeks or something.'

'What did Diamant want to talk to you about?'

Now Tim stood up, Storey wondering whether the man would come clean or lie, and whether Tim would even know the difference.

Chance said, 'I don't have to tell you anything, *Mister* Storey. You get that? Not constable or sergeant or inspector. Mister. You're working for us, allegedly, and I think I've had enough of defending myself. I don't even know what I'm defending myself against, but you're making me feel guilty when I haven't actually done anything. Does that seem right to you?'

Storey stood up too and was about to reply when the studio door opened with a sucking sound behind him and he turned around. Geneva Chance had entered, looking from Storey to Tim and back again, her eyes wide. Then she said to her brother, 'They've found Dad,' and went straight out of the door again.

Storey didn't know what had happened , but he knew it was bad.

OUTSIDE THE STUDIO a police Volvo was now parked behind his own and the front door of the house was open. Geneva Chance was striding ahead of them towards the house. Over her shoulder she said, 'Two policemen came in and started asking Adam and me when was the last time we'd seen Dad. Then they said they'd found a body they thought might be him.'

'Found him where?' Storey asked.

'They haven't said. I got the idea it was dumped, you know, not collapsed on a street or anything.'

Tim said, 'How do they know it was him?'

'I don't know!' she said, turning to glance at him over her shoulder, her eyes flashing. 'They asked if there were any other family members so I came to get you and Adam went to find Johnny.'

Storey said, 'Perhaps I should go.'

'Don't you dare. You're involved now.'

Tim and Geneva were surprisingly calm, Storey thought. It was that time when you didn't believe the worst had happened and were thinking up reasons for it not to be true.

Inside the house, Storey heard the policemen's voices before he saw them: that quiet, no-nonsense tone he remembered from his own time acting largely as an observer while more senior people talked to victims, or sometimes villains they were trying to pacify.

Adam and Johnny and two other men in shirtsleeves and ties were standing in the front room. When Geneva arrived, entering first, Johnny stepped forward and put an arm around her.

He said, 'I can't believe it, can you? When did you see him last?'

She shrugged him away, saying, 'Don't do this, Johnny.'

He dropped his arm. 'Do what?'

'Pretend you liked him.'

'Don't say—'

Geneva turned to the policemen, both in their forties with serious faces and greying hair. 'He made us a stew last night. He cooked for us most nights. Then he went back to his cottage. I haven't seen him since. Have you checked he's not there?'

Without answering, one of the policemen noticed Storey hanging back and said, 'Who are you, might I ask?'

'Never mind,' Geneva said. 'Friend of the family. Can we go and check my dad's not home?'

'We can't all go,' the same policeman said. 'I have to tell you it might be a crime scene and we don't want everyone trampling over everything. We've got a crew on its way.'

'I'll go,' Storey said, lifting his chin towards the other policeman, adding, 'I know the drill. Why don't you come with me?'

The policeman looked at his colleague, who nodded, saying, 'Wear your gloves.'

LEADING THE POLICEMAN across the lawn towards Bill Chance's cottage, Storey said, 'How did you find him?'

The other man said nothing for a few strides, then said, 'You're Paul Storey, aren't you? What the fuck are you doing here?'

'Does it make any difference?'

'If you're involved it might do. You get your sweaty fingerprints on everything, don't you? Just because you're bosom buddies with Jackie West you get away with all sorts of shit.'

'And here I was, thinking I was being helpful.'

'Dougie won't like it if you get in his way.'

'That wasn't part of my master plan. So where did you find Mr Chance?'

'This it?'

The policeman had ignored him because they'd arrived at the cottage, the policeman approaching to peer through the window of the ground floor and then stepping back to look up at the one immediately above them. Storey noticed that the graffiti had been scrubbed off, leaving a blurred red mark in which he couldn't make out any words.

Storey went around the corner and knocked on the front door, noticing the policeman pulling on white latex gloves. He nodded towards the door knob. 'Want to give it a go?'

The man stepped forward and the knob turned and he pushed it open but stayed outside. He called Bill Chance's name but there was no reply. He leaned forward and called louder.

'You can tell it's empty, can't you?' Storey said. 'It sounds empty. You want to check inside?'

'No, we're pretty sure it's him.' He closed the door and turned back to face Storey square on. 'Someone called it in to Crimestoppers. Other side of Coventry, through Ansty, just past the golf course, the man said. This was two o'clock in the morning. An officer goes out, finds him in a ditch, stark bollock naked, as described.'

'Already dead?'

The policeman said nothing.

Storey said, 'And the caller identified the body despite him being naked?'

'By name. Which is weird, unless he's the murderer, which I doubt. Woman who took the call said he sounded absolutely terrified, as if he knew who did it but didn't want to say. So Mr Smart-Aleck, figure that one out.'

THE FORENSIC TEAM arrived twenty minutes later, driving their van across the lawn to park twenty feet from the back door and cordoning off the cottage, though who they were protecting it from was hard to see.

Storey stood outside and watched until Geneva Chance came from the main house and walked towards him, her head down. He thought she looked pale and beaten down. He said, 'How are you doing?'

She stood next to him, watching the forensic team unloading equipment. 'Those policemen keep asking me that. I wonder if they ask the boys the same thing. Do I look as if I'm more likely to burst out crying than them?'

'Have they told you how he died?'

'They say they can't be certain what the actual cause of death was, but it looks like he's got several knife wounds in his stomach.'

'Has anyone told them about the graffiti on the cottage yet?'

195

'I haven't. They want to speak to me later. I'll mention it.'

'Do you think they're connected—the graffiti and your father's death?'

She sighed. 'You tell me, you're the expert.'

They were both quiet for a minute, then Storey said, 'You've all seemed to take the news in your stride. What you said in there, about Johnny not liking him. Was that true?'

Now she looked up at him, her blue eyes clear.

'It was true. It's true for all of us. None of us liked him. Which is hard to deal with when it's your dad.'

Storey let that sink in for a while in case she wanted to add anything. He glanced at her but she was still watching the forensics officers move back and forth.

He said, 'Did the police say they had any suspects?'

She turned to look up at him properly, her face a curious mixture of anger and shame, her blue eyes dark but without tears. She said, 'No, but they'd be stupid if they weren't thinking about us, wouldn't they? That van and those people in white suits aren't there for nothing, are they?'

CHAPTER TWENTY-SEVEN

THE TWO POLICEMEN were roughly the same age but one acted younger and kept looking at Geneva as if wanting to check she was actually there in the room with him. He was called Preston. He had coarse skin and lifeless hair and his bottom lip stuck out as though he'd learned to pout early and now couldn't stop himself. The older one was almost nice-looking, with short hair greying at the sides, a straight nose and a cupid's bow mouth. He was Reed. Preston and Reed, like an upmarket men's tailor.

They were talking to each other, comparing notes while sitting on her sofa, and in the end she just left—if they wanted to talk to her they could come and fetch her.

She went into the kitchen and found Adam leaning against the counter with a glass of water in his hand. Through the windows she could see the front of the white forensic van parked outside her father's cottage. Its back end was out of sight, behind hedges. It gave her an odd feeling to think these strangers were going through his place, rifling his clothes, peering into the corners of his life.

Adam said, 'You're not sorry, are you?'

'What—about him?' She thought for a moment, trying to work out what her feelings were. Then she said, 'I don't like to think of him naked in a ditch. That doesn't seem right somehow.'

'Have the police said anything to you about who did it?'

'Nothing. You?'

Adam shook his head. 'What are we waiting for?'

'They're going to ask us questions.'

'Well I can't tell them anything.'

'Can't or won't?'

'What's that supposed to mean?'

'You know what it means,' she said. 'You're as bad as Johnny, pretending you liked him when that's a pack of lies. Where is he, incidentally? And Tim?'

'They got permission from the cops to go to the studio. To spend time commiserating with each other. They're probably rehearsing.'

Geneva said, 'Is that a good idea? Makes us seem … callous.'

'The police have seen it all before. They'll put it down to shock, it's a coping mechanism or something. What are we going to do about Storey?'

'What about him?'

'Johnny thinks it's all connected—the robbery, the graffiti, now Dad being murdered. We should just tell the police about the guitars and the graffiti and pay Storey off and let the police deal with the whole thing.'

'I thought he didn't want the theft to get out.'

'Only because he didn't want to deal with the police and journalists and so on while we were recording. It's too late for that now.'

'And what do you think?'

'He might be right. You know Dad was mixed up with some dodgy people in Spain, who he pissed off. I wouldn't put it past them to do something like this. First the guitars to let us know they're on the way. Then the graffiti to tell us they can get in when they want.'

'Then they take him somewhere and stick a knife in him? Just because they were pissed off?'

'You have to see it from their perspective—'

'On which you're a great expert all of a sudden.'

'—they've seen him as someone who kept bragging about his money, about his kids, us ... you know what he could be like. Pretty unbearable once he'd had a drink. Maybe he got drunk and said too much, or propositioned one of the gangsters' wives. He didn't have any limits, did he?'

'No,' Geneva said. 'He didn't.'

SHE HATED THIS—the thing they couldn't talk about. The thing they all knew but none of them could say out loud. They trod on eggshells around her if they came anywhere near the subject.

Were they embarrassed? Were they upset?

Despite knowing her brothers all of her life, she still couldn't read them. They formed a men's club to which she had no access. She couldn't get in. She'd forced her way into the group, using her singing ability as a way to gain entrance to the club, and they let her in sure enough ... but that was for public consumption and didn't change their attitude towards her when they were off-stage. Yes they were happy enough for her to be in the band, but it wasn't full membership, and she knew why: somehow she was tainted. What her father had done to her when she was fourteen had somehow coloured their view of her. They knew he was to blame, and had punished him by withholding any feeling or affection for him while still allowing him to be part of their lives. But she sometimes wondered if she'd been punished more—she was the innocent party but she was treated as if she were the guilty one.

At least that's what it felt like.

So what would they say to the police, now? Would it all come out and drag her through the gossip rags, just when she was thinking of changing her life for good? Or would the police investigation uncover other secrets that no one knew about Bill Chance—perhaps not even his children?

———

NOW PRESTON, THE policeman who stared, walked into the kitchen before she could say anything more to Adam. He said to her, 'Can we have a chat? Just get some basics down before you make a formal statement down at the station. It's all pretty standard.'

She said nothing but nodded and walked past him out of the kitchen. What a bitch she was being.

Reed was standing in the living room, staring out of the window across the lawn at the high wall that protected the house from the road. When she came in, he said, 'Did he have his own transport, your dad?'

'What's that got—'

'I was just wondering how he got out there. The middle of nowhere, really. Empty road, past midnight. Could he have driven there? Though, granted, we didn't find a car.'

Geneva sat down, wondering what she felt in the face of being questioned. She hadn't done anything wrong, so she shouldn't feel guilty … so maybe she should feel sad? Or angry?

And then she realised she didn't feel anything. Was this the numbness that was supposed to come with bereavement? Or was it something else? Was she really dead to any emotion towards her father? It was complicated by the fact Reed's question seemed irrelevant, almost childish. Maybe he was trying to trick her because they'd surely know by now whether or not he had a car and where it might be parked.

It was all a mess.

She said, 'Bill hadn't driven for years. When he was in Spain he used taxis all the time and since he came back he hasn't bothered. He never went anywhere anyway.'

Preston had come in behind her and closed the door. Now both policeman sat facing her across the glass coffee table.

They asked her where she'd been the previous night and what she'd done, and asked her again when she'd last seen her father. They asked about his routine, about his cottage and when he usually went to bed. They asked whether she'd heard anything unusual last night, like a car arriving or leaving, and she told them she'd gone to bed at ten o'clock and her room was at the back of the house and she wouldn't have heard any traffic even if she'd been awake. The double glazing was very good.

'So as far as you were aware, you'd all eaten together and then he went back to his house on the grounds. You went to bed a little later and didn't hear anything unusual.'

She thought for a moment. Then she heard herself saying, as if the words were coming from someone else, 'You should know I didn't get on with him, my Dad.'

There was only a brief hesitation before Reed said, 'Oh, why's that?'

She thought for a moment, turning things over in her mind, scenes coming back to her from twenty years ago. She said, 'After our mother died he went to pieces. He didn't know how to do anything. My brothers had to hold it together for all of us. He lost his job, couldn't pay the mortgage ... so Adam and Johnny started playing gigs to earn money. Then Tim joined in and eventually me. It brought him round, gave him something—I don't know, a direction, perhaps. And then he wanted to take charge, be our manager. Tell us what to do. But Adam and Johnny were independent by now, they didn't like being pushed around and although Dad was big, Adam was bigger, so Dad started to take it out on me, and on Tim to a certain extent.'

'He beat you?'

'Not exactly.'

'What then?'

She couldn't say it, not to these two middle-aged men in their dark trousers and shirt-sleeves. It wasn't because it seemed like an act of betrayal ... it was just banal. She would come across as yet another victim of abuse, another sufferer, and she didn't want that. She didn't want to be pitied. She'd fought her way out of the depressive episodes that used to haunt her and had even written a song about it … She couldn't bring it all up again unless it was on her own terms.

She said, 'It was more psychological. Mind games. Trying to assert himself over us and prove he was still the parent. Does that make sense?'

Neither policeman answered, then Reed, the one she thought of as the senior partner, said, 'What was his state of mind, would you say, last night? Was he particularly happy or upset about anything?'

'Perhaps worried.'

'Why? Worried about what?'

She told them about the red paint graffiti that had appeared on the side of the cottage and described what it said.

'It called him scum?'

She nodded.

'What did you make of it?'

'We didn't know what to think, except maybe someone he'd met in Spain was getting their own back.'

'Why would they do that?'

Geneva said, 'I wasn't the only one who didn't get on with him. He'd spent a lifetime compiling a list. This might turn out to be harder than you thought.'

CHAPTER TWENTY-EIGHT

STOREY HAD DECIDED he needed to talk to Odeta again, look in her eyes and see what kind of person she was. Given recent developments it would also be interesting to see if he could find any link to Bill Chance's death. And he admitted to himself he wanted to see if he could push the woman into saying something she didn't want to.

So when he left the Chances he drove back into Coventry and parked outside Odeta's shop for a while, seeing a couple of people go in and one come out again after five minutes. Wednesday afternoon, it wasn't that busy.

He couldn't help thinking about Geneva and her brothers, how they'd responded to their father's death. The police could have announced they'd found an old tramp dead in the woods for all the impact it had on them. Geneva had said none of them liked him but that didn't seem much of an excuse. He was a human being who'd been living amongst them until the night before. Were they all really that cold? He was sure the policemen would pick up on it, too, which might make life difficult for them in the weeks to come. He'd be interested to know if the forensics team had found anything in Chance's cottage.

Finally he climbed out of his car and pushed into the shop, from light to dark, taking a moment to adjust, looking around. He wanted Diamant to be there. He wanted to have an argument with someone, to feel justified in being angry, maybe get involved in a fight …

Odeta was standing behind the counter at the far end, her arms crossed, staring at him, her black hair uncombed … or had she styled it like that deliberately, he wondered, to play on the idea that she was wild, untamed? He didn't know her well enough yet to guess how calculating she was, either in business or in her personal life. Perhaps she thought she was seductive when in fact it came across as desperate.

He crossed to the counter, saying, 'You remember me? I came in a couple of days ago looking for guitars.'

'I remember you. The tall man, looks like a policeman. Did you find the guitars?'

'Would it upset you if I said yes?'

'Why would it upset me?'

'You would have lost a sale.'

Odeta shrugged. Storey realised her dark eyes gave nothing away. He supposed years of bargaining had made her a tough negotiator and also made her cautious.

She said, 'So you haven't found them. And you come back here to ask again, to see if we were lying. Isn't that true?'

'I spoke to Diamant Monday night, did he tell you? Great name, that, incidentally. I suppose it means

Diamond, does it?' Odeta said nothing. 'Anyway, when I was talking to him I had the idea there was something else I could buy from you, if I asked.'

'Buy what?'

'Put it this way, I saw a man from your club giving another man a package that could have been drugs.'

Now Odeta unfolded her arms and moved along the counter to deal with a customer wanting to buy a Samsung tablet. She lifted the bar in the counter and passed through and went to the glass cabinet where it was displayed and took it out for him to inspect. Then she came back and faced Storey again.

She said, 'I will talk to Diamant and ask what he meant. I don't understand anything you've said.'

Storey had the sense there was nothing he could do to pressurise this woman. Having had the life she'd had, a verbal threat from someone she didn't know wasn't going to worry her.

He said, 'I heard about your husband. I heard he was murdered. That must have been tough for you, not long in the country, trying to learn the language, our customs, how we did business. And all of a sudden you're the one in charge with people depending on you.'

'I'm still alive, aren't I? I'm making a living. I integrate with the community, they all know me. I give money to the church every Sunday morning.'

'But it must be difficult for a single woman in your line of work.'

Now she was smiling at him, knowing he was trying a different approach because none of his others had worked so far. She said, 'What line of work is that?'

'Buying and selling. Dealing with importers, or with bad clients who try to rip you off.'

'I think, Mr Storey, that you are trying to tell me something without telling me something. We are friends here. You can speak to me directly to make everything easier to understand.'

'No, I don't think I can. I used to be a policeman, did you know that? You probably did if you've done your research on me. You said I looked like one and you were right. Well we were taught not to make any charges unless or until we had the evidence to back it up.'

'That sounds like a good instruction.'

'But I have to say Diamant was more flexible, more open. I thought I could make a deal with him. You're not as flexible, are you?'

'I'm the boss. Do you understand that, Mr Storey? I'm the one who makes the decisions. And because of that I have the responsibility. My husband, Toni, was only a year older than me when he died but he looked ten years older. The responsibility of coming here and looking after me and our friends made him look like an old man. Tired. So I don't have time to be flexible. I don't have the energy.'

Storey leaned over the counter and lowered his voice. 'So if I wanted to buy, let's say, some Class A drugs, you'd be the one bringing them into the country? Perhaps fetching them yourself from London, or maybe giving out a telephone number so I could call and arrange a meeting, and a sale?'

She stared at him, her eyes flicking from his face to the customer still playing with the tablet in the shop behind him, checking the customer's actions, making sure he wasn't about to make a dash for the door with the tablet tucked under his arm.

She said to Storey, 'We are a respectable business. I've enjoyed our conversation but it has nothing to do with what we sell. Here we sell things that people have brought to us in order to be given money. In my club we sell alcoholic drinks and play music loudly. That is all.'

'That's a shame, then, because I heard you sold drugs to people and that you might be holding on to two guitars for someone, guitars that are worth many thousands of pounds.'

'We have no guitars here.'

'That's what you keep telling me. The question is, do I believe you?'

'And what is the answer?'

'I'm sorry to tell you no, I don't.'

<hr />

DIAMANT WAITED UNTIL the man Storey had left before coming through the back door behind the shelves. He'd heard the man's voice and wanted to hear what Odeta said to him, how she'd handle it. He thought she'd done well — kept him at a distance and not given anything away. Played what the English called a 'straight bat', a defensive stroke with a cricket bat that gave no chances to the fielders to catch the ball.

Now he came up behind her as she finished a transaction for the sale of a tablet, letting himself be known by touching her on the arm. She didn't respond. The seductive persona she used upstairs in her apartment was not on display when she was being a professional. That was okay: he understood. In fact he preferred it. He became confused when she changed her manner towards him. It made him feel as if he was trying to catch up with her in a game whose rules he didn't understand.

She waited until they were alone at the counter, then turned to him, saying, 'You leave me out here to deal with this Storey by myself.'

'I'm sorry—'

'He thinks he knows something about us, about me, and I cannot let that happen. Do you understand?'

'Do you want me to hurt him?'

'I would like very much for you to hurt him. Do you think you can do it?'

He frowned at her, wondering why she would doubt him. 'He will be easy. He's tall but he's thin. I can perhaps break a bone or two.'

'Will you let him know it is you?'

Diamant paused. This was a good question. If Storey had been a policeman then perhaps he would still know policemen, and it might make life difficult for him and Odeta just at the point when their new system was beginning. The three brothers were nearly ready to move into the house in Ryton and it might not be a good idea to attract attention.

He said, 'There is a consideration.'

'What?'

He explained his thinking to her and watched as her face darkened.

'So you refuse to do anything about him?'

'I didn't say that. But I have a choice of two methods: I can wear a mask and injure him in a way that he doesn't know what has happened, or why. Or I can talk to him reasonably, let him know he's in danger and he should stop visiting us and looking for the guitars.'

'Which method do you think you'll choose?'

'I don't know yet,' Diamant said, still thinking. 'I have more to consider.'

———

SHE WAS STILL watching him and now she said, 'There is something else on your mind. Tell me.'

For the thousandth time he was amazed at her ability to know when something troubled him. Perhaps there was some witch's blood in her after all, as some of Toni's family members had said when he married her.

He said, 'The other night you said you would visit the Chance people to make them an offer about the guitars.'

'I did.'

'So when is this going to happen? We have two tactics available to us—we could use the fact that Tim Chance buys and uses drugs, and they should pay us for that information; or the fact that we have their guitars and we know their value. If they want them back, then they should pay us a portion of their worth.'

'We have been very fortunate. This is the advantage, Diamant, of expanding the business. Many different opportunities come your way.'

Diamant saw that she either didn't understand the problems or she didn't want to see them. He said, 'My question is, which approach are you going to take?'

'As part of your education I asked you to decide what I would do. Do you remember?'

She was enjoying this too much. He felt like a child again, but one about to fail a test.

He said, 'I think using blackmail is dangerous. Tim Chance is a pop star and if he's caught using drugs then I don't believe anyone will be troubled by it. People expect that pop stars use drugs.'

'And your concerns about my other option?'

'If we tell them we have their guitars they could report us to the police. Though the fact Tim Chance is a customer of ours might prevent them doing so. But I don't think they will agree to buy them back from you.'

'What else?'

'You said you would make them an offer of some kind. I haven't been able to understand what you mean. If they pay you for the guitars, that is good, but it's not probable. And I have the feeling you have something more in mind.'

She smiled one of her bitter smiles, those that brought ice into the dark centres of her eyes.

She said, 'Yes, I have something more in mind. You will discover soon.'

———

HE STAYED WITH her at the counter for a while and they talked about the new stock and what had been sold during the day. Diamant liked it when they spoke casually about the business of the store—it made him feel comfortable. Whenever Odeta started talking vaguely about her plans he became worried. He began to think she was hiding his future from him and he didn't like that. It was unfair of her when he put so much of his time and energy into making their current situation work.

So now this unclear talk of what she was going to say to the Chance people worried him. She thought she was being clever but it was the wrong time to be clever—there was too much at stake with the telephone drug delivery service they were setting up. Why would she place it at risk? Why wouldn't she tell him what she had planned?

NOW HE WAS in the Jaguar, driving home: a small apartment in the centre of town. As he drove he wondered if she was getting greedy, moving away from the influence of Ari Sallaku in London and beginning to think only of herself ... that was it, he realised. She was going to establish her own system, maybe even involve Maltin Lami, the hard man from Albania who had helped her ten years ago. Why wouldn't she? It would be easy to deceive Sallaku. London was a long distance from this small part of Coventry. She could say what she wanted to Sallaku and he would have no way of checking on her. Before he knew it, Lami and Odeta would have set up a system to rival London and there would be little he could do. It was her way of making her own reputation. Forget about Toni, look at *me!*

Diamant pulled into his parking slot and killed the engine. He looked at the inside of the Jaguar and realised it didn't stand comparison with the Mercedes Tim Chance had been driving. This was the cheap Jaguar, a ten year old X-Class, and it showed—there was no luxury in it at all. The seat in the Mercedes had fitted itself to his shape and all the furnishings had looked expensive. This piece of shit Jaguar was hard on his backside and had no elegance.

He realised he wanted what Odeta wanted—to get his hands on more money, to buy the best things and not the second-best. Perhaps he was as greedy as she was.

But there were easier ways for him to earn this money. He would contact Valmir, his cousin in London, and an associate of Ari Sallaku, and see what he thought. Perhaps he would have some ideas.

First, though, he must consider how to deal with Paul Storey.

CHAPTER TWENTY-NINE

KEN TALBOT LAY back on his bed and stared up at the ceiling. He hadn't slept in what was it, now, thirty-six hours?

The face was still there, right in front of him. Wherever he looked the face looked back. Inescapable. The eyes were wide open and scared, even though the pupils were blank, without light. The mouth was slightly open as if trying to say something, perhaps name the people who'd inflicted this indignity on him.

But Talbot already knew that, didn't he? He'd practically seen the whole thing ...

HE STOOD UP from the bed and walked down the short corridor to his study. He wanted to check the news sites again. There'd been nothing in the Coventry Telegraph but perhaps it was too soon. He'd reported it in the early hours of Wednesday, the police would have been there within an hour or two. They'd find the body, look around, investigate the area, then take him at his word and find the address of the Chance family and someone would go tell them. Then they'd have to identify the body.

They'd do all of this, presumably, before letting the press know. If they'd needed to identify the corpse maybe they'd have asked for help in the local press and TV — was anyone missing? Did anyone see anything that night? And so on. But if they already knew the body's identity perhaps it went a different way. Especially with a famous family like the Chances: keep it quiet, don't make a stir, don't encourage gawkers and the press to come round to the house or the place where the body was found.

But he was guessing. He had no idea what the real sequence of events would be.

He just knew he had to tell someone …

He went over it in his mind one more time. Following the two brothers, keeping a distance but feeling mildly excited, wondering where they might be going. It was a divergence from his vigil over Geneva but it was gone midnight and he knew she'd be in bed by now; she was an early-to-bed person. She'd said so in many of the interviews he'd read.

Tim's courtesy Mercedes was white, which made it easy enough to follow and eventually they hit the Hinkley Road going out to the motorway and Talbot began to worry they were heading for Birmingham, though where they might be going at nearly one o'clock in the morning, he had no idea.

Instead they went over the motorway junction, quiet at this hour, and took the narrow road through Ansty, turning right onto the even smaller lane towards the golf club. After a few hundred yards he saw Tim's brake lights brighten and he pulled up, switching his own lights off. Using the binoculars he always kept in his glove compartment, he saw Johnny and Tim climb out dressed in white outfits that almost glowed in the moonlight and open the boot ... and then lift out what Talbot knew immediately was a body. It was a full moon and the August sky was clear and he saw them count one and two and three and between them swing the body almost casually into a hedgerow.

They stripped off the outfits, which he realised were made of paper from the way they tore, and pushed them into a carrier bag which they put back in the boot.

When they climbed back in the Mercedes he reversed his own vehicle twenty yards and swung into the opening of the drive of the golf club and ducked down. Fifteen minutes later he realised they must have continued along the lane instead of turning back, eventually driving past the Rolls-Royce factory and taking a roundabout way home.

He sat for five minutes waiting for his heart to stop thumping. He thought he could almost hear it in the quiet of the car. He was in the countryside, at one o'clock on a summer's night, with nobody around, and he thought he'd just seen a dead body being dumped in a ditch.

What did people do in these situations?

WHAT HE DID was go and verify it. If he'd gone home without knowing for sure he'd have believed he was a fool and a coward for not checking.

What's more, a dread rose in his chest about who it might be. He was sure the body was too large to be Geneva. Could it have been Adam? It was big and heavy enough, judging by the efforts of the two other brothers. But would they really have done that to their own brother? Unthinkable.

So he needed to check. Then he'd decide what to do. Perhaps he would even *know* what to do, as if seeing the body close up would release some secret knowledge of how to continue.

He drove slowly towards where he thought they'd parked. He remembered it was just past a signpost for the golf club. He found it and stopped the car, leaving the engine running and the headlights on.

He finally climbed out, into the open air, one of the warmest nights of the year, the weatherman had said. Talbot leaned against his car and breathed deeply. The air was almost sweet. Ahead of him the moon turned the tarmacked road into a silver river snaking between the hedgerows. A bird called—he had no interest in birds and had no idea what it was.

Then he stood up and walked along the yard-wide strip of grass lining the tarmac. The other side of the grass was scrub, then a slight ditch and then taller hedgerows.

He saw the body straight away.

It showed pale white in the ditch, against the bushes, and he saw it wasn't Adam—the shape of the body was soft and curved, without Adam's muscular build.

He looked both ways up the road and then stepped from the grass and into the scrub on the far side, his feet scrunching through dry twigs and branches. From there he could peer down at the body, and immediately recognised Bill Chance, the children's father.

He'd landed on his back, his head staring up at the skies, his right arm bent awkwardly beneath it as if he'd just taken the opportunity to lie down and watch the planets as they moved between the stars.

Talbot recoiled, the expression on Chance's face now permanently burned in his memory: fear, surprise ... and love.

SINCE HE ARRIVED home he'd stayed indoors, not sleeping, his browser permanently open on the Coventry Telegraph's site and constantly refreshing it. He didn't know whether he wanted to see a story on the body or not. If there *was* a story he'd feel vindicated, believing he'd done something useful and that his obsession with Geneva Chance had been beneficial. If there *wasn't* a story he'd feel relieved ... he could perhaps imagine it hadn't happened and he'd hallucinated the whole thing.

And yet he wanted the story to appear. He wanted to know what happened next. Did the police have any clues? Would they suspect the Chance brothers of murdering their own father? Would they question them? Visit the house and find evidence ... ?

Of course! That's why the brothers were wearing white paper decorators' overalls. They must have killed him somewhere—perhaps even in the house—and were intent on leaving no clues, no blood spatter, no clothing hairs, nothing from their own persons other than what you'd expect from everyday contact with his children. So then burn the overalls and the plastic bag they were stuffed into. And—damnit!—it was Tim's courtesy car. Talbot would bet any money it was due to be taken back to the garage the next day and his own car, a black Mercedes, returned to him. So any stray fibres or hairs would stay in the white Mercedes or, more likely, cleaned out when it was valeted.

And that meant it was all planned. It wasn't an accident, a bit of rough and tumble with dad that went wrong. Johnny and Tim had thought it out, murdered their father and dumped the body without any clothing, perhaps in the hope no one would recognise him. If it weren't for him, Ken Talbot, they might have done it. Sure, a body would have been found eventually. And Bill Chance's going missing would have been recorded with the police. So they would surely have put the two events together … he'd just shortened the timeline.

… And then the same question kept coming back to him: *What should he do?*

Yes of course he should go to the police, admit to being the anonymous tipster and then explain what he was doing at one o'clock in the morning following the two brothers along a country lane. Would the police believe him? Or would they take one look at his online history, his Facebook group for Geneva, his various posts, the photos in his own study for God's sake, and think he was an oddball, a nutter, crying out for attention because in fact he was the perpetrator, not the witness?

He didn't want to take that risk. He didn't want the exposure, the explanations, the changes to his routine …

But he couldn't keep it to himself, could he? So not the police and definitely not the press or television. Then who?

———

HE WENT BACK to his bedroom and laid down again on his back, staring up at his ceiling. Then he realised he was mimicking Bill Chance's final position and shifted his bulk until he was face to face with the wall. This was what it would be like in prison, he reminded himself: lying on a bed staring at a blank wall.

The idea crept up on him slowly and then became insistent.

Fifteen years ago, when the obsession had first begun, he'd written a fan letter. It was the only time he'd put anything in writing and in fact he hadn't expected anything in return. He just wanted to express his appreciation for what the group meant to him.

But he got a reply. It was hand-written and was very kind, thanking him for his interest and hoping that he liked the next album.

He'd been delighted and carried the letter with him until it started to fray at the edges, at which point he'd bought a cheap frame from Boots and put it behind glass.

The letter had been so kind, and returned so quickly, it spoke of someone who could never have inflicted physical injury on someone else—certainly not the gaping wounds he'd seen on Bill Chance's torso.

Yes it was a risk but who better to talk to about this? After a day and a half thinking about what he'd seen, he'd convinced himself that it was only Johnny and Tim who were in play. No one else from the Chance organisation could be involved. That explained their secrecy, their planning, their flight into the country at one o'clock in the morning. Perhaps this was the only viable way of getting rid of their father's body … they could hardly cremate it in the back garden.

He turned over and struggled up from the bed. If he got through this he would definitely start that diet. He'd read good things about the 5 and 2 regime and thought he could give it a go.

First he had to set himself straight with this business.

He walked back to his study, pulled open his desk drawer and took out a small black address book. He'd had the house telephone number for a while but never used it — it was a secret he could keep to himself. Something to have in reserve. He opened the telephone book and pulled up the dialler on the phone and dialled the number.

It was answered after two rings by exactly the person he wanted to speak to: not Johnny, not Tim. Thank Christ for that.

He said, 'Hi, am I speaking to Adam Chance?'

CHAPTER THIRTY

THEY WERE SITTING in Stef's apartment, Liam thought, as if they were waiting for the gas man to call. Nothing they could do until Johnny had brought the money. So they sat in the two chairs, Liam texting Jen, Stef staring at him as if he couldn't believe his eyes.

Liam knew he was being stared at but didn't care. He was getting to like having an advantage over Stef. He'd taken a risk by stealing the guitars from the flat and taking them to the exchange shop but it was working out okay. He was showing he could play with the big boys, too. Word would get around that he wasn't just muscle, but he could think tactically. Or was it strategically? He always got those two confused.

He looked up from his phone and said, 'What do you think of Johnny Chance, then?'

Stef's expression didn't change. He had those dark eyes and the sharp cheekbones like a chisel staring at you. He said, 'What difference does it make what I think of him?

You've pissed him off so he's not going to work with us again, is he?'

Liam almost laughed. 'What the hell … did you think he was going to be like a regular customer? Want us to do a bit of burglary for him now and then?'

'You don't get it, Liam. That's why you're going to struggle at this.'

'What are you talking about?'

'Rich people have all sorts of things they need doing — things they can't or won't do themselves. Even if Johnny Chance didn't need us again, he might have a friend who wanted something. Beating up an agent, perhaps. Stealing a contract from someone's safe … I don't fucking know, do I? But you haven't built any trust at all. I'm not saying Chance is particularly trustworthy, but you've proved that we aren't, either. So we're fucked as far as him or his friends are concerned.'

Liam felt the hair on his arms prickle. He hated it when people criticised him, even if there was some truth in what they said. He knew he could be over-sensitive — it came from the way his dad always kept him down, he knew that. But he was going to prove them all wrong. He'd found something he was reasonably good at and he was going to come out on top, one way or the other. One of the ways you did that was by sticking to your guns, being persistent. So he said, 'You didn't answer the question.'

'Say it again.'

'We know we can't trust him, but what's he like apart from that? Is he a rich knob, given he's been famous since he was a teenager? Or can you have a conversation with him, go down the pub for a drink?'

He thought Stef would laugh but he didn't. He answered as if he'd already given the question some thought, his face a still mask.

'He's like all rich people: he's only interested in himself.'

'Fuck me, then I must be rich too and I never knew.'

'Not the same thing, dickhead. Well actually it might be. Rich people are usually rich because they've robbed someone. They might not have done it on purpose, like we do. Or even knew they were doing it … as far as they were concerned, they were just making money. Not taking it from anyone.'

'You're making this shit up. You read too much.'

'I should stop talking, it's like trying to train a chimpanzee.'

'… Who knows where the guitars are. Let me get this right. You're saying I'm not rich because I'm not really interested in myself. That doesn't make sense. Everyone's interested in themselves but not everybody's rich.'

'A tough one to figure out, isn't it?'

THERE WAS A knock on the door and Stef went to answer it. He came back with Johnny Chance behind him, using his tough-man slouch in his skinny jeans and black leather jacket. Liam thought the jacket was probably worth more than he'd see in a couple of months working at Ikea.

Liam said, 'We were just talking about you.'

'Sad lives you've got.'

'Wondering how far we could trust you not to fuck us up.'

Stef had taken his seat again and Johnny looked around then pulled over an upright chair and sat on it, looking down at him.

Johnny said, 'You can't trust me at all, can you? Though as far as I can see, you're the one in charge here. I'm just the bag man.'

He pulled a transparent sandwich bag from his jacket pocket and threw it at Liam, who caught it. He saw it was full of banknotes, mostly fifties and twenties.

He said, 'I don't have to count this, do I? I wouldn't want to be embarrassed in front of the people I'm going to see.'

'It's all there, what I said. A grand.'

'Easy come, easy go.'

'If you say so.'

Johnny turned to Stef. 'You're not saying anything today.'

'Glad you noticed. It's all down to my partner now.'

'You talk about trusting me, I've seen nothing yet to make me trust you.'

Stef shrugged and Liam said, 'What was it all about, anyway? Why did you want the guitars stolen? Is it an insurance scam?'

''Fraid not. But if I told you, I'd have to kill you.' He grinned without any humour in his eyes.

Liam felt his heartbeat flutter: not because he was afraid, but because here he was, dealing with Johnny Chance, someone who'd been famous as long as Liam could remember. And he had the advantage over him. It felt good.

'So we go to all the trouble of stealing them,' Liam said, 'then you want them back again within a week. Why not wait longer, till you're sure there's no come-back from the cops or the insurers or anyone else?'

'I don't have to answer your questions, but just to keep you quiet I'll tell you: it's that trust thing again. I don't trust either of you, so I'm going to stash the guitars somewhere safe myself. I should never have let them out of my control.'

Liam grinned back at him. 'That's what you get when you deal with crooks—crooked deals. I don't know what my partner said to you but the guitars were never in danger of going anywhere. I would have got them back when you needed them. I know a lot of people in Coventry, I could be very helpful to you—'

'Liam … ' Stef said.

'Fuck off, Stef. Mr Chance here deserves to know what we could do for him, given the opportunity. We're not just burglars, we can be anything you want. Enforcers, you know, beating people up. Or stealing specific things for you, like from a safe—'

Johnny didn't seem to hear him. Now he was standing up, brushing down the front of his jeans, looking at Stef rather than Liam. Liam noticed the lines on his face, the tiredness in his eyes. It surprised him. Then Johnny turned to him, saying, 'You don't know me. You don't know what I've done and what I can do. Don't get in a fight with me, do you understand?'

Liam also stood up and stepped closer. He was several inches taller than Johnny and he looked down at his upturned pale blue eyes. Then he reached into his pocket and pulled out a black USB memory stick.

He held it in front of Johnny's nose, saying, 'I thought you might like this back. Like a gesture of goodwill.'

Johnny snatched it from him, turning it over in his hands as if checking it was the right one.

He said, 'Did you open it?'

'It was blank.'

Johnny had put the stick in his pocket and was now staring at him. He said, 'That's interesting.'

'Why?'

'Because I don't believe you.'

'Well then,' Liam said. 'You'll just have to trust me, won't you?'

CHAPTER THIRTY-ONE

STOREY WONDERED WHY they'd chosen this place to meet. The Chace Hotel had an old-fashioned feel, with half-timbered beams on the outside and high ceilings, wooden floors and lots of wood panelling on the inside. Not the kind of place you'd expect a pop group to choose. No flashing lights, no juke box ... or perhaps his ideas about pop groups were old fashioned.

He sat in a corner of the bar waiting for them to arrive. The phone call had come from Adam Chance a couple of hours ago, saying they wanted to meet him. Not at the house, which was still full of police and forensic staff, but at this hotel out near Stonebridge Highway. He didn't say why.

Storey had guessed what they wanted to talk about but had decided to keep an open mind—people could surprise you.

At eight o'clock it was still sunny outside and the bar was beginning to fill up with a serious crowd—delegates from the business courses running in the conference rooms, a couple of American visitors, a party of middle-aged women celebrating a birthday.

Now the Chance brothers were coming through the wide doors, all three of them, a feast of denim and leather. What made them look like pop stars and not like men who worked underneath cars or in warehouses? Was it the quality of the denim and leather? The attitude they showed, owning the room as soon as they walked in, because they were now the most important people in it? Or maybe it was just expectation—they looked like pop stars because he knew they were.

Tim peeled off to go to the bar and Johnny and Adam sat down facing him, crossing their legs, brushing their trousers as if it were a family trait.

Adam said, 'Thanks for coming. Short notice, we appreciate it.'

'Where's Geneva? Is she not a part of this?'

'She's never part of the business end.'

'So this is business?'

'What did you think it was?'

Before he could reply Tim arrived with drinks for the three of them. He portioned them out then sat down. They all drank, Storey watching them, trying to gauge where they were. Whose idea was it? Who was the leader? Adam was the eldest but Johnny had the sharpest tongue and was probably the quickest witted.

Johnny said, 'So, Mr Investigator. What have you found out? Do you know who nicked my guitars?'

'I suppose the mourning period for your father's over, then, is it?'

'Leave him out of it,' Tim said. 'None of your fucking business.'

'Was your dad house-proud?'

'What?'

'Did he like cleaning, mopping floors, getting in the cracks and winkling out the dirt?'

'What are you talking about?'

'It's just that when the policeman opened the door yesterday, the door to your dad's cottage, the smell of bleach was really strong. I thought maybe he liked cleaning. Doing a thorough job.'

Adam leaned forward. He said, 'You saw him in the house, didn't you? Cooking. Peeling vegetables. As it happens, he was very domesticated. He kept our place and his own spotless. We even had to sack the cleaning woman because there wasn't enough for her to do.'

Storey nodded. 'Very good.'

'So,' Adam said, 'do you have anything to report? Any news about the guitars?'

Storey took a pull from his own drink. 'Not in so many words, no. A few ideas. Clues, you might say.'

'Like what?'

'Much too vague to bother you with. I need to do more digging first.'

Tim said, 'So you know something but you're not gonna tell us? Why's that? Aren't we paying you?'

'Technically, no. I haven't seen any money yet.' He paused. 'Tell me, do you really want the guitars back?'

'What kind of fucking question is that?' Johnny said.

'Frank Lamb told me you didn't want to report the theft. You've not exactly been hustling me to find out what I've been doing, until tonight. I'd say you were reluctant to talk to me or tell me anything. Which you must admit is a bit weird.'

Adam said, 'We've been a bit busy. Rehearsing, recording. Now with Dad … Plus, we've got a tour in a few weeks' time. It was Larry Lamb's idea to get you in and we never agreed to it, you're right. But it was always going to be a distraction. That's why we didn't report the theft in the first place. We haven't got the time.'

Storey took another drink and looked at each of them in turn. The likeness between them was disturbing because they were distinct in every way except their looks: the square chin, the pale blue eyes, the short straight nose …

He said, 'What do you want? Why are you here?'

Johnny reached into the pocket of his leather jacket and pulled out a transparent bag filled with notes. He dumped it on the table between them, where it settled awkwardly. He said, 'We're dispensing with your services. You haven't come up with anything and now, with Dad dead, the police are taking over.'

'They are? You've told them about the stolen guitars?'

'Yeah, and they've got a theory,' Tim said, grinning and looking at his brothers. 'They reckon it was all part of a pattern leading up to his murder.'

'What kind of pattern would that be?'

'First put the frighteners on us by nicking the guitars, just to show they can. Then they come in and write some graffiti on the cottage walls. Letting us know who the real target is. Then they take Dad out and knife him.'

'That's a big escalation there, at the end. You'd have thought there'd be another couple of steps in between before ratcheting up to murder.'

'It's their theory. Take it up with them.'

'Did they come up with it of their own accord?'

Adam leaned forward. 'What do you mean?'

'You didn't give them any tips in that direction?'

'Why would we do that? We're musicians, not detectives.'

Storey shrugged. 'It just seems early for them to have a theory, before they've really had time to work on it. For example, the break-in to the studio was a set-up, wasn't it?'

'What do you mean?' Johnny said.

'The burglars didn't break in. Someone helped them crack the electronic code for the studio door—or even gave it to them. Second, do the police have a theory about how your dad was taken out of the grounds? You can only operate the gate from inside the house or if you've got the electronic gadget in your car. Your dad wouldn't have been in any state to be taken over the wall ... so how did they get through the gate? Do the police have any ideas about that?'

Tim said, 'Why don't you ask your friends in the cop shop? They didn't tell us anything, as if it were a bloody state secret.'

The doors of the bar opened and a large party of young men came in, talking loudly. Storey and the three brothers turned to look at them as they went to the bar to order.

Storey said to the brothers, 'Have the police released the body yet? For burial?'

'No,' Adam said. 'Why?'

'Just wondering. Because he was murdered they'll hang on to him for a few days, while they investigate. Looking for all that CSI stuff—material under his fingernails, fibres in his hair, that sort of thing.'

Tim said, 'They won't find anything like that.'

'How do you know?'

'Stands to reason. He was found naked, wasn't he? Sounds like the men who killed him got rid of any evidence.'

'Men?'

'Must have been more than one, mustn't it, to get him out? Dad was a big guy.'

'I suppose so.' He took another swig from his glass, noticing the brothers had barely touched their own. They were concentrating on him. He added, 'It's amazing what forensics pulls out nowadays. Did you see the equipment they took into his cottage? They'll find a fly's leg if it's out of place.'

Johnny pointed to the bag of money on the table. 'Are you going to pick that up?'

Now Storey leaned back and stretched, showing he was comfortable. He said, 'I like to stick with a case, as we investigators call them. Why don't you wait until I've found the guitars before you pay me? How's that?'

'We can't let you in the grounds again,' Johnny said. Storey saw a coldness come into his eyes. 'There's too much going on. The police are all over us. It won't be long before the press are on it and everything goes to shit. And if you're there, the notorious Paul Storey, it'll just make things worse.'

Storey thought for a moment, looking at the men at the bar, still making a noise and patting each other on the back. Perhaps they were a sports team celebrating a win. He said, 'I can live with that. Incidentally, does Geneva even know you're seeing me tonight?'

'Like we said, she's not involved in the business dealings.'

'Maybe not, but she's involved in all this, isn't she? The theft and the murder of your father. You can't keep her out of it.'

'That's exactly what we're going to do. If you want this money, you've got to stop talking to her. Call it a condition.'

Storey stood up and looked down at them. 'I think that's up to her, don't you? Call it a suggestion.'

He walked out of the bar.

CHAPTER THIRTY-TWO

BACK WHEN HE used to work in an office, Ken Talbot would tell the woman in the cubicle next to him about the first time he saw Chance play.

'It was a club in Tile Hill,' he said, 'off Broad Lane. Used to have talent nights every other Friday. These four skinny kids came on, looking like nothing, like a strong wind'd blow them away. Two at the front, the boy and the girl, Johnny and Geneva, they sparked off each other like they'd been doing it forty years. He'd stand back a bit and play something, a lick on his guitar—they were doing Eurythmics covers, stuff like that—then Geneva'd come forward and belt out a line like Annie Lennox, only Annie Lennox who'd swallowed a bag of nails, all gravelly and mean.'

'I love the Eurythmics,' the woman said.

'Then I watched them get bigger and bigger, they went to London and got a record deal and started turning up on TV shows. Not everybody liked them but I suppose because I'd seen them at the beginning I felt some kind of connection with them.'

'Really?' the woman would say, looking at him oddly.

'I've been to see them twenty-three times,' he'd say. 'Never been disappointed.'

'Lucky you,' she'd say, and turn back to her monitor.

NOW HE WAS waiting for Adam Chance to arrive at his flat so he could tell him he'd seen Johnny and Tim dump the body of their father in a ditch.

Was he mad?

What did he expect Adam to say? Thanks for the info, I'll get back to you on that.

He was more likely to get angry at him, threaten him, swear at him …

Talbot was surprised Adam had even agreed to come. If he'd been in Adam's place he would have laughed at him and hung up. Or reported him to the police.

But Adam Chance was known to be the sensible one, the one who acted least like a spoiled pop star and most like a real human being. He'd earned sympathy when his wife, Angie, had run off with someone else, and he was usually the one the girls said they'd most like to marry. While Johnny was the one they'd most like to fuck. So when Talbot spoke to him, telling him what he'd seen, part of him wasn't surprised when Adam asked who he was and where he lived …

And twenty-four hours later he was wearing his best trousers, an ironed shirt and clean shoes, waiting for Adam to arrive. He'd mopped the bathroom and wiped the bath.

Put Harpic down the toilet. Wiped the surfaces in the kitchen. Made his bed and tidied his study. Who did he think was coming—the Queen?

It was after nine thirty, getting dark, when the knock on the door came. At last.

He opened it and there was Adam Chance, in person. Tall, good-looking, broader in the shoulders than he would have thought. Denim jeans and shirt with a leather jacket over the top. A silver ear-ring in his left ear, like a pirate. And wearing a thin white scarf around his neck despite the hot weather.

Talbot's throat was dry but he thought he managed to appear casual: 'Adam, come in.'

'Is it Ken? Glad to meet you.' And there he was, holding out his hand for Ken to shake, feeling his own hand soft and pudgy against Adam's firm grip.

Adam said, 'Do we go through there?' Pointing with his eyes to encourage Talbot to let him in.

Talbot stood back, then closed the door behind Adam as he walked along the corridor, past the old framed posters of the band's tour dates, through to the small sitting room, newly vacuumed and smelling of one of those air-fresheners with wooden sticks poking out of the top of a bottle.

Adam made himself comfortable, still smiling, while Talbot offered him tea or coffee.

'No, that's okay,' Adam said. 'Tell me something about yourself. You mentioned in your phone call that you wrote to me years ago and I replied. So you've been a fan a long time.'

Talbot sat facing him and told him the story of when he'd first seen Chance, in the pub in Tile Hill, and how he'd followed their career ever since. 'To be honest,' he said, 'I think when I was younger I had a bit of a crush on Geneva.'

Adam laughed pleasantly, showing his film-star teeth.

'You're not alone!' he said. 'I doubt we'd have been so popular if Geneva wasn't singing with us. The thing is, both women *and* men like her. Of course the men fancy her but the girls want to be like her. Did you fancy her, Ken?'

'I'd be lying if I didn't! She's very attractive.'

'Yes,' Adam said, 'everyone thinks so, don't they? She's a very pretty girl. So you've been to see us play, then?'

Talbot said yes he had, then asked if Adam wanted to see his mementos. He could have the tour if he liked.

'I'd like that,' Adam said, standing up. 'Where do we start?'

Talbot led him back down the corridor to his study and showed him inside, pointing out the photos he'd stuck on the wall that morning—the official band photos, not the private ones he'd taken himself. Then he opened a drawer and showed Adam the tickets to the gigs he'd seen over fifteen years ago, the print fading, the prices seeming ridiculously cheap.

'My word,' Adam said, 'you were a fan, weren't you?'

Talbot felt himself blushing and wondered whether he should be doing this … it was now beginning to feel odd. A little childish. The sort of thing a grown man nearly forty years of age shouldn't be doing. If it were Led Zeppelin or The Who it might be different. But Chance was a pop group, like Take That or The Spice Girls … he felt his credibility draining away just at the point he needed it most, talking to a member of the group about the most unbelievable thing he'd ever witnessed.

Adam said, 'So how does your wife or girlfriend feel about all this?'

A dagger into Talbot's chest. He put a bright look on his face. 'Not married! I lived with a woman for a couple of years but we split up. Flying solo at the moment.'

'Me too!' Adam said. 'Great, isn't it? No one to tie you down or tell you to stop watching television … all that shit they put you through.'

Talbot knew he was being kind but went along with it, laughing in a conspiratorial way as he ushered Adam back to the sitting room.

Now Adam was saying, 'So look, you started to tell me something pretty incredible on the phone yesterday. What's all that about?'

Talbot sat opposite him again, feeling the size of his buttocks on the sofa, comparing them to the lithe man facing him, feeling underpowered and, admit it, a little stupid.

He told his story, fudging the part about watching the house at midnight in case he caught a glimpse of Geneva by saying he was returning home from a night out when he happened to recognise Johnny and Tim pass in front of him at a junction. Given it was almost one o'clock he thought it would be fun to follow them and see what they were up to.

'So you were alone in your car?'

Talbot nodded. 'Yes, no one else saw them as far as I know. You know what Coventry's like. Traffic all day long till ten o'clock, then it goes dead. So one o'clock in the morning there was nobody. Nobody with me and not many, if any, out and about.'

'Okay,' Adam said, leaning forward. 'Then what happened?'

Talbot described following them out of the town, over the motorway junction and through Ansty before they turned towards the golf course.

'The golf course?'

'Yes. They drove past the entrance and I have to tell you, I was really beginning to wonder what they were up to now. At first I thought they might have been going to the golf club for a private do ... or perhaps going on to Birmingham.'

'But they stopped.'

Talbot said yes and then described what he'd seen and, afterwards, what he'd found when he went back to the place where they'd parked.

When he stopped talking there was a pause. Then he said, 'I was waiting to see it on the news. I was sure someone would find him.'

'It was definitely Tim and Johnny?'

'I've been a fan for nearly twenty years. I'm sure it was them. And it was definitely your dad.'

'Yes, it was, wasn't it?'

Adam leaned back and let out a deep sigh. He seized the ends of his scarf and wafted them in front of him. 'Wow, that's some story. My poor old dad, what a way to end up, eh?'

Talbot nodded, thinking Adam was reacting oddly to what he'd heard. It was probably shock.

Adam said, 'So eventually you reported it.'

'I didn't know what to do at first. Then I called it in, anonymously. There's a number on the Internet for anonymous tips. I just mentioned the body and who it was. I didn't say anything about Tim or Johnny.'

'Why not? You're a witness.'

Talbot shrugged. 'Dunno. I suppose with my connection to the band … it felt like a betrayal. I'm still not comfortable talking to you about it, to be honest.'

'It was my dad, man!'

'I know, I know … but I didn't know that what I'd seen was right. I couldn't believe that Johnny and Tim had … you know. So what options were left? Had they found the body and for some reason wanted to dispose of it by the roadside? That didn't make any sense. Nothing made any sense.'

Adam was nodding. 'I get that. There are times when nothing makes sense.'

Talbot said, 'So I presume the police have been in touch? I mean, I haven't seen anything on the news or in the papers, but I can't believe they didn't find the body.'

Yes,' Adam said, 'they found the body. I had to go over and identify it today. Nobody else in the family wanted to do it.'

'So Tim and Johnny haven't said anything?'

Adam shook his head. 'You wouldn't expect them to, would you? In the circumstances.'

'Did they not get on with Bill? Do you think they had a row or something?'

'No idea.'

'How … how is Geneva taking it?'

Adam looked at him fiercely. 'How the fuck do you think she's taking it? It was her dad.'

'Yes, sorry, sorry … thoughtless.' He paused. 'Have the police said anything about suspects?'

'No, nothing. They're still in the house, doing forensic stuff. God knows why, he wasn't killed there, was he?'

'Maybe not.'

'Maybe not?' Adam said sharply.

Talbot realised he'd made a mistake. He hadn't mentioned following the two brothers from the house, the body already in the boot. So he should have no reason for believing Bill was murdered there, should he? But how else to explain the fact that Johnny and Tim were disposing of the body? How would they have found it if they hadn't been there when the murder was committed?

Talbot began to feel uneasy about the situation he was in. He hadn't really thought it through. Perhaps he should try to get a sense of Adam's thinking ...

He said, 'So what are you going to do?'

Adam had been looking away, and Talbot thought he saw a deep sadness in the other man's eyes. He understood it. He'd been responsible for bringing news to Adam Chance that he would now have to process on top of the murder of his father. His two brothers might have been involved in the murder of their father. Life wasn't getting any easier for him.

Now Adam was standing up and Talbot struggled to his feet to see him out. Adam said, 'I'll have to talk to the boys first, won't I, before I say anything to anybody. You've not mentioned it to anybody else?'

'Absolutely not. I wanted to keep it in the family, so to speak, honour your father's memory. I thought you'd be the one to talk to.'

'Good. I'll talk to the boys and after that I'll bring the police in.'

He started walking down the corridor to the front door, Talbot thinking it had gone better than he thought. Much better. Adam was always the sensible one. He'd understand what he had to do.

Half-way along the corridor, Adam stopped. 'Oh, I forgot to tell you. You know that letter you think I sent you fifteen years ago? It was probably my Dad who sent it. We had so much correspondence, he dealt with all that stuff. We just signed them at the bottom. Ironic, eh?'

Talbot felt the bottom fall out of his stomach. That was so disappointing …

Adam went on, 'But to compensate I brought a present for you.'

'Me? No, really … given the circumstances …'

'It's nothing,' Adam said, unfurling the thin white scarf from around his neck. 'I thought you should have this.'

He held the scarf out so Talbot could read it like a banner. It read 'No Chance, 2000AD', a remnant from the tour. Talbot already had one, but not one that had been on Adam Chance's shoulders. He felt himself blushing again as Adam stepped forward and wound it around his neck.

'No, really …'

'It's okay,' Adam said. 'You should have this. Let me …'

Now he was standing even closer and was working his way round so he was standing behind Talbot, who thought the scarf was a bit tight.

He said, 'Could you loosen—'

Whatever Adam was doing behind there, he wasn't listening. Talbot realised Adam had looped the scarf round but still held both ends—which for some reason he was pulling. Talbot brought his hands up to the scarf and tried to put his hands underneath it, next to his neck. But his hands were too fat to slip them between the scarf and his skin.

He felt himself lurching, now, losing his balance and only kept upright by Adam's strong hands on the scarf. Damn, he was definitely falling, this was awkward. He needed to get his feet underneath him but Adam kept jerking him backwards, as if he were deliberately trying to keep him off balance. Why would he do that? Why doesn't he let go, give me a bit of air?

He was feeling faint now, too, starting to see little black triangles everywhere, as if he were looking through a kaleidoscope that was constantly changing ...

And he was seeing the walls of the corridor at odd angles, the framed posters of the band, of Geneva, of himself in front of the Hammersmith Odeon when he went down to London to see them play to a packed house. Mostly screaming teenagers, of course, so he stood out like a pervert amongst all the youngsters a head shorter than he was ... but he didn't care, he was seeing Chance, live, at one of the biggest venues in the country, watching Geneva Chance singing her heart out, looking at him as she did so, singing her song just for him ...

If he drifted off to sleep now he'd remember that moment perfectly. That would be nice.

CHAPTER THIRTY-THREE

DIAMANT DIDN'T LIKE leaving Kostas in charge on a Saturday afternoon: it was one of their busiest times. But Odeta had been firm—she wanted to go see the Chance people *now*. She had made her plans and she didn't want to wait any more.

So Diamant had checked Kostas knew how to work the till and the credit card machine, again, and told him that if anything of high value came in, he was to take delivery and tell the seller to come back on Monday morning for the valuation. They would only be gone an hour.

He had asked one of the other brothers to follow Tim Chance home one night, so he knew the address, and now they approached the high walls and the black gates, slowing down to see if they would open.

They didn't.

So he climbed out of the Jaguar, leaving Odeta sitting as upright as a queen in the passenger seat, staring ahead and seeing nothing, while he approached the gate post and found a button and the speech mechanism.

A voice he could not understand because of electronic crackle said something to him. He said, 'I am Diamant Dushku and I am arrived with Odeta Morina to discuss business with the Chances.'

Another noise that he couldn't understand and then the gates began to open inwards. He climbed back in the car and drove through. He parked behind two other cars on the driveway, neither of them the white Mercedes belonging to Tim Chance that he envied. Perhaps he wasn't home.

Odeta waited for him to walk around and open the passenger door for her, still establishing her position, and the door to the house was now opening. He had looked at pictures online and recognised the oldest brother, Adam, and the youngest, Johnny, as they came out and stood on the top step. Behind them the house was very large and modern with lots of glass and roofs. It seemed they still had some money.

There was a noise to his right and he saw that the sister, Geneva Chance, had come out of a building that was attached to the back of the garage. She was slim with short hair and he liked to look at her. She stared back at him but didn't move.

Now Odeta walked towards the two brothers, and Diamant followed. He admired her confidence, her willingness to place herself in difficult situations. He still had no idea what she was going to say to the brothers but was interested to find out.

And then Tim Chance appeared behind his brothers, coming to a halt as if he'd run to the door. He stared at Odeta and then stepped forward.

'What the fuck are you here for?'

Odeta glanced at Diamant, saying quietly, 'This is Tim Chance?'

He nodded and she turned back to them.

'I suggest we go inside to have the conversation. I have an offer to make to you.'

Tim looked as if he wanted to come down the steps and punch her, but Adam put a hand on his shoulder and all three brothers then turned and went back inside, Adam waiting by the door to see Odeta and Diamant in.

NOW THEY WERE seated like cousins visiting at Christmas, Odeta and Diamant on a small sofa, the three brothers in chairs and on a longer sofa facing them. Diamant wondered if they would ask whether they'd like tea.

Adam Chance was doing most of the talking, getting them into the room, asking them to sit, now looking at them expectantly. Tim still seemed angry and the young one, Johnny, stared with dark eyes at Odeta and then Diamant, then back again. Diamant supposed this young one had been in many fights.

They did not seem like musicians. They did not seem peaceful or friendly, as he supposed musicians to be.

They seemed disturbed and on edge.

Adam said, 'My brother tells me you run a night club in Coventry. He also says that this gentleman—' nodding towards Diamant '—has information about some guitars that were stolen from us a few days ago. So can you tell us what this information is or what you'd like from us?'

Odeta had said nothing so far. Now she turned towards Adam and said, 'You are Adam Chance. I have read that you are the sensible one of the brothers. They say Tim Chance is wild and difficult to control.'

Johnny Chance said, 'What do they say about me?'

'That you are the dangerous one, the one most likely to take risks. And the most creative.'

Johnny grinned. 'I'll take that. So, Mrs Gypsy Woman or whoever you are, what can we do for you?'

'We have two pieces of information that are useful to us, and also possibly to you. The first is that Mr Tim Chance is a user of cocaine. Please do not ask how I know. But I'm certain that you know this too.'

She let that hang in the air and no one argued with it or denied it. She nodded as if satisfied, then said, 'The second piece of information is that we know where your stolen guitars are and can recover them for you. For a small fee.'

'How small?' Adam asked.

Now Odeta took her time, folding her hands on the lap of her black skirt and looking at each of the brothers in turn. She said, 'I am a small businesswoman, with a shop and a nightclub in Coventry. And now I would like to get into show-business.'

———

DIAMANT HAD BEEN watching the brothers. Now he turned to stare at his boss. What was she saying? What could she mean?

Adam Chance said, 'That sounds … interesting. What exactly do you mean? What kind of show-business?'

Odeta smiled one of her rare smiles and said, 'I do not sing nor do I play an instrument. I'm not interested in performing. But I am, I think, a good businesswoman. I would like to become involved in your marketing. Specifically, your clothing and products. Diamant, show them your tee-shirt.'

He stared at her even harder. Then he pulled back the sides of the thin canvas jacket he was wearing so they could all read his tee-shirt: 'Odeta's Man'.

Odeta said, 'You see the gold lettering? I worked for a month with the printer to achieve that shade of gold. And the ... what do you call it? The typeface. He made adaptations to it so there is no other typeface like it. This is the kind of expertise I can bring to your marketing.'

Diamant saw that Johnny Chance was having difficulty holding back his laughter, lowering his head and shaking it and coughing at the same time. He wondered if Odeta saw this and he also wondered what she would think of this behaviour.

As for himself, he did not know what to believe. It was so different from what he expected that he couldn't organise his thoughts to make sense of it. Instead he kept his face serious, as if he'd known all the time that this was her offer.

Odeta was continuing: 'I know you have professionals to do this kind of thing, but I am saying you can dismiss them. I and my company will be responsible for all products, tee-shirts, calendars, pencil cases, diaries, everything of that nature.'

Adam said, 'That's a nice offer. What if we can't do it? We have contractual obligations we can't just cancel.'

Odeta smiled at him again. 'As I mentioned we have two pieces of information. If you cannot cancel your other obligations and allow me to manage your marketing, the first of those pieces of information, concerning Tim Chance's drug addiction, will be revealed to the press. This might damage your reputation, especially amongst younger women. As for the second piece of information, the location of your guitars, well that will remain with me. And at some point in the future those instruments will find their way into the possession of a collector who will have paid me many thousands of pounds.'

Johnny said, 'What if we just tell the police about you? We reported their theft the other day. They might arrest you for blackmail. How does that sound?'

Odeta was still smiling. 'But we know they weren't stolen from you, don't we? We share a connection.'

Diamant was still watching her. How did she arrive at that idea—that the man Liam Fisher had stolen the guitars with the Chances' agreement? Was she just trying it to see what kind of reaction it got?

In fact none of the brothers disagreed with her, at least directly. Johnny said, 'We have someone looking for them. Someone private.'

'I know. Mr Paul Storey. Has he delivered them to you?'

'Not yet.'

'And he will not. He is a fool and his connection to this situation will soon be ended, in any case. Now, shall we discuss how to make this work?'

———

ODETA STILL WORE a plain gold ring with a single sapphire set into it on her right hand. It was the only thing of Toni's that she kept. After his murder she burned his clothes, his papers, anything that belonged to him except the photos of their wedding. It was as if she never wanted to see anything belonging to him again.

Now she sat in the passenger seat as Diamant drove them home and she moved the ring around on her finger with her other hand, back and forth, as if making some kind of connection with her dead husband. As though she wanted to contact him and tell him, I did it. I created my own business.

Diamant had decided that he would talk to her directly, tell her he thought her idea was crazy, that she knew nothing about marketing, about pop music, about the world in which the Chances operated.

But she was so pleased with herself he found it hard to open the subject. Instead he asked her why she thought Liam Fisher had stolen the guitars with the Chances' knowledge.

She said, 'Because he brought them to us and not to someone who would sell them abroad. If he knew their value he would find someone in London who had a client for this kind of material. That is not you and me, Diamant.'

'You could have shared your thinking with me,' he said. 'I could have asked Liam Fisher directly.'

'I don't need to tell you everything. That is why I continue to be the leader of our enterprise.'

'You could have told me about the marketing idea, too.'

'Yes,' she said, 'I could.'

Diamant felt himself growing tight across the chest and he wanted to hit her. Instead he breathed deeply and said nothing. He sensed her looking at him but didn't return her gaze.

Finally she said, 'I do not need your approval, Diamant, for what I've decided to do. I would like you to agree with me, but it's not necessary. You can run the telephone line for drugs with Kostas and his brothers and I will deal with the Chance brothers. How strange, eh, that there are two sets of brothers here! It's like it was planned that way. Perhaps Toni is up there taking care of us, what do you think?'

Now he glanced at her. 'I'm not sure Toni is in a position to take care of us.'

'What, you think he's somewhere putting coal into a fire, forever and ever?'

This was the opening he was looking for. He said, 'Toni knew what he was good at. He knew how to run the organisation. He knew how to lead men—when to command and when to ask.'

'This is not about Toni, is it?'

There she was, doing it again, anticipating what he wanted to say.

'It's moving away from what we know,' he said. 'The timing is delicate. We need to make sure the telephone business works, that everyone knows their place and their responsibilities.'

'Diamant, I believe you're turning into a leader at last. I must have taught you well.'

'You taught me to concentrate. You taught me to listen to my instinct, and my instinct is telling me that working with the Chance brothers is dangerous. They are dangerous.'

'What makes you say that? They make music and sing. That is all they've ever done, since they were children.'

'Yes,' he said. 'But perhaps they are bored with that now. Perhaps they want something else in their lives.'

Again he knew she was looking at him, he felt her eyes on his face … and then she shifted her position, turning slightly away to look through the passenger window. She said, 'We will not talk of this again. You seem to forget I've been training you, feeding you like you might feed a plant. I expect you to take over from me, Diamant, when I move into different areas of my life. You have been loyal and honest and worked hard. I have enjoyed working with you, and to be honest I thought our relationship might develop into something a little more.'

'I'm—'

'But now I realise that you don't want me and you have no girlfriend. I don't blame you for being gay, it's something we cannot help.'

'I'm not gay!'

'Please don't argue with me. It's obvious now I've realised it. Your ridiculous shoes, your jewellery, the way you always smell like a woman. You even walk a little funny.'

'Odeta, I swear to you—'

'We won't talk of it again. I will tell no one, unless you want me to. Perhaps one of Kostas' brothers is that way inclined. I could arrange a match.'

Diamant opened his mouth and then closed it. He'd seen her in these moods before, when nothing could persuade her from her position. It was better to say nothing and let it blow away. She would have forgotten in a few days.

As they neared the shop, Odeta said, 'Have you done anything with Mr Paul Storey yet?'

'No,' Diamant said. In fact Storey had been on his mind as something he should deal with this weekend.

But now he didn't feel like telling Odeta anything. She said, 'It would be better if he was dealt with before I started working with the Chance brothers. It would be ... cleaner.'

'I know.'

'So you'll take care of it?'

'I said I'll take care of it.'

He stopped the car outside the shop and stared through the windscreen, unsure of the feelings that had suddenly begun to rage in his chest. He was angry, but he didn't know who with. He was confused, but he didn't know about what. The world had become more complex and difficult to understand in the course of one afternoon.

He looked down to see Odeta had placed a hand on his knee. But he knew it wasn't a sexual advance. It was a calming gesture. She had seen into him again and recognised he wasn't at peace. Damn her cleverness! He could never escape and feel something she didn't already see and understand.

Did nothing ever surprise her?

———

KOSTAS WAS ALONE in the shop, sitting on a stool and looking at a car magazine. He stood up when Odeta and Diamant came through the door and placed the magazine on the counter.

Odeta said, 'Has there been some business?'

'I sold a small television and a PlayStation 3,' Kostas said. And some games for the PlayStation.'

'Anything else?'

'Yes, someone arrived to take something back.'

'What?' Diamant said. 'Who was it?'

'He was a big man with a bruise on his nose,' Kostas said, perhaps already sensing trouble. 'He had a ticket. It was legitimate.'

'Yes, but what was it for?'

'He wanted the guitars. The two guitars that were in the stock cupboard. He paid in full, in cash.'

He pressed a key on the till and it opened and he pulled out a wad of notes.

Diamant couldn't bring himself to look at Odeta. He knew for once she'd been surprised by events. And it wouldn't be making her happy.

CHAPTER THIRTY-FOUR

THERE WERE MORE people in the cemetery than Storey would have liked, but it was Sunday afternoon so perhaps he should have expected it.

He knew his way to his father's grave without having to think about it and when he arrived he looked around before squatting to rearrange the remains of the flowers he'd left the previous week. They'd wilted in the heat but still had colour and shape so he left them where they were. Perhaps change them next time.

He'd been coming to visit regularly since the burial but what had happened to Bill Chance had given him more incentive. He'd stayed away from the Chances since he'd met the brothers in The Chace Hotel a couple of days before—partly because they'd told him he wouldn't be allowed into the house and partly because their attitude had pissed him off. With Frank Lamb still in America and Geneva out of touch, he felt his connection to the family and to his 'case'—if he could call it that—was more or less broken. So he'd stayed at home, done his laundry, went shopping. Lived an ordinary life for three days and given no thought to how he should deal with the Chances.

Now, staring down at the marble headstone with his father's name and dates on it, he thought about Bill Chance and how he'd ended up, thrown naked into a ditch in the middle of nowhere. His own father had died of cancer, painfully despite drugs, but at least he was warm and knew where he was. He couldn't imagine what it would have been like for Bill, his life draining from him through the cuts in his abdomen.

Who had done it, and why? How had Bill been taken from his house and why was his murder so apparently brutal?

Storey had resisted the desire to call Jackie West and ask whether she knew anything. Instead he'd kept an eye on the local television news and Internet sites, waiting for Bill's name to pop up next to the name of someone who'd been arrested as a suspect in the murder. He knew little about Bill's past apart from what he'd been told by the family … maybe it *was* disgruntled gangsters from the Spanish Costa, people with underworld nicknames wearing lots of gold who'd borne a grudge against Bill for several years and finally found a way to extract a humiliating revenge.

Or perhaps it was closer to home … someone Bill knew and had annoyed since coming back to the UK.

Storey couldn't stop himself contemplating whether Bill's own family could be involved. Their cold-heartedness when they'd learned of his death was chilling, but as Geneva had said, they didn't like him. They'd lived with him and funded him, but perhaps that was as far as their filial duty went. You couldn't be forced to like your own family, and why should they fake it in these circumstances?

Did he really believe the brothers or Geneva would be involved? Certainly it would be relatively easy for the brothers to kill him and get him out of the house before dumping him … but what would be their motive? Dislike? Was that a strong enough emotion?

There had been times when he hadn't got along with his father—the period before he'd decided to join the police force, for example, when he'd appeared to be drifting. His father had always had a trade and couldn't understand why his son wasn't built the same way. He'd ask pointed questions about whether Paul was still renting a flat or had he put down the deposit on a house yet. Or he'd suggest he could lend Paul some money if he wanted to retrain as an electrician, plumber, dentist … anything.

So when Paul decided he'd join the police force his father was apprehensive but glad he'd finally found a direction. He'd be okay now, set up for life. Something his generation seemed desperate to ensure.

And now it was all up for grabs since he'd quit as a specialist firearms officer to return to Coventry and start again.

Doing what?

Still looking. Waiting for something to come along that was both exciting and low-profile. He'd had enough of high-profile, though everything he'd been involved in since coming home had thrust him, eventually, in front of a photographer or a journalist with a microphone.

'Do you know what, Dad?' he said to the gravestone. 'I wish I were a plumber, now, or an electrician. Then I wouldn't know all these weirdos or have all these secrets.'

But even as he said the words he knew he also enjoyed the haphazard nature of his life, the impossibility of knowing what he'd be doing one day to the next, the varied and unusual people he met every week.

He wasn't sure he could give all that up for a career looking into people's drains.

IT WAS LATE afternoon when he arrived home, parking the Volvo on the main street and crossing the twenty yards or so of grass to get to the front gate.

He unlocked his front door and went in, and was immediately aware that someone else was in the house. There was a strong scent, something sweet but not quite a woman's perfume. He called out, 'Hello, who's there?' and then things happened very fast.

First, Diamant Dushku appeared in the doorway to the living room, pointing a handgun at Storey's midriff.

He was probably expecting Storey to put up his hands, the normal response to show surrender. But Storey was on alert as soon as he entered the house and knew that surprise was actually on his side. For one thing, Diamant hadn't cleared the doorway fully and the sphere of action of his right hand, holding the gun, was restricted. Secondly, he probably wasn't aware that Storey was comfortable around guns and knew Dushku wasn't holding it in a practised way.

Storey took half a second to size up the situation then took one step forward, pulled Diamant's gun-hand towards and past his waist, twisting it hard so he gave up the gun, then levered Diamant's fingers back so he went to his knees to avoid them being broken. Diamant grunted and at that point Storey let go of his hand.

He slipped the magazine from the gun, a Glock 19, put the magazine in one of his trouser pockets and the gun in the other, then helped Diamant to his feet.

The man was flushed, a layer of sweat breaking out on his forehead. He put a hand on the door frame to steady himself and said, 'That was very good. I didn't know you were an expert. I would have been more careful.'

STOREY SAID, 'COME in and sit down.'

He went into the sitting room and waited for Diamant to come in. Eventually the other man stepped through the doorway and pulled himself to his full height. He walked to Storey's sofa and sat down. He said, 'What are you going to do with me?'

'How did you get in?'

'Your door is easy. I have a plastic card—I push back and forward and lean against the door and it comes open. I do it often. You need a better lock.'

Storey remained standing so Diamant wouldn't think he had an advantage. He said, 'Is this what you do for Odeta? Is that why you're her man?'

'Odeta and I are nearly partners. We run the business together.'

'So this was your idea to come here? What were you going to do?'

Diamant moved and sat on the edge of the sofa, his knees high and his hands dangling between them. He shrugged. 'I had not decided. You saw that I came to the door when you arrived—I didn't shoot you in the back like a coward. I thought I might talk to you.'

'Perhaps you were going to threaten me. Perhaps you and Odeta thought I was getting too close to understanding your business. The drugs. The stolen property.'

Diamant said nothing and looked around. Then he said, 'This is an old man's house. The pictures on the wall, this old-fashioned seat, the pattern in the carpet. Why do you live here?'

'In my house I ask the questions.'

'You are going to shoot me if I do not answer?'

Storey took the magazine and weapon from his pockets and slid the magazine back into place. He remembered the familiar feel and the weight in his hand. It was both comforting and disturbing at the same time. He said, 'I don't shoot people now, unless they really deserve it. So what did you want to talk to me about?'

'I have to tell you to stay away from Odeta and me. She is becoming angry. She wants to hurt you. She thinks you have shown a lack of respect for her work.'

'And do you think that?'

Diamant paused. 'I think you had to do your job, for the Chance people. I understand that. Odeta takes things personally. She expects people to have respect but she doesn't do anything to earn it. I have seen this more and more in the last year.'

'Do you have the guitars?'

'No, we don't have the guitars.'

Storey was sure he heard the word 'now' in the sentence, though Diamant hadn't said it. That made things difficult. If the Albanians didn't have them, who did? Was there a whole group of players he knew nothing about? He said, 'Do you know who *does* have the guitars?'

'No. We are not interested in these guitars. We have other interests, business interests.'

'Who with?'

Now Diamant looked up at him almost smiling. There was an odd expression on his face. He said, 'With the Chance brothers. We have an agreement with them. We are going to be their marketing people for their new tour. We will be selling tee-shirts and mugs and calendars and pens with the Chance brand on them. It is Odeta's speciality.'

'Are you serious?'

'We signed the contract yesterday afternoon. Everyone is very happy.'

Storey sat down in the armchair next to the television. Facing him, with his body folded at the waist, Diamant looked older and more out of shape than when he was standing. He wore tight black jeans that gave him the appearance of being slim, but the tee-shirt he wore couldn't hide the bulge of his belly. Storey also noticed Diamant was wearing cherry red shoes with white tips and elaborate stitching. Weird.

Storey said, 'I want to give you some advice, Diamant. You're a big man and you look fierce with the hair and moustache and everything, but you're too soft for this business. Don't look at me like that. You can't help it.'

'I have killed men.'

'Really? Where?'

'In Albania. It was political. I was seventeen.'

'This is different. Running a crime gang in the UK needs you to be much more ... scary. I've heard you Albanians can do it, but personally I don't think your heart's in it.'

'Are you saying I'm gay?'

Storey frowned. 'Where did that come from? You're not, are you?'

'Of course not.'

'I didn't think so. I've seen the way you look at Odeta. You know she doesn't look at you the same way, I suppose.'

'She doesn't?'

Storey shook his head. 'Sorry. You're an employee as far as she's concerned.'

Now Diamant leaned back in his seat. 'She thinks I'm gay because I haven't asked her for sex. Sometimes when we're alone she acts ... differently. As if she'd accept me if I tried to take her. But ...'

'But you see her husband standing there.'

'Yes! Exactly! I'm excited by the thought of having her, but when she shows her legs or her chest I become confused and don't know how to act. Then she thinks I'm gay and wants to introduce me to other men.'

'Leave her. Set up your own business. An honest one. Be a cab driver, anything. You don't need to be a criminal. You'll get deported if they catch you.'

Diamant slumped on the sofa. 'I know. I worry about it. I like my life here and I don't want to return to Albania.'

'Do you have family there?'

'A brother and a sister. And the son of my sister. He wants to come here but I tell him no, it's not safe. I don't want him to work in our business.'

Now Storey stood up. 'Good advice. Go back to Odeta and tell her you talked to me and I listened.'

'What will you do?'

'I'm still looking for the guitars. I'm interested to know what happened to them.'

'Can I have my gun back?'

'No, you can't.'

'It's my favourite gun. I could fight you for it.'

'I think we've established you'd lose. Now go home. Talk to Odeta.'

'She'll want to know I hurt you.'

'Tell her what you want. She probably won't see me again.'

CHAPTER THIRTY-FIVE

STEF WONDERED WHY he was nervous. He never felt this way before a job. It wasn't his way. So why was his mouth dry and his palms wet? It didn't make sense.

He glanced over at Liam, texting again, laughing at the things Jen was sending him, not a care in the world. He'd brought the guitars in twenty minutes ago and now he was looking forward to pay day. They'd phoned Johnny and he was en route, cash in hand.

Liam put his phone down and looked at him. 'Cheer up, Steffie. It's party time. I just told Jen to book us a dinner tonight. Why don't you come with us?'

'Why, you want to throw another beer mug at my head?'

Liam grinned. 'We're over that, now, ain't we? Best of mates. Which reminds me, I was going to ask … what have we got lined up next? Is there any way we can get something else out of the Chances? I think deep down Johnny likes me—what do you reckon?'

'Was there really nothing on that USB stick?'

The grin still there. 'Would I have lied to him? The almighty great Johnny Chance?'

'What was it? Bank details or something? Passwords?'

'I never said there was anything on it, did I? You're making shit up now.'

'If he finds out you took whatever was on it, then wiped the stick, he'll kill you.'

'That squirt? I don't think so. Let him try.'

'Don't push him.'

Liam shook his head and glanced around the room.

'You didn't answer my question—what's lined up next?'

'Nothing,' Stef said. 'Lying low. Don't overdo it. Enjoy your life instead of worrying about the next score.'

'Jesus, who are you, Jeremy fucking Kyle? You still haven't told me how much the Chances are going to pay to get their guitars back. If it's not enough I might have to pursue other areas. Know what I mean? Ikea doesn't pay me enough to buy a house and keep Jen in vodka tonics. I'm going to have to supplement my income. You're my first port of call but I might have to widen my net.'

Stef closed his eyes, then opened them slowly. Not much longer now. 'You do what you have to do. You're freelance, like me.'

'Definitely,' Liam said.

THERE WAS A knock on the door and Stef went to answer it. Johnny Chance stood on the doorstep in a white tee-shirt and what looked like new jeans, freshly pressed. No leather jacket, no jewellery. He nodded at Stef then brushed past him into the room.

Stef saw that Liam had stood up—asserting his size again. Wanting Johnny to know who was in charge here. If they'd had horns like deer, Stef thought, they'd be locked by now.

Johnny said, 'Where are they?'

Liam pointed to the corner of the room where the large bag containing both guitars lay on the floor. Johnny picked up the bag, laid it on the sofa and unzipped it. He unwrapped the acoustic guitar from its blanket and looked it over, peering in the sound-hole, checking the back for marks, then holding it so he could look down the fretboard. He put a foot on the sofa and played a few chords with the guitar laying across his thigh, adjusting the tuning on a couple of the strings between each chord.

Liam said, 'All right? They haven't been touched since we put them in there. Except when I looked to see what the rattling was and found that memory stick. Stef kept that bit of information to himself. I wondered what he was looking for when we were in that studio. See, it was me who actually nicked the guitars in the first place, wasn't it?'

Johnny was ignoring him, standing the guitar so it leaned against the arm of the sofa while he picked up the Fender and went through the same process. The sound that came from the strings was tinny and indistinct because it wasn't connected to an amplifier, but Johnny still retuned and strummed a few chords, holding his ear close to the strings to hear them more clearly.

Finally he stood straight, saying, 'Okay, they're good.'

'So when do we get paid?'

Stef watched it play out and couldn't stop it. He saw Johnny pick up the guitars, one after the other, and wrap them and lay them back in the soft case before zipping it up. Then he picked up the case and walked it around so it stood by the front door. He was rolling his shoulders, his expression blank.

He approached Liam and looked him up and down, as if he were weighing him up, Stef thought, working out how much of a threat he was. Liam was probably a stone or two heavier than Johnny but wouldn't be as lithe, as quick in his movements. Muscular but slow.

Now Johnny was saying, 'You know, I've come across people like you all my life.'

'Oh yeah?' Liam said. 'What kind of person's that, then?'

'People who've got one skill and think that means they're a genius. You're big and you're cunning, but that's all you've got, isn't it?'

'You reckon?'

'Yeah, I reckon. You could have been one of our roadies, back in the nineties. Only roadies are really smart. They have to be. They have to do a bit of this and a bit of that as well as having some brawn—or at least the brains to work out how to move stuff, heavy stuff, without damaging it.'

'So you think I'd have made a good roadie, is that what you're saying?'

'No, the opposite. I'm saying you wouldn't last five minutes. The others would laugh and throw you off the bus.'

Stef watched Liam take this in, his eyes glittering, his arms and hands moving restlessly.

Johnny judged it perfectly. He took half a step back and reached around to his back pocket, saying, 'But you talked about getting your pay.'

'You're damn right,' Liam said.

Johnny said, 'Well this is it,' and even though Stef was waiting for it, what he'd discussed with Johnny on the phone, he didn't see it happen. He thought they'd agreed he would go first but he realised in a rush that Johnny *liked* it. His anger was so great he couldn't control it.

So Johnny brought his hand around from his back pocket but instead of holding a leather wallet he held a curved eight-inch knife. Liam was still staring down into Johnny's eyes, trying to intimidate him while he thought of something to say, but then he frowned as Johnny's knife penetrated his stomach.

His face seemed to expand, the eyebrows rising, his cheeks puffing out, his mouth widening as he let out a roar and pushed Johnny away. It did no good because Johnny took only a single pace back then stepped forward and slashed at Liam's stomach again.

By now Stef had taken out his own knife and crossed the carpet and pushed the blade into Liam's side, beneath the rib cage, pushing as hard as he could and watching the blood start to slide along the blade towards the handle. He worried about the stains on his rug and the sofa, especially as now Liam was reaching for Johnny again, shouting, 'You little fucker!' and trying to grab the other man around the neck.

Stef slashed and stabbed at Liam's side, avoiding the blows Liam was using to try to swat him away, the three of them now moving backwards and forwards as if they were dancing ... and then Liam had pushed Johnny away so that he tripped backwards on to the sofa, landing on it but then rolling immediately to one side as Liam tried to fall on him.

Stef went for his back, stabbing Liam under the shoulder blades, the knife so slick with blood he had to change his grip. And now Johnny was up again and stabbing Liam in the neck, in the side, a raw manic energy coming from him, his voice guttural, saying, 'Die, you bastard, fucking die …'

And then it was over and Liam was still, face down on the sofa, the blood pooling on the carpet and on the seats of the sofa, splashes visible on Johnny's tee-shirt and, Stef supposed, on his own clothes too. He had no idea how he was going to clear up the mess. He knew Johnny Chance wasn't going to help.

The two of them stood upright, panting, staring down at Liam's broad back.

'Fuckers take a long time, don't they?' Johnny said, turning to him.

'I don't know,' Stef said. 'That was my first.'

Johnny grinned, saying, 'Not mine. Nor the last.'

Stef was saying, 'What do you mean?' when he felt something in his abdomen, thinking, Shit, Liam must have got me with something. Then looking down and seeing Johnny Chance's curved blade sticking in his stomach, Johnny's hand gripping the handle tightly, and feeling something more as the other man moved the knife back and forth, as if he were sawing.

So that was what he meant by it not being his last, Stef thought, glad to have worked it out, glad of the explanation, and waiting for the pain to start.

Here it came.

DIAMANT HEARD THE lift descending and stepped around the corner. He breathed deeply and waited. Don't be impatient, he told himself. And don't move too soon.

Odeta had said the first priority was to get the guitars back, so he'd looked at the paperwork the man Liam had completed when he deposited the guitars and found the address he'd used. Diamant had driven there immediately and arrived just in time to see Liam walk up the steps to go in to the block of flats, which was only five storeys high and seemed badly constructed, the walls patched and crumbling. There was something about the way Liam approached the building, looking around, moving aside to let an old woman leave through the door ... the woman not seeming to recognise him or give him any acknowledgement. This confirmed it for Diamant—Liam didn't live in the flats: when he had searched for Liam's address on the contract agreement he'd found several agreements in his file. Diamant noticed the address Liam had written this time, for the guitars, was different to the address he'd used before when selling items to the shop. Perhaps he'd moved. Or perhaps he was using someone else's address.

Diamant stayed in the Jaguar and waited.

Twenty minutes later he watched from across the road as Johnny Chance arrived in a BMW with a stripe down its side, a vehicle he'd seen parked in front of the Chance garage the other day. Chance glanced around before going through the glass doors. This was another confirmation. The Chance brothers had arranged to have the guitars stolen and Liam Fisher was probably the thief. Now Johnny

Chance had arrived to take them back. Diamant didn't understand the reasons for this theft and return, but the deal Odeta had arranged with the Chance brothers depended on the threat of selling them elsewhere. So he needed to recover them.

Perhaps, he thought, this was why the brothers had agreed so readily to Odeta's offer—they knew where the guitars were and were going to recover them without his or Odeta's help. They were treating them, the poor, backward Albanians, as idiots.

Well he would turn the tables on them. He would arrange things so the brothers would have to deal with him, not Odeta. He would show these sophisticated British men that he could make plans too.

———

Now the lift had reached the bottom floor. Forty minutes had passed since Chance had arrived and no one else had left. Diamant had concealed himself next to a heavy green door leading from the fire stairs. The door was around a corner and concealed from anyone leaving the lift and walking to the front exit. Perfect.

He heard the doors of the lift open and the light footsteps of a small man. Then he saw Johnny Chance emerge bit by bit into his sight—he was carrying the same large bag that Liam had brought the guitars in when he first sold them to the shop. His hair was wet, as though he'd taken a shower, and the white tee-shirt he'd worn when entering the flats was stained pink and was also damp.

Strange.

Before Chance reached the front door, Diamant stepped from behind and placed the barrel of his remaining Glock at the base of Chance's neck, reaching around to put his hand over his mouth at the same time.

Chance stopped dead.

Diamant said nothing. He didn't want to give away his identity with his voice, though in the end he knew it wouldn't matter.

He took his left hand from Chance's mouth and reached down to take the bag from the man's hand, lowering it to the ground. Chance began to say something but Diamant jabbed him in the back of the head with his gun's barrel and the other man stopped talking.

Afterwards he realised he should have thought through his plan but it was too late now. Leaving the guitars on the floor, he placed his left hand over Chance's eyes, then turned him with the gun barrel and twisted his hand so the man was pointing back towards the lift, which had closed its doors.

Still standing behind the shorter man, Diamant pressed the button for the fifth floor then put his hand over Chance's eyes again. The doors opened almost immediately. He was pleased to see that his precautions were needless because there were no mirrors on the sides of the lift. He pushed the barrel until Chance walked into the lift and kept the barrel in place until the doors began to close again. Before the doors caught on his arm, he withdrew it and turned away.

Now he turned swiftly, picked up the bag as he went, and left the building. He crossed the road and climbed in the Jaguar. He wondered whether Chance would realise immediately that he was alone in the lift ... obviously there was no gun-barrel being held to his head and neither were his eyes shielded. He would turn at once but have to wait until the lift reached the top floor before he could bring it down again, by which time Diamant would be gone.

And Chance would have no idea he'd been robbed by one of those stupid Albanians ...

He grinned to himself as he drove away. He would enjoy telling Odeta that part of the story.

CHAPTER THIRTY-SIX

MONDAY MORNING STOREY decided he was going to see the Chance family one last time. If the brothers didn't want him to work on finding the guitars then he wouldn't. He'd present his invoice, return the device that opened the gates, and maybe say a proper goodbye to Geneva while he was there.

None of it sat well with him but with Diamant and Odeta involved, and the murder of Bill Chance, it was getting too complicated for him to deal with when the police had more resources.

Perhaps he'd drop them some helpful tips.

So he sat on his sofa watching the 8 a.m. local news and eating breakfast when a story came up that caught his attention, though at first he didn't know why. It was a report on a murder that had taken place on Friday of a local man in his flat. The body had been discovered by a neighbour who hadn't seen him in a day or two and was worried because they talked frequently. The dead man had given her a key some while ago for security reasons, so she let herself in and found him lying in a heap in the corridor. At first she thought he'd passed out or had a heart attack, but police investigation over the weekend discovered that he'd been strangled.

A picture of the man was shown on screen at the beginning of the report, followed by exterior film of the man's apartment block, its entrance hidden by a blue forensic unit's awning.

It was only when the man's image was shown again at the end of the report that Storey recognised him: the overweight fan who'd accosted Geneva Chance that Saturday afternoon in Coventry city centre. The same round face and pink cheeks and the urgency in his eyes.

His name was given as Ken Talbot.

Storey changed his plans.

———

IT TOOK FOUR attempts before Jackie West answered her phone, saying, 'Sometimes I think you believe I'm your sidekick.'

'That man strangled in his apartment.'

'Don't tease.'

'I met him with Geneva Chance one afternoon.'

He explained the circumstances, how the man recognised Geneva straight away, asked for her autograph, told them to remember his name. And he had.

There was silence at the other end of the line before she said, 'And this helps me how?'

'There's a lot of death taking place around the Chance family at the moment. Their father, now this guy. I thought you should know. I don't want you accusing me of keeping information from you, do I?'

'Are you saying we should look at the Chances for these two murders?'

Storey's turn to pause. 'I'm not sure that's what I'm suggesting. They had no reason to kill Talbot as far as I can see. Why would they? He's a fan, not a stalker.'

'Do you think Talbot might have killed Bill Chance and somehow they found out and this is their revenge?'

'Unlikely. Talbot was too big to go climbing over walls, in and out of the Chances' property, to get to Bill's house. And probably too clumsy to kill, strip and dump Bill Chance by himself. He was a big guy. On the other hand, there's nothing to say Bill didn't leave the property under his own steam and was killed elsewhere. Everyone's being a bit vague about that.'

'So do you have any other theory?'

'Not my job to have theories. I'm just passing on useful information. Has anything come back from forensics yet? There was a strong smell of bleach in the house but that doesn't necessarily mean anything.'

'You know perfectly well that even if I had information on the investigation, I couldn't tell you. Don't play dumb.'

'Sometimes I can't help it. I'll take that as a no.'

'I've got to go. I'll send someone to ask some questions. Now, I don't suppose I have to tell you to keep your nose out of this?'

'Of course not,' Storey said, trying to remember the name of the road where Talbot had lived.

HE FOUND THE road and once he found the road he found the house—the blue forensic awning was still standing outside the entrance and there was a police Volvo parked outside. As they'd been working since Sunday morning, activity had calmed by now, the police having knocked on all the doors they could find, and there was just one uniform leaning against the side of the police car watching traffic slow down and encouraging it on its way.

Storey pulled in at the end of the road and waited. It was a residential area in the north of the city, near Longford Park, whose vivid blue floodlights rose high above its small car park. In Talbot's building there were six flats that used one communal entrance, currently hidden by the blue awning. One of the windows displayed a Brexit Now! poster but the others were hung with simple net curtains. He realised anyone entering the building before dusk stood a chance of being seen, and dusk was currently just before nine o'clock. So whoever came to see Talbot, and murder him, would probably have arrived later in order to remain hidden.

He was watching the building through his windscreen, so didn't see the person who approached from behind and knocked sharply on his side window. He switched on the engine so he could lower the glass. A woman in her late sixties or seventies, wearing a headscarf, said to him, 'Are you from the papers? Because if you are you can bugger off. We've had you here all weekend. There's nobody in.'

Storey was already smiling, saying, 'No, I knew Ken, Mr Talbot. I couldn't believe it when I saw it on the telly. Then I wanted to see it for myself.'

'Well you can still bugger off, we've got nothing to say. We've told it all to the police.'

'I appreciate that. Did you know Ken?'

'Me? No,' the woman said. 'You need to talk to Joyce. They're all down at the Community Centre, having tea. It's been laid on.'

'Joyce?'

'Joyce Matthews. You know, the one who found the body. She's a bloody celebrity now, and don't she know it.'

THE WOMAN'S DIRECTIONS took him back towards the centre of town for half a mile and then he saw the sign for the Community Centre and pulled into the car park. The building was single storey and painted white and looked like a temporary structure long past the date it should have been knocked down.

The entrance door led to one large room where half a dozen tables were filled with older men and women drinking tea and picking ginger biscuits from cracked plates. At one end of the room was a hatch where the drinks were served and Storey crossed to it and asked for a cup of tea. Leaflets on the counter advertised forthcoming jumble sales, guitar lessons and the local amateur dramatic company's production of Separate Tables.

He picked up his tea cup and saucer and leaned in to the hatch. The volunteer was in her thirties and looked capable and friendly. Storey said, 'I don't suppose you know where Mrs Matthews is, do you?'

'Are you from the papers? She doesn't want to talk to any more reporters, it upsets her.'

'No, I'm not from the press. I knew Ken Talbot slightly.'

'Oh,' she said. 'That woman in the bright red cardigan over there. You wouldn't think she was trying to keep a low profile, would you?'

Storey went to the table where the woman was sitting and found an empty chair at the end. He didn't look at her but stirred sugar into his tea and looked around aimlessly. A pair of elderly ladies were talking to Joyce Matthews and there was a man who looked as if he was in his seventies reading a newspaper and paying no attention.

As he hoped would happen when a stranger arrived, they began to drift away—first the man, who folded his paper and left without looking at anyone; then the two women, who hauled up large bags of shopping and told Mrs Matthews to look after herself before glancing at Storey and walking away.

He moved closer to her and knew she was watching him. She was a comfortable looking woman with watery eyes and permed hair the colour of the tea she was drinking.

She said, 'Are you one of them reporters? I've said all I'm going to say to you.'

'No, I'm not a reporter,' Storey said. 'I met Mr Talbot once. When I was with Geneva Chance.'

He knew the calculated guess he'd taken was right when her eyes lit up and she leaned towards him.

'You did? Where?'

Storey explained where he was when Ken Talbot had approached Geneva, adding, 'He seemed like a big fan.'

'Oh, he was! In fact—' She stopped dead and her mouth fell open. 'Oh dear, I've just remembered something.'

'What's that?'

'I feel so bad, I've got to tell the police about it.'

'You can tell me if you like. I work with the police. I can contact an inspector as soon as you tell me what the problem is.'

Now she was weighing up, looking at how he was dressed, thinking about how he'd approached her, what his general attitude was. The calculation was over in two seconds.

She said, 'When I went round on Sunday it was because I hadn't heard anything from him in two days. He'd told me he was going to have an important visitor, but he didn't say who.'

'You didn't see anyone?'

'The police say he was murdered Friday night, don't they? I was at the Bingo then.' She shuddered. 'So when I got back he was probably already dead.'

'So you went around on Sunday ...'

'Yes, because I'd tried to phone him to see if he wanted to come and have a cup of tea. Secretly I thought he might tell me who his visitor was.'

'Very clever.'

'Well I knocked and knocked and I even went out to check his car was there, and it was, at the end of the road. Which I thought was a bit odd. So eventually I went and fetched the key and opened the door. And there he was, just inside, lying on the floor. I thought he'd passed out or had a heart attack so I called the ambulance and they told me he was dead.'

Her eyes had glazed over as she relived the experience. Storey pushed his impatience down and said, 'So what was it you've forgotten to tell the police?'

She raised her head and looked at him. 'It was you mentioning Geneva Chance reminded me. In the corridor he'd lined the walls with photos of her—well, her and the group. And posters of their tours, years ago. In fact he had photos everywhere, and now I think about it I don't remember seeing any while I was waiting for the ambulance to arrive. I was too shocked to think straight. The photos were on his walls, in frames … everywhere. But they'd all gone. Someone had taken them. Is that a clue, do you think?'

'I'm sure it is,' Storey said. 'I'm sure it is.'

———

HE WENT OUTSIDE to call Jackie but his phone rang before he could dial.

Of course it was her.

He answered, saying, 'Hello, sidekick, how can I help you?'

'And here I was,' she said, 'thinking I was going to help you. Again.'

'How's that?'

'Are you still looking for the guitars or have you given up?'

'It depends.'

'On what?'

'On whether I think I can get paid, for one. Have you got something?'

'It seems there was a bit of a fuss in a pub last week— The White House, on the Keresley Road. Do you know it?'

'Never heard of it.'

'Two blokes got into a row and started fighting and our trusty men in blue put them in the cells for the night. It was only because the girlfriend of one of them argued their case that we didn't take it any further. Not that I suppose either of them would press charges, as they were apparently mates. And the landlord didn't seem to care.'

'And I'm interested in this because?'

'Because the girlfriend, a Jennifer Slattery, said they were arguing about guitars. I must have mentioned it to someone, because I'm a good girl, and it's come back to me this morning.'

'You're a very good girl,' Storey said. 'But why are you telling me instead of following it up yourself?'

'Because I've got enough on my plate and because if you look at it, it doesn't mean anything. Two guys banged up for fighting. It might be something or nothing. And you're my go-to man for something or nothing.'

'What if I end up face down in the Coventry canal?'

'Then I'll give myself a really hard time for an hour or so. Do you want the names and addresses or not?'

He wrote them down and hung up, wondering why he hadn't told her what Joyce Matthews had said about the photos.

Sometimes he confused even himself.

CHAPTER THIRTY-SEVEN

THE FIRST NAME Jackie had given him was Stefan Malyzs, who lived in a block behind the faith church at the bottom of Ansty Road that Storey remembered used to be a bowling alley. For some reason he never understood, the roads there were all named after poets—Longfellow, Coleridge, Browning.

He parked opposite the apartment block and watched it for fifteen minutes. No one went in or came out. It had five floors and was probably considered swish forty years ago. Now it was just dirty and run down.

Jackie had told him that Malyzs and the man he'd been fighting in The White House both had records, Malyzs having served a couple of years for forgery, the other man, Liam Fisher, being a petty crook and occasional brawler.

Storey thought about what he would say to them. Could he ask them directly about the guitars, where they were hidden, and who was paying them? Or maybe he should bring up Odeta and Diamant and ask what their connection was to the Albanians? Or just ask outright how much the Chance brothers had paid for them to steal the guitars?

Any of those questions would probably get a reaction and he could take it from there, wing it as he usually did.

IT DIDN'T QUITE go like that.

First thing he noticed was the door was open. Not a lot, but not on its catch.

He knocked and the door swung open. He called Malyzs' name out loud, saying it again as he stepped into the flat.

It was surprisingly well-decorated—neutral colours, wooden floors, paintings on the walls.

Left, he could see a toilet through an open door. Right, at the other end of the corridor, another door, perhaps a bedroom. The corridor turned left, perhaps to a kitchen.

Straight ahead, through another doorway, and he was into a large, light room with tall picture windows and more tasteful artwork on the walls. A large sofa and a matching armchair. A couple of bookcases filled with a mixture of hardbacks and paperbacks.

And on the carpet, the bodies of two large men lying side by side like soldiers sleeping.

THERE WAS BLOOD everywhere—on the sofa, on the chair, on the pale rug, and on the bodies of the men themselves. One of the men was dark haired and had a strong nose and well-defined cheekbones. He looked about fifteen years older than the other man, perhaps more. He would be Stefan Malyzs. Jackie hadn't said anything about his nationality but his name sounded Polish, an idea which his looks confirmed.

Storey had a feeling that meant something ... but he didn't know what. He told himself to leave it alone — if it meant anything, it would come.

The other man, Fisher, was covered in knife cuts — his face and arms had bled and it looked as though he'd been knifed in both the stomach and sides. Malyzs seemed to have bled only from his stomach, as though one cut had been enough to finish him. Fisher was the bigger man so perhaps he'd fought harder.

Judging by the pallor of their skin they'd been there a while.

Storey stepped back and quickly searched the flat without touching anything, pushing open doors with his elbows and trying to avoid stepping in places where blood had pooled. He noted a trail of blood leaving the main living room and being tracked down to the bathroom. Inside, a white towel was stained pink and had been discarded on the floor of the shower. Someone had cleaned themselves off before leaving.

As far as he could see, there were no guitars. He couldn't be sure because they could be in a cupboard or under a bed, but they certainly weren't openly visible.

So was this Diamant's work? Had Malyzs and Fisher stolen the guitars from the Albanians and Odeta found out and sent Diamant round to strike a deal? He wasn't sure Diamant was capable of this degree of butchery — not because of any moral qualm, but because of sheer incompetence. Two men the size of Malyzs and Fisher should have been able to stop Diamant because he didn't know what he was doing. Maybe if he'd surprised them or attacked them from behind … but Fisher at least had fought wildly and with Malyzs along to help they could probably have disarmed Diamant and dealt with him.

No, this savagery was the work of someone cunning and lithe. Someone full of rage.

———

HE LEFT THE apartment, closing the door to the same position he found it by wrapping his handkerchief around his finger and pulling.

Then he sat in his car and called Jackie West and told her what he'd found.

'Both of them dead?'

'Laid out on the floor, blood everywhere. Looks to me like they'd been knifed. Defensive wounds on Fisher's arms.'

'Jesus God,' she said. 'Are you still there if I send round a team?'

'No,' he said. 'Previous appointment.'

'You're lying to me, Storey, I know it. What are you up to?'

He said, 'I wish I knew.'

'Did you touch anything?'

'Please.'

'So no guitars, stolen or otherwise?'

'Not that I could see.'

'We should talk to the Chance people, though, shouldn't we? I could do without all this going on right now. We're really stretched. Just when I think I've got some pegs in the ground, everything shifts and I've got to re-schedule.'

'What did you just say?'

'I'm trying to organise a diminishing number of coppers to cover an increasing number of crime-scenes.'

'Something about pegs.'

'Just stay there, will you, until the team arrives? You can show them in. Tell them you spoke to me. After they've finished laughing, give them a statement.'

But Storey barely heard what she said. His mind had finally created the spark that made the connection.

CHAPTER THIRTY-EIGHT

HE PARKED ON the street outside the Chance house and took the electronic door-opener from its place on his sun-visor. He then climbed out and pressed the button so the doors opened and walked inside. The usual two BMWs were parked outside the garage, suggesting everyone was home. It was several days since the body of Bill Chance had been found and there was no longer a police presence. Presumably they'd found nothing. Perhaps the bleach that he'd smelled when Bill's cottage door was opened had done its job and removed all traces of blood … if, as he thought, this was where he'd been murdered.

But he still found it difficult to believe the Chance brothers were involved in the murder. With what motive?

And then Ken Talbot, a loyal fan? What could he possibly have done to rouse one or more of the brothers to kill him?

And whoever had murdered these two older, overweight men … did they also knife the younger, fit and strong Stefan Malyzs and Liam Fisher?

If not the brothers, then who? The Albanians? Diamant, or Kostas?

Too many victims. Too many suspects.

WHEN HE RANG the bell there was a long pause before Adam Chance opened it. The usual smile was gone, Storey noticed, and instead of standing back to let Storey in he stepped forward to block his entrance.

'We told you we didn't want to see you again.'

'Didn't work, did it?' Storey said, walking up the steps quickly and pushing past, almost daring Adam to physically stop him.

He walked across the wide hall and looked in the downstairs rooms until he saw Johnny and Tim were sitting outside on the patio, stretched out on loungers and drinking. The sun was directly overhead by now but they were sheltered by large cantilevered sunshades.

'Afternoon, boys,' he said, aware that Adam had followed and was standing behind him. 'I see you're still in mourning.'

Tim sat up on his lounger but Johnny stayed where he was, looking up at him through dark glasses, a reddish glow on his skin. He said, 'Yeah, we're in the sun. On tour in three weeks, gotta look healthy after all those months in the studio. What the fuck're you doing here, anyway? We kicked you out.'

'Brought you this,' Storey said, tossing the electronic door gadget to him. Johnny let it bounce off his stomach and fall to the floor.

Now Adam came around from behind and sat at a small table containing glasses and carafes of water. Storey shifted his position so he was looking at all three of them, though Tim avoided his eyes and sucked on a plastic water bottle.

Storey said, 'Thought you should know I haven't found the guitars, though I came close. You don't have to pay me anything.'

'Good, because we weren't going to,' Johnny said. 'You've done fuck-all and our dad was murdered on your watch.'

'Pity about that,' Storey said. 'I liked him. Seemed eager to please.'

Tim snorted into his water bottle then wiped his face. 'You don't know what you're talking about,' he said.

'So tell me.'

Tim stared at him for a few seconds, then shifted his gaze again, staring straight ahead with a muscle working in his cheek.

Storey moved to the edge of the patio and looked out over the garden.

He said, 'Last time I was here there were some lads packing up a tent. Hard workers, weren't they? They'd pegged it all out and now they were packing it all up.'

'Have you finished your business here?' Adam asked.

'Nearly. I was just wondering … I understand the people you used for the marquee were Polish. Frank Lamb told me that. He was very impressed by them. How did you come across them, out of interest?'

'No idea,' Johnny said. 'They just turned up one morning and got to work.'

'Were they locals? Did you talk to them?'

Now Johnny stood up and walked towards him. 'I might have had a word,' he said. 'It was my party, after all. Least I could do was show them pop stars weren't all bastards. Be friendly. Make a good impression. Why all this interest in some random Poles?'

Storey grinned. 'It's amazing when something turns out not to be random, though, isn't it? For example, when I said I nearly found the guitars, the truth is I think I found the people who stole them. Couple of petty crooks. Let's call them Stefan and Liam. I went round to see them today, see if they still had the guitars.'

'And did they?' Adam asked.

'They might have done, at one time. But they couldn't tell me because they were lying on the floor surrounded by blood. Someone had been very handy with a knife. Cut both of them up. Now it's possible they knifed each other, but in fact there were no knives in close proximity, shall we say. And they were lying next to each other as if they'd been laid out.'

'Any idea who might have done it?'

'None at all,' Storey said. 'But it's very suspicious, isn't it, that they were both knifed to death and your dad seems to have died in the same way. Looks like there's a desperate knife-murderer on the loose.'

Now both Tim and Adam stood up, their faces blank. For a moment Storey wondered whether he'd pushed too hard. He could perhaps handle one of them but three would be a test.

Adam said, 'We'll be very careful in future.'

'Yeah,' said Tim. 'Now fuck off and don't come back.'

'Don't you want to know where your guitars are?'

'I thought you said you hadn't found them.'

'Doesn't mean I don't know where they are.'

'So do you?'

'I'm not sure.'

Seeing them all take a half-step towards him, Storey knew he was even closer to the edge now, feeling the anxiety and fear coming off them no matter how confident they tried to play it.

Johnny broke the atmosphere by turning away, walking to the table and filling a glass with water. Drinking it while staring straight ahead. Perhaps calming himself down.

He said, 'You just like winding us up, don't you? You haven't got any idea where they are.'

'Have you?'

'Me? Why should I know?'

'I thought you might take a guess. Or Tim there. Seems very friendly with some unsavoury Albanians. I don't know—Poles, Albanians ... Coventry's nearly as diverse as London these days. Do you ever look at the Coventry Telegraph online? They have a regular rogues gallery of people caught and sent down for various offences. These sad faces staring out at you, their sentences listed underneath. White people, Middle Eastern, some Europeans ... all of them caught and now having to spend time at Her Majesty's pleasure. Makes you think, doesn't it?'

Johnny took another swig from his glass, saying, 'Stupid bastards.'

'Why's that?'

'Shouldn't have let themselves get caught, should they?'

'Well that's the thing I can tell you,' Storey said, 'from my long time in the police force. No crook ever thinks they're going to get caught. And they're always wrong.'

———

ADAM WALKED HIM back through the house and paused to press a button to open the electronic gates. He said, 'I can't work you out, Storey. We all thought you were working for us but I'm not sure now. Am I right?'

'A payday would have been nice but hey, things change. Turns out I didn't like the job much.'

'Are we going to see you again?'

Storey looked at the man—tall, confident, good-looking, rich. He must have thought he had everything when he was twenty-five years old. So why was he so ... what? Anxious? Fearful? There was a jitteriness in his eyes that Storey hadn't noticed before. Or perhaps it hadn't been there. He felt he could stick out a finger and knock Adam Chance over with the slightest push. Fragile, that was the word. They were all fragile, like flowers past their best just waiting for the leaves to turn brown and drop off. Waiting for the end.

He said, 'I can't make any promises. You and I both know there's more to come.'

Adam stared at him, his eyes still moving around, unable or unwilling to focus on anything for longer than a second or two. He said, 'Family's an amazing thing. I'm guessing you don't have one.'

'Not one like yours, that's for sure.'

He left through the front door before Adam Chance could finish his threat.

HE'D ALMOST PASSED through the large black gates when he heard Geneva Chance calling his name. She caught up with him and pushed him through into the road and out of sight of the house.

She said, 'What are you doing here? They told me they'd sacked you.'

'They tried but it didn't take. Besides, I had to tell them something.'

'Can we go somewhere?' she said, her hand on his arm.

'I don't think that's a good idea at the moment.'

She flinched almost imperceptibly and he knew she was hurt. He was struck how often he was doing that nowadays—recognising he'd said something he'd later regret. Perhaps he was growing up. Or developing a conscience. Trying to make it up to her now, he said, 'Don't you want to know what I told them?'

'I've got something to tell you first.'

'Go on.'

'Day before yesterday two people came here, a man and a woman. I was coming out of the studio and I saw them arrive. Dark skin but not African or Indian, looked middle Eastern or Greek, something like that. Wild black hair, the pair of them. He had a long moustache and wore bright red shoes and she wore a black skirt. In this weather.'

'Did you talk to them?'

'The boys took them inside. To be honest I didn't want to know.'

'I know who they were. I spoke to the man yesterday. He told me they're working for you now. Selling your merchandise—tee-shirts and so on.'

She frowned. 'First I've heard of it. Who are they?'

Storey gave her their names and Geneva said, 'So it doesn't sound like they're even English. What's going on?'

Storey shrugged and told her the woman, Odeta, owned a cash exchange shop on the Foleshill Road. Perhaps she wanted to get into merchandising.

She said, 'That's crazy. We've got a company in London does all that for us. We've used them for years. They've already got the tour posters and everything else printed up, ready to go. We went down a couple of weeks ago for publicity photos. What's Johnny playing at?'

'You'll have to ask him yourself. If I were you I wouldn't trust Odeta and Diamant to sell popcorn in a cinema.'

Geneva thought about this for a while, then sighed and let it go. She said, 'Are you coming to the funeral?'

'Your father's?'

'Day after tomorrow. The body's been released now. Frank Lamb's made all the arrangements from the States, bless him.'

'I can't promise to make it.'

She didn't seem surprised or disappointed. He thought again how small she was, but unlike her brothers she seemed stronger after all the turmoil in her life.

She said, 'I'd like it if you came but I'd understand if you didn't.' She touched him on the arm and he felt again the electricity between them. She added, 'So go on, why did you want to talk to my brothers?'

Storey was reluctant to tell her. He thought it had been a mistake on his part to tell her about Diamant and Odeta, so adding in Stefan Malyzs and Liam Fisher seemed like a further act of cruelty, dragging her into a world where she didn't belong. But he couldn't tell her brothers something and not tell her as well. She deserved that, however difficult it might be to hear.

He said, 'I think I found the people who stole Johnny's guitars.'

'Who?'

'I'd rather not give you their names.'

A hardness came into her eyes. She said, 'Listen—don't treat me like a child. My brothers do that and I don't like it from them and I don't take it from anyone else. If you've told them you can tell me.'

He knew she was right. He had no obligation to protect her and besides, what was he even protecting her from? It would be all over the news soon. So he explained who the burglars were, describing how they'd been found dead in the apartment belonging to Stefan Malyzs, though the guitars were still missing. He didn't tell her he was the one who'd found them.

She was shaking her head before he'd finished. 'Oh, God, I had a feeling it would end up like this.'

'What would?'

'I don't know. It all just seemed so … so petty and vindictive. The theft. And the guitars were worth so much. As soon as anyone found out it was always going to get messy.'

'You've never heard of these two men?'

'Me? No, why should I?'

'I think it's possible Stefan worked here, putting up and taking down the marquee for your brother's birthday.'

Now her head was down and then he realised she'd begun to cry. She lifted a hand to her eyes and sobbed quietly. 'We can't get out from under it,' she said. 'Everything's shit, the whole thing's shit ...'

'From under what?'

She moved her hand to cover her mouth and shook her head. Then she glanced up at him, her eyes fierce again, and said, 'I can't tell you. I can never tell you.'

'You can tell me —'

But she'd already turned and run back through the black gates into the safety of the house and garden, Storey watching her run and feeling his own heart beating a little more quickly because he'd seen into the passion that she'd kept from him.

From everyone.

CHAPTER THIRTY-NINE

ODETA HAD CLOSED the shop for the afternoon and told Diamant to come upstairs to talk to her.

She was always so secretive, Diamant thought, keeping her thoughts and ideas to herself and then placing them before him like a winning hand in a game of poker — What do you think of that?

In the past he hadn't known what to think. She had always been ahead of him with new ideas and new plans, leaving him to talk to Ari Sallaku in London to see whether he would agree. Sallaku wouldn't talk directly to her, but he usually agreed with her suggestions. It was her idea to open the club as a way of cleaning some of the money they earned. It was her idea to create the telephone line selling of drugs because she'd read about it in the newspaper. And he already knew her next idea was to begin selling Black Mamba and Spice because there was a ready market for it, though the last thing he wanted was a line of teenagers lying on the pavement outside the shop, their heads sunk into their chests as if they were asleep—or dead.

So walking into her apartment he wondered what she wanted to sell to him this time. How surprised would she be when he said no to her? After all, he'd heard back from his cousin Valmir in London, with very exciting news.

And instructions.

———

HE WAS GLAD to see she was still dressed for business, though her expression was playful. She said, 'Have you spoken to Paul Storey?'

Diamant felt himself turning red at the memory of his meeting with Storey but calmed himself, hiding his face by walking around her to sit in one of the comfortable chairs. He said, 'We won't see Paul Storey again.'

'Good. Did you hurt him badly?'

'No, I thought I would talk to him instead. He's a reasonable man, and besides, he knows policemen in this city. I didn't want to attract their attention by hurting him.'

'You believe he is frightened of you?'

Diamant looked at her and felt a strength in himself. He said, 'Aren't you?'

She frowned and sat facing him. 'Why should I be frightened of you? Don't you like me any more?'

He didn't know how to answer that so looked away, feeling her gaze on the side of his face. He knew this conversation would end in a particular way but he didn't know how to get there. Toni would have known. He could have learned a lot from Toni had he stayed alive.

Odeta said, 'Do you hear that?'

Now he did—a knocking on the door downstairs. The metal shutters were down on the windows and on the door but someone was still trying to enter. He said, 'I'll go.'

———

THE SHOP WAS dark with the shutters closed, with only shards of daylight coming through gaps in the metal, but he knew his way through the counter and across the floor, around the display cabinet in the centre.

He had a sense even as he was moving the bolts and unlocking the door that he shouldn't do it … but he was Diamant Dushku, soon to be an important man, so he had no fear. He pulled the door open far enough to see outside.

At first the dazzling daylight blinded him, but then he began to focus. The person standing there was Paul Storey.

Diamant hesitated a moment too long and already Storey was pushing against the door and now he was in the shop, saying, 'Glad I caught you in, Diamant. Where's Odeta?'

'Not here.'

'You're such a terrible liar. Does she have the place upstairs? I saw a couple of people moving about—that was you two, wasn't it? How about you take me to see her?'

'What do you want?'

'I'll tell both of you, then I don't have to repeat myself.'

Diamant felt the weakness in his own expression, the dryness of his lips, the swallowing. He hoped Storey wouldn't see these things in the half-light. He said, 'I told her about our conversation. I said we wouldn't see you again. I told her I frightened you so that you wouldn't come.'

'Do I look as though I'm frightened?'

'I have another gun.'

'I've got one too, remember? Yours.'

This man was impossible to deal with, Diamant thought. He could not be argued with and seemed to have no fear. He respected that while at the same time hating it.

Finally he said, 'Follow me. Don't touch anything.'

'I'll follow your aftershave then I won't get lost.'

ODETA HADN'T MOVED when he walked back into the apartment, Storey behind him. The sun had moved lower in the sky and the room was half in shadow, but Diamant still noticed the slight movement of her mouth as she recognised the other man.

'Mr Storey,' she said. 'I didn't expect to see you again. I don't like the fact that you are here, but never mind. Did you find the guitars?'

Diamant turned and watched Storey take in the room, a professional. Seeing the doors to the bedroom and kitchen and bathroom and noting they were closed. Looking around for possible weapons. Moving so he was at least a couple of metres from both him and Odeta. Then Storey said, 'It seems they were probably stolen by a couple of men you might know.'

Odeta was very good. 'Men we might know? I don't understand. Are they people who work for me?'

Storey's face was calm, Diamant thought. He'd never noticed it before but his eyes were still and he seemed to think before he spoke. He was never surprised and never angry. Now he said, 'Their names are Stefan Malyzs and

Liam Fisher. They were found dead in Stefan's flat. I think they were contracted to steal the guitars and I think they brought them to you to look after.'

Odeta turned to Diamant. 'We don't know anything about this, do we, Diamant?'

'We have told him many times that we have not seen the guitars.'

'So you've never met Stefan or Liam?' Storey asked him directly.

'Why do you think I am lying to you? Why don't you believe us?'

Storey nodded. 'That's a very good question. Why don't I? Maybe it's because I think you've been lying to me from the beginning, from the first time I mentioned the guitars. Something passed between you two when I mentioned them. I haven't been able to shake off the idea that you knew something then. And of course you're in this business to make money, so why wouldn't you take the opportunity to take the guitars and sell them?'

Odeta said, 'I'm interested ... how did the men die? I have seen nothing on the television about it.'

'They were only discovered today. Stabbed multiple times. The younger one, Liam, had really put up a fight.'

'You talk as if you were there.'

'I saw them. I saw the place.'

'But you didn't see myself or Diamant there.'

'No, I didn't,' Storey said. 'And to be honest I don't think you had anything to do with killing them. I don't think Diamant's capable of it.'

'You don't know what I am capable of.'

'Big words, Diamant. But you and I both know big words are not enough.'

Odeta said, 'You can search the building if you would like. We don't have the guitars here. Or anywhere.'

Storey turned to look at the room again. 'You wouldn't keep them here anyway. It's too dangerous. If they turn up I recommend you give them back.'

'So if you don't believe we killed these men, and you don't believe we have the guitars here, why have you come to talk to us?'

'I'm just shaking an apple tree,' Storey said. 'See if I can make some cider.'

'I don't understand.'

'I know. That's part of the fun.'

———

DIAMANT WALKED STOREY out and locked the door behind him, then went back upstairs, his heart heavy but not fearful of what Odeta would say.

As he expected she was walking backwards and forwards, her arms folded, her face white with anger. He had seen her like this only a few times and it used to frighten him. Now he knew he had been frightened because of the force of her will, not because she could do anything to him. He had always been the tool she used to express that will, but that was changing.

She saw him and said, 'You lied, Diamant. You stood in this room and you lied to me. You said you had frightened him and he would not come again to talk to us.'

Diamant walked to the table, pouring himself a drink, thinking now this room could be his. He had always liked the place and it would be good to live so close to the work.

Perhaps later he could find somewhere outside, in the country, with fields and sheep and cows.

Odeta was saying to him in Albanian, 'Are you listening to me? Look at me when I'm talking to you.'

'We speak in English,' Diamant said. 'That was your rule. One of your many rules.'

Her face turned dark. 'What are you talking about?'

'Since I've been working for you there have been many rules. It seems to me that I have to learn these rules and obey them, while you break them when you like and even make up new ones when it pleases you.'

Her black eyebrows moved even closer together. 'Have you been drinking? Why are you talking to me like this? What are you going to do about Storey? We can't allow him to look at us any more. We don't know who he talks to, who his friends are. We don't know our enemy, Diamant, and—'

'I know him,' Diamant said. 'We had a long talk yesterday. He wanted me to give up this work and drive a cab.'

Odeta crossed to the table and poured herself a drink, shaking her head. 'Toni was right—you cannot trust people who serve you longer than five years. They become bored or want more than they have. You and I have to talk, Diamant.'

'Ah, Toni,' Diamant said. 'Your husband, your great love. The man who brought you to this country and then started sleeping with other women.'

Odeta turned to him, her eyes widening. 'What do you mean? What other women?'

Diamant breathed deeply. This was the time.

'There was the blonde girl who worked in the shop when we first began. She opened her legs for him after the first week. And the girl who worked in the newsagents at the weekend. She was next.'

'Stop! Stop! What are you saying?'

'I'm telling you what you already know, Odeta. What you have always known. You watched and you waited, learning how to be English, how to run a business. And when you thought the time was right, you cut Toni's throat and blamed it on the Kosovans. No one believed you'd do it yourself, not even the British police—you played your part well.'

He thought she would continue the argument but the fire in her eyes dimmed and she sat down, arranging her heavy skirt over her knees. She said, 'How did you know?'

'I found the knife. You had cleaned it of blood and placed it back in the drawer. But there was still blood in the places where the blade meets the handle. I threw it away before the police arrived.'

'So you looked for it as soon as you saw that Toni was dead? Already you didn't trust me?'

'That was one of the lessons Toni taught me—never trust the people closest to you. He didn't listen to himself. Besides, he was too clever to have been caught and murdered by Kosovans. He would have cut out their tongues while they pleaded for mercy.'

'I miss him now. I was angrier then. Toni and his blonde girls. I was too dark for him, too limited. Not adventurous enough in the bedroom.'

'He would have been proud of your success.'

'Do you think so? I have tried to think all the time, to do better and make the business grow. I'm sorry I have made your life hard in these ten years. But you seemed to enjoy it.'

'No,' he said, 'I didn't. And that is why things are changing now.'

'What do you mean? What things? Now you have the guitars we can continue with our contract with the Chance people. We can expand the business into marketing, leave this dirty shop behind us. Of course the telephone drug sales will begin soon, and I still want to move into this other drug, this Black Mamba ...'

Diamant put his glass back on the table and stood in front of her. He wondered what she saw. She had been cruel about his shoes, and the way he walked, and the man Storey had said that his hair and his moustache made a false impression on people.

So who did Odeta think he was? Would she understand what he was about to do to her?

She was looking up at him now and he thought he saw some fear in her eyes. That was good. His cousin in London had said she must be afraid. She must feel fear. This would be her real punishment for acting against Ari Sallaku. And afterwards, he would receive his reward.

Odeta said, 'Diamant, I think we should open the shop for the evening. Will you go down and unlock the doors, or shall I do it?'

She tried to stand up but Diamant pushed her down in the chair.

'No,' he said. 'We won't be opening up again this afternoon.'

'Why not?'

'Because I have something to teach you. Something that Toni would have taught you, if he was still alive. But because he is dead, I must become the teacher. And I'm very good.'

CHAPTER FORTY

IT HAD BEEN going through Tim's head for hours now, since Storey had shown up and more or less told them he knew they'd done it. Done everything—stolen the guitars, murdered their dad, the two thieves Johnny had hired, the man Adam had strangled … What was in his head was a phrase: 'going to get caught'.

He said out loud, 'We're going to get caught,' and Johnny thumped him on the arm.

'For the thousandth time, we're not going to get caught. There's nothing. No evidence, nothing connecting us to any of these people.'

'The Albanians.'

'Well we're going to sort them out, aren't we? That toe-rag Diamant was the one who robbed me yesterday. I recognised his aftershave. Smells like one of those candles Genny puts in the bathroom.'

They were in Johnny's bedroom, waiting for Adam to finish his exercise routine downstairs. Tim hated this room—posters on all the walls of Johnny at the front of the band trying to look like Jimmy Page or Clapton, the guitar hero. He could just about see himself behind his drum-kit on a couple of them, but it was all Johnny, Johnny, Johnny. It always had been and always would be.

He said, 'It was a stupid fucking idea anyway.'

Johnny was looking at his iPad. 'What was?'

'Having someone steal the guitars.'

'Jesus, not this again,' Johnny said, throwing the iPad on to his bed. 'How many time do I have to tell you? We couldn't just knock off the old man without setting up a story, could we? Otherwise it would be random. Unbelievable.'

'You reckon what you came up with was more believable? Old crooks from Spain who didn't like him, setting up a ... what ... a gangland hit? Our dad?'

'I didn't hear you disagreeing at the time. You could have said something, or come up with your own idea.'

'Perhaps I should have done.'

'Perhaps you should have seen that crank following us when we ditched Bill. You were driving, that's down to you.'

'It was dark, how was I supposed to see anything?'

'We were in the fucking country at one o'clock in the morning ... how many car headlights do you expect to see in the rear-view mirror at that time of night?' Now he snorted and reached for his iPad again. 'The first time you come up with a plan for *any*thing I swear I'll give up the guitar and learn the bagpipes.'

Tim said nothing but looked at Johnny resentfully. He *did* make plans, occasionally. He had to think clearly about when he went to the club to buy his stuff. He talked to his accountant from time to time to make sure he had enough money in his current account to keep functioning.

But Johnny was right on the whole: he lived from day to day and let other people do the thinking. He was cool with that. Except when it got them into the shitty situation they were in now, with 'going to get caught' rattling around in his head every thirty seconds.

He said, 'Do you think we should do something about Storey?'

Johnny looked up again. 'Are you kidding? He's been all over the press, even the police who came here knew him.'

'But he seems to know what we've been doing. He knows more than he said.'

'Oh don't be such a fucking cry-baby. All he's been looking at is the guitars, right? When we get them back we'll say they were thrown over the wall or something and he'll have to give it up.'

'I don't think he'll give it up.'

'All right!' Johnny shouted, flinging his iPad away. 'Just shut the fuck up about him, will you? We'll do something. Let me work it out.'

'You don't need to shout.'

'It'll all be over soon and we'll go on tour and the album will be released and we'll be on television again and everything will be just lovely. Is that okay?'

'You don't need to shout. I've got a headache.'

NOW ADAM CAME in, his face flushed and his hair still wet from the shower he took after exercise. He said, 'Children, keep it down. Your sister's down the corridor, if you've forgotten.'

'This moron wants us to do something about Storey. I've told him it's too risky.'

Adam shut the door behind him. 'The worst we do is pay him something to keep his trap shut. We don't touch him. For one, I think he wouldn't be that easy to put down. Second, he's too well-known to the cops. They'd take it seriously.'

'What I said,' Johnny said. 'It's all coming to an end now. The last thing we want to do is stir things up again. After tonight, that is.'

Tim looked at his brothers and wondered when they'd grown so confident in their own decisions. Their plans. He'd never been certain about anything, which is why he'd gone along with it, the Plan. The Revengers, they'd called themselves. Taking the long view, working things out till they'd reached this situation. One or two wrinkles had cropped up—the Albanians, and Storey—but they'd still managed to pull it off.

He said, 'Why do we have to get the guitars tonight? There's no rush.'

Johnny said, 'Because I don't want that bloody Albanian sleaze-bag to think he's got one over on me. I've waited twenty-four hours, just to give him a sense of security. But tonight I'm getting them back and this time I'm keeping hold of them. And you're coming because you're my brothers and you love me, right?'

'Right,' said Tim, wondering whether he meant it.

CHAPTER FORTY-ONE

BY NINE O'CLOCK Geneva was dressed and ready for bed. If anyone had asked what she was thinking, she'd have said, 'Too much'. The house was falling apart around her. No one was cooking or making any effort to keep the place tidy, and she was damned she was going to do it just because she was a woman.

And she was in a constant state of Pissed Off. The sooner she could find somewhere else to live, the better.

She was even considering not going on tour. If she thought about it, she was only doing it out of boredom anyway. It was Johnny's idea, as usual, but she had no real stomach for it. She'd rather work on her own material now. Having had her song stolen seemed to have flipped a switch in her head—she was coming up with ideas for songs all the time. She'd even re-recorded the one that had been taken and liked the quality in her voice better.

If she could find her own place she'd build her own recording studio and get Pete in to work with her. Her brothers would have to survive without her.

———

SHE LAY ON her bed in her dressing-gown listening to the low drone of the boys' voices down the hall. They'd been arguing, as usual, but laughing, too. She'd barely spoken to them since Bill's death, largely because she didn't want to say out loud what she'd been thinking.

It was another reason to leave.

She knew there'd been no love lost between Bill and the boys, especially when she'd let slip to Johnny what Bill had done. It was amazing she'd been able to keep it in all those years—was it ten, or twelve?—without them suspecting anything. She'd read all about it, of course. The self-blame. The feelings of worthlessness. The anger that seemed to have no direct outlet.

She'd never known whether Johnny had told the others and had been too ashamed to ask. Since that time he'd been angry, too. Even angrier than he'd been before. She wondered if the fact neither of them had maintained a sexual relationship with anyone else had been the result of what Bill had done to her when she was fourteen.

She could still feel her father's hands on her arms. It was only once, but she'd never forgotten.

And it seemed neither had Johnny.

———

SHE TURNED THE light out and tried to sleep but her brothers were still talking and eventually she couldn't stand it any more. She got out of bed and put on her dressing-gown and walked down the corridor to Johnny's room.

She knocked and went in.

All three of them looked at her.

They were dressed to go out: heavy shoes and jackets, despite the fact the temperature must still have been in the mid-twenties.

The sun had set half an hour before but there was an afterglow and they hadn't yet switched on the lights. Johnny was lying on his bed staring up at the ceiling. Adam and Tim sat in the two expensive armchairs Johnny had brought back from Peter Jones in London, now faded and threadbare. All of the bedrooms were big enough for double beds and some furniture and had both walk-in wardrobes and en suite bathrooms. Big enough for family conferences.

Surprised, she said, 'Where are you going this time of night?'

Johnny was the first to answer: 'Out.' Giving it a hard, don't-bother-asking edge.

'Is it about the guitars?'

'Why do you say that?' Adam asked.

'Storey told me he found the people who stole them.'

'Storey Storey Storey,' Tim said. 'Got a new boyfriend, have we?'

Adam raised a hand to calm his brother down, then said, 'Did he say who they were?'

'No,' she said, wondering why she was lying. 'Just that they were dead. And the guitars weren't there.' And then

315

she couldn't help herself, it came out before she could think: 'Did you kill Dad?'

The brothers looked at each other, then Johnny said, 'Why would we do that?'

'You know why.'

Johnny stared at her for a moment then looked back up at the ceiling. 'It's a mystery,' he said. 'I suppose the police will catch them eventually. Don't tell me you're sad.'

She couldn't answer that and she realised Johnny knew it. To say yes would be to undermine the basis of the relationship they'd shared during the last ten years—with Johnny knowing first and then, she supposed, Adam and Tim. The thing that kept them close, even living in the same house. To say she wasn't sad, on the other hand, would be to admit a deadness of feeling that seemed unhealthy, even if justified, and he knew she couldn't do it. Not yet, not even after twenty years of living with the memory.

Adam said, 'You should go back to bed, Genny. We won't be out long. Back before midnight.'

'Where are you going? And don't say Out.'

Now Johnny swung his legs from the bed and stood up. 'Actually we think we know where the guitars are. We didn't need Storey to tell us. So we're going to have a conversation with a man about getting them back.'

All three were standing now and Geneva knew how hopeless it would be to argue with them. Thinking what else she could throw at them, she said, 'Why have you given marketing to those Albanians? What's that all about?'

Johnny stopped as he was passing her, taking her hand. 'It's just business,' he said. 'Everything's just business. Making money. Paying for us to carry on living this life of helpless luxury, indulging our every whim and satisfying our every need. How did you find out about that?'

Tim said, 'Look at her—Storey told her. How the fuck did *he* find out?'

Johnny was nodding. 'He's clever, I'll give him that.'

Adam said, 'Don't we always do the best for us, in the end? Doesn't it all work out?'

She pulled away from Johnny's grip, saying, 'Work out for who? I've made a decision—I'm quitting. Leaving this place.'

'And?' Johnny asked.

'Yes, and leaving the band. I can't do it. You'll have to get someone else to go on tour. Blame it on Dad's death. Or cancel it altogether, I don't care. You've still got the album.'

'Great,' Tim said. 'That's us screwed. No one will ever book us again.'

Johnny said, 'It's more serious than that, isn't it, Genny?'

She turned away from his face, only inches from hers.

'Go to your business,' she said. 'Go murder some more people.'

SHE WATCHED FROM her bedroom as they drove out of the gate in one car, turning towards the city.

Despite the heat she felt cold gripping her limbs and a sense of hopelessness in her chest. She wanted to cry and she wanted to be angry. She wanted to hit someone and she wanted to curl up in her bed and go to sleep.

She couldn't do anything. Her mind was a mess. She knew some things she shouldn't know, and there were things she didn't know but wished she did.

She found her phone and called Storey.

———

SHE SAID, 'WHERE are you?'

'At home. What do you need?'

'I need to be told I'm not going mad.'

'Is there any evidence you are?'

She paused. 'I think my brothers killed our dad. Tell me I'm going mad and it's not true.'

Now it was his turn to be silent, Geneva wondering whether she'd gone too far, involved him in a secret she should have kept to herself.

Then he said, 'You're not mad. What's your evidence?'

'Nothing. Their attitude. The things I know.'

'What do you know?'

She was hesitant again. She'd seen it in their eyes, she realised, just tonight: the guilt. She'd asked them outright and they'd looked at each other like kids caught stealing apples. Then they'd brazened it out and moved on as if she hadn't asked.

She said, 'They think they've done it for me.'

'They murdered their father for you? How does that work?'

She felt the heat in her face, the awful thickening in her throat that came whenever she tried to talk about it. 'Bill raped me when I was fourteen. Just once. He apologised the next day and was mortified. I didn't know what to do or who to talk to. So I kept it inside and carried on as if nothing had happened.'

'But eventually you told your brothers.'

'Yes, I told Johnny ten years afterwards. When we were successful and rich and blah blah blah. Bill must have guessed or found out they all knew because he moved to Spain soon after. We had nothing to do with him except giving him a pension. Then a couple of years ago Adam suggested we have him back, put him in the cottage. So he was exiled even though he was here. He was insanely grateful, did all the cooking, looked after the house ... all that shit.'

'How did you feel about it?'

'I didn't know what to feel,' she said. 'I hadn't forgotten what he'd done. Of course I hadn't. I still dream about it, awful dreams. But it was like something that happened to someone else. We'd had all the success and people liked me and I'd survived. I wasn't going to be imprisoned by it.'

'But you were living with your brothers in one house and never went out, as far as I could see. Isn't that like being in prison?'

'You don't get to scold me.'

'I'm sorry,' he said. 'This isn't why you rang me, is it?'

'Yes ... no. I think Johnny might be about to do something stupid.'

'Where is he?'

'They've all gone out, the three of them. They said it was business but what business would they be doing at ten o'clock on a Monday night?'

'Do you know where they've gone?'

She hesitated again. What did she want to happen? Whose side was she on? And was there even a side? She said, 'I think they've gone to see the Albanians. They talked about getting the guitars back and, I don't know … we talked about the Albanians doing our marketing and there was just something in the air.'

'That's what we policemen call a clue. I'll go and see if anything's happening. You stay there, okay?'

'Storey?'

'What?'

'Don't hurt them. They were doing it for me. I think they're angry for me. It's my fault all this has happened.'

'Don't say that. Never say that. They're responsible for what they do, not you. Now just stay there and I'll call you later when I've found out what's going on.'

He hung up and she stared at the phone.

Then she scrolled through her contacts list and called a taxi.

CHAPTER FORTY-TWO

DIAMANT WAS SAYING, 'I didn't mind when you killed Toni, because I thought I could take over. I knew Ari would never let a woman lead our organisation, but I didn't know how much respect he had for you. You are a very good talker. You can persuade people to do what you ask them to. I was often surprised that I did the things I did, just because you asked. Are there witches in your family? No, don't answer, you will only lie. In addition to persuading, you are good at lying. I have seen it every day, in the shop, when you are talking to customers. I have learned a lot from you. I would have learned a lot from Toni, but I understand why you had to sacrifice him.'

It was getting dark outside and he walked to a table and turned on a lamp. Odeta was seated on an upright chair that he'd moved into the middle of the room. She followed him with her eyes, saying nothing.

Diamant sat opposite her, admiring her calmness. He supposed she thought there was a way out, an opportunity to escape, but he had his instructions.

He said, 'I have been talking to my cousin, Valmir. Do you remember him? He visited three years ago. He works for Ari in London. He's a small man with a nose like a bird … a beak, they say—curved and long. He's learning English at night school. So, I have been talking to him and he has been talking to Ari. That is why we're in this situation, you and me. He has given me clear instructions. He has tired of you, Odeta. He thinks you are more interested in this shop than selling the drugs. And now there is this "marketing" for the pop group. He thinks you have lost your way, and I agree with him. Ten years is a long time to run an organisation, even a small one, so he would like me to end your connection to him.'

He stood up again and turned on another table lamp, wondering whether he was putting off the moment. He felt her eyes following him around but she said nothing. He sat down once more, knowing he had her full attention.

'He wants you to feel pain. I don't know why, but I think it's to be a lesson to the others. To me, of course, and to Kostas and his brothers, and to the other organisations in the country. That is why—' he gestured to the camera he'd set up on a tripod—'he has asked me to film it. It was fortunate that we had a tripod in the shop, eh?' He grinned at her but was unsurprised when she failed to return it. 'Always lots of photography equipment,' he said. 'Men buy these things for their holidays or their weekends and never use them. Strange. So anyway, in a moment I will begin recording and then the lesson will begin.'

He stood up and showed her the weapon he had in his left pocket, then walked to a side table, opened a drawer, and took out a knife.

'Do you recognise this? This is the knife you used to slit the throat of Toni. I know I told you I threw it away but I lied. I took it home and hid it. Luckily the police never came to search because they would have found it. So, here it is. Can you guess why I have brought it with me today? No? You have very little to say now. Perhaps you would like to call me a gay again. Or laugh at my shoes, or the way I walk. No? Okay.'

He walked to the camera, a modern Nikon that could film in high definition, and bent down to look at the dials and the screen on its rear. He'd practised earlier in the day so knew what to do.

'There, we are now recording.' He walked towards her, turning the knife in his hand. 'The first lesson—did you hear that?'

He stopped and listened. He heard it again.

He said, 'Someone is trying to break into the shop. Wait here.'

HE HAD HIS gun and his knife as he went down the stairs to deal with the burglars in the shop, so he wasn't worried. It had happened before. It was usually someone drunk, someone who had been in the shop earlier in the day and wanted to take something without paying.

But the defences were strong—metal grills came down over the two large windows, protecting the glass though you could still see the display. And the door was protected by a separate iron gate that came down from above so burglars couldn't even get to the door, which was recessed behind it.

What he'd heard was the sound of breaking glass, which could only happen if someone had found a weakness in one of the windows, perhaps with a sharp object pushed between the gaps in the grill. But what would be the point? They still couldn't get past the grill and into the shop.

Before he reached the bottom of the stairs he heard more glass breaking and the sound of a voice.

The voice was saying his name, over and over. But not saying it properly ... saying 'Diamond, Diamond, are you in there?'

He recognised the voice at once. It made him angry and it made him strong. Perhaps this night many situations would be resolved.

———

HE TURNED ON the light in the shop immediately—in the past this had scared off burglars. But of course the Chance brothers were not burglars. They were here for other reasons.

When he turned on the lights, he switched on the illumination over the outside of the shop as well, so now he could see the faces of the brothers. The young one, Johnny, had his face pressed against a hole that he'd made in the left hand window. The glass hadn't shattered but the hole had spread cracks outwards, and Diamant knew the entire window would have to be replaced. More expense.

He stood in front of the hole, saying, 'What is it you want? It is late.'

Johnny said, 'Sorree ... we need to talk to you and Odette or whatever the hell her name is. Are you in for business?'

Diamant stared at them for a moment, the three faces lit from above so their expressions couldn't be seen. All right, he said to himself. This is when it's decided. Their future and mine.

He said, 'I'll open the door.'

'Jolly good show!'

He moved to the side and slid back the bolts on the door and opened it, then pressed the mechanism that raised the grill over the front.

The three brothers stood in the entrance, waiting for the grill to rise enough for them to step through.

They waited until it finished its travel, then Johnny came through first, followed by the one called Tim and then Adam. Johnny said, 'You look tense, Diamond. Nervous. But we come in peace. We want to talk about music.'

Diamant said, 'We will go upstairs. It is more comfortable.'

'Glad to see you're taking it sensibly.'

Diamant saw the look that passed between the three brothers, but as he already did not trust them it made no difference.

He said, 'We will talk upstairs.'

———

DIAMANT GESTURED AND they all moved to the back of the store and through the hatch in the counter, which Diamant had left upright. Johnny whistled at the electronic equipment on the shelves but said nothing except, 'Through here?' when he found the opening for the bottom of the stairs.

Diamant nodded and they all walked upstairs, towards the lights of Odeta's apartment.

He watched carefully as Johnny reached the top of the stairs and entered the apartment, then slowed. He heard, 'What the fuck …' but Adam and Tim kept walking and pushed him further inside.

Diamant reached the top of the stairs and closed the door behind him, seeing the room almost as they had seen it. A large, oblong room with old furniture and many lamps. Rich carpets on the floor and expensive velvet curtains at the windows. A large mirror on one wall and two large and comfortable sofas, with a space between them.

In that space, Odeta was strapped to the upright chair beneath the ornate chandelier, grey gaffer tape over her mouth, her ankles strapped to the legs of the chair and her arms tied behind her.

Her eyes flashed furiously at the Chance brothers and then at Diamant, who said, 'Odeta and I have been talking. Well, I have been talking and she has been listening. We have agreed that we don't want to be involved with the marketing of your music, but we are going to keep your guitars.'

Johnny turned. 'I'm glad you said that, Diamond, because it proves something. It proves you have the guitars. It was you who robbed me the other day, wasn't it? I smelled you. I can still smell you. You smell like a woman, did you know that? I don't know what you're wearing, but I think you picked it up from a flea-market without realising it's a woman's perfume, not a man's aftershave. Perhaps it's one of the things about living in Britain that you don't understand.'

'There are many things,' Diamant said, 'that I don't understand about living in Britain. Why you have Lords and Ladies who pretend to be better than the rest of you. Why you get drunk whenever you can. Why you believe politicians. But I do understand your attitude to money — you all want as much of it as you can get. This I have learned, and copied. And unfortunately Odeta has stopped me getting the money I want, so I am punishing her.'

Now Adam Chance said, 'We don't know anything about that. We just want the guitars and we'll be gone. If you don't want to handle the marketing, that's fine with us.'

'Why do you want the guitars? Why are they so important?'

Johnny smiled, saying, 'It's me, really. You hurt my pride. I had it all planned out. They were just a ruse, a trick, a way of making it seem like we'd had real burglars so the cops would think our dad was in trouble … oh, fuck, it's too complicated to explain.'

Still smiling, he pulled his knife from his trouser pocket and took a step towards Diamant, who reached behind him and took his second-favourite gun, the Glock 17, from the back of his waistband.

Johnny stopped dead and Tim said, 'Oh, shit.'

Johnny said, 'You're not going to use that, are you? I've seen you in operation. You don't have the guts to shoot us.'

'Perhaps not,' said Diamant, 'but do you want to risk the gamble?'

He saw the boys' attention shift before he heard anything. Their eyes had flicked past him to the door. He turned and stepped back, gripping the Glock, and saw a young woman standing in the opening, her eyes wide, and it was a moment before he recognised her.

Then Johnny said, 'For Christ's sake, Genny, what are you doing here?'

Before she could reply, Diamant stepped towards the brother closest to him, Tim Chance, and placed his Glock against the man's head.

Everyone turned to look at him.

He said, 'Now let's begin the negotiations.'

And that was when Geneva Chance screamed.

CHAPTER FORTY-THREE

STOREY ARRIVED JUST in time to see Geneva Chance entering Odeta's shop. The windows were barred but the door grill had been raised. Previous arrivals. She went in tentatively, as if she were treading on broken glass, or perhaps trying not to disturb whoever she thought was inside.

Looking up, Storey saw several shadows moving around in the large room upstairs. So everyone was here.

He hoped they were staying calm, but with Johnny and Diamant in the same room there was no guarantee of that.

He crossed the road and went in.

THE SHOP WAS empty, but he could hear muffled voices upstairs. The hatch on the counter at the far end was raised so he went through it and approached and walked past the storage shelving to the back of the room. Here there was an open door and he presumed Geneva had just gone through it and up the stairs. He remembered from his previous visit that the staircase led directly into the large sitting room. When he arrived he'd be facing the windows and everyone would be to his left, either sitting on the couches or standing facing each other. To his right would be a display cabinet containing some photos and little porcelain objects—plates and figurines. To his immediate left, against the wall, would be the long table beneath a tall mirror.

It had gone quiet on the second floor, with only Diamant's voice speaking. Storey wondered if anyone was armed. Diamant had said he had another gun and it seemed the boys preferred knives, if the fates of their father and the two burglars, Stefan and Liam, were proof of anything.

So depending on how the meeting was going, Diamant was likely to be in charge. Perhaps that was why he was doing all the talking.

Then he knew Geneva had arrived in the room because he heard her let out a single scream. It wasn't a scream of pain or terror—more like a release of frustration.

Nevertheless he took the stairs two at a time.

———

HE ARRIVED AT the top and halted: it was quiet again. Now he didn't want to rush inside and panic everyone into shooting or throwing knives at him. He waited a moment, listening hard, then stepped through the doorway.

Everyone was standing except Odeta, who was tied to a chair, gagged, her eyes wide. She seemed unhurt. Johnny and Adam were facing up to Diamant, Johnny with his knife in hand, a grin on his face. Diamant was behind Tim Chance, holding a gun into the man's side. Geneva was just inside the door, her back to him, and she didn't acknowledge his presence, though she must have heard him running up the stairs.

He didn't know what he'd expected to see, but this wasn't it.

He said quietly to Geneva's back, 'I'm here.'

He thought she might turn and look at him, or step further into the room. But she said, 'I know,' and didn't move.

'Are you hurt?'

She shook her head. Then said loudly, to the rest of the room, 'But I'm really pissed off.'

Johnny said, 'Genny, take a pill. We're having a business conversation. Storey, fuck off, you're not needed.'

'Says the man whose brother's got a gun pointed at his intestines. You sure you can handle this?'

'You have no idea what I can handle,' Johnny said. 'Ain't that right, brothers?'

Adam and Tim both nodded.

Johnny said, 'Let's see what the gypsy woman has to say,' and tore the gaffer tape from Odeta's mouth. She yelped and took several deep breaths and spoke very fast, releasing what Storey thought was probably a stream of Albanian swear words.

Diamant said, 'Oh, you shouldn't have done that.'

Ignoring him, Geneva walked up to Johnny and slapped him in the face.

He said, 'You do that too often, sis. You can quit it now.'

'You stupid bastard,' she said to him. 'I didn't want any of this. All of it just so you could get your revenge on Bill. I wish I'd never told you. I wish I'd kept quiet and been the good little girl and you'd have stayed normal and decent.' Now she caressed his cheek and seemed on the verge of crying. 'But you had to be the white knight, killing the dragon. Getting yourself into all this shit just for me.'

Johnny frowned, saying, 'Are you kidding?'

'What do you mean?'

Johnny glanced at his brothers and said, 'You think you're the only one he raped?'

CHAPTER FORTY-FOUR

GENEVA STEPPED BACK and raised a hand to her mouth.

'Oh my god ... oh my god ...'

Adam said, 'You were the last, not the first. That was me.'

Geneva said, 'Why didn't you say something?'

'Why didn't you?'

That hung in the air for a moment, then Johnny said, 'None of us knew about the others. Bill was clever like that. Separated us all out, made us keep quiet. Stopped with Adam when he started on Tim. Then stopped with Tim when he started with me. We didn't talk. We felt guilty. Thought it was our fault.'

'I know what that feels like.'

'It wasn't till you told me, and I told the others, that it came out he'd done it to all of us.'

'Why didn't you tell *me* then?'

Adam said, 'Because we're stupid. We wanted you to think we were strong. That we had your back. And I suppose we were ashamed.'

'My god, I had no idea.'

Adam went on, 'Then we came up with the plan and brought him back from Spain. Making him feel comfortable again.'

'You were setting him up,' Geneva said. 'I never saw it. I didn't understand what you were doing. I thought you were being forgiving and I was a hard bitch because I couldn't do it. I could barely look him in the eye.'

'We didn't tell you,' Johnny said, 'because you would have stopped us. You're better than all of us. And we didn't want to be stopped.'

Diamant had been looking at them in turn. Now he said, 'So you are all gays? I did not expect that.'

Johnny turned on him fiercely. 'Keep your fucking mouth shut, Diamond. You don't know what you're talking about.'

Storey felt himself tense up, sensing a shift in the atmosphere. He was surprised to see Odeta relax in her chair, shaking her head to loosen her shoulders as if she were preparing for something.

He said, 'Diamant, put the gun down. You're not going to shoot anyone here.'

'Why do you think so?'

'There's no need. Just give these people their guitars back and let them go.'

'You think I can't kill anyone? You think I'm a weaker man than this one?' He waved his gun towards Johnny Chance.

'What do you mean?'

'When I took the guitars from this one, he had just murdered the man called Liam Fisher. I saw him go up in the building after Fisher but only this one came down. I think he showered in the man's room, or the room of his friend, perhaps, but I saw his shirt was pink and he smelled of blood. He had tried to clean himself but it's not easy.'

Storey knew it was true. He'd seen the bodies.

Now Odeta was laughing and Diamant turned towards her, his gun still pressed into Tim Chance's side. 'Why are you laughing, old woman?'

'Because you try so hard to be a man. You rob a man from behind his back so he can't see you. Now you're holding a drug addict by the neck and waving a gun around like a big man. You are half the man Toni was. You are nothing without me.'

'Let's see,' Diamant said. He raised his Glock and shot her between the eyes. The back of her head exploded across the room behind her. The chair she was tied to fell backwards and Diamant said, 'No, I still feel the same.'

Then several things happened in quick succession. First, Johnny made a growling sound and lunged forward and stabbed Diamant in his side, Tim squirming out of the way while trying to grab Diamant's gun.

Diamant flung Tim to one side with his right hand and pushed Johnny away and raised his gun and fired one shot at Johnny. Then Storey fired Diamant's Glock, his favourite gun, hitting Diamant in the throat. Diamant crashed backwards against the long table, his eyes widening, and fell to the floor. His hands went to his throat and he tried to draw breath.

Behind him, Storey heard Johnny's voice saying, 'He's got me, the bastard's got me.'

When he turned he saw Johnny was holding up his left hand. It was covered in blood and missing two fingers. The pain had yet to hit him and he stared at the ruined hand as if it belonged to someone else.

Storey put the Glock in his pocket and breathed in. Taking inventory, he saw that apart from himself, only the Chance family was still alive.

Lucky Chance indeed.

Then he heard the police sirens. He'd been beginning to think Jackie West hadn't picked up her voice-mail.

But she always picked up, eventually.

CHAPTER FORTY-FIVE

AND DIAMANT'S CAMERA had caught it all.

The Nikon DS5600 captured everything in high definition, wide-angle, autofocusing, and with perfectly adequate sound and colour representation. The film was damning. Almost everyone who was guilty proved it, everyone who was innocent had it proved for them. Storey hoped the film wouldn't be leaked but given the high profile of the Chance siblings thought that was a slim hope.

———

THREE DAYS LATER, with her brothers still in custody and alone in the house, Geneva called Storey, saying, 'Have you seen YouTube?'

Believing the film had got out, he felt his stomach sink. He said, 'Not lately. Cat videos aren't my thing. What should I look for?'

'Not look. Listen. I'll text you a link.'

A moment later his phone pinged and a link was displayed in his text app. He clicked it and a YouTube page opened and after a moment a video began to play. The video was a static image of Geneva Chance, and the song was her song, the one she'd played for him, her strong voice sounding mournful and lost. He wondered whether she sounded so forlorn because he knew her family and her history.

But then decided no—it was the power of the song itself.

Letting the song continue, he scrolled down the page ... over two million plays in the last three days. It was a viral hit.

This time he listened to the words. Of course the song was about her father, but now he understood it. It was a cry of pain and rage and regret ... but no forgiveness. What she'd kept inside for twenty years had finally come out. He hoped it would give her some release.

———

HE RANG HER back and she answered immediately.

He said, 'So one of the burglars found the stick and put the song up on YouTube before he died. Probably thought he was being clever. Are you okay with it?'

'I suppose. Did you read any of the comments underneath?'

'No, I didn't want to know what they said.'

She gave a small laugh. 'They think I posted it because Bill's dead. That I wrote it after he died, as an elegy or something. Must be more bloody ambiguous than I thought.'

'Can you get YouTube to take it down?'

'Why should I? I was frightened of everyone knowing about me, frightened of Bill hearing it and … I don't know what. Now it's done I'm past it.'

'Do you know why the burglars took it?'

'I think it was Johnny. He set up the whole burglary thing to make it look like a threat, didn't he? That and spraying the side of Bill's cottage. I've been going over and over it in my head—why they did it. How they set it up. I was wondering why they got those two men to steal the guitars and then wouldn't let Larry report it. If the idea was to set it up so that there was some kind of plot against Bill, why wouldn't they let the police know about the burglary?'

'Did you work it out?'

'I think so … they were just laying the ground, weren't they? Making up a story that someone would put together later.'

'That's why Johnny kept tabs on Stefan and Liam—he wanted his guitars back eventually, presumably a long time afterwards so he wouldn't have to explain to the police where they came from because it would all have died down. His mistake was in letting them steal the expensive ones. That put a whole new slant on the theft.'

'That's what I thought,' Geneva said. 'But it had to be the expensive ones, didn't it, or else the theft wouldn't have worked as a warning that the bad guys were serious. Stealing cheap gear wouldn't have had the same effect.'

'Have the police said anything about the guitars?'

'Yes, they found them in Diamant's own flat. Along with thousands of pounds' worth of coke, in a wardrobe.'

'My police contact told me they're tracking it back to its source. They think there's a guy in London who's been shipping it in. And there are three brothers up here who were connected to Diamant and Odeta. Another three brothers.'

She was quiet, then, and he said, 'So you think Johnny was the one who told them to steal your USB stick, too?'

'I remembered something,' she said. 'The night it was stolen, I hadn't left it in the studio. You remember me telling you sometimes I forgot and left it there but I usually took it back to my room?'

'I remember.'

'Well when it was stolen I was confused. I didn't find it in my room, where I thought I'd taken it, so then I thought I *must* have left it in the studio ... and it wasn't there either. So naturally I presumed the burglars must have taken it. I couldn't believe I'd been that stupid but after the theft and everything I convinced myself that's what happened.'

'So now you think Johnny took it from your room in the house and left it in the studio to be stolen.'

'The others are sharing the blame but it's him. I think he found the song some while ago, played it, and he was threatened. He's the song-writer, not me. Plus, he'd have known what the song was about as soon as he heard it. It was a childish thing to do but who said he was rational? Perhaps he thought if it was stolen I'd give up on it.'

'He must have thought you had other copies, though.'

'Perhaps he looked and couldn't find any—which is no surprise, because there weren't any. He should have just wiped the stick if he was worried, but maybe it looked more realistic if it vanished along with the guitars. Perhaps he hoped I'd forget about it. Got it out of my system and wouldn't bother recording it again. Especially after Bill's death.'

She sounded weary but somehow relieved and Storey recognised the lightness of tone that sometimes emerged from victims of crime when they realised it was over and they'd survived. He said, 'So what's happening next?'

'You wouldn't believe, Larry Lamb's getting enquiries about me doing a solo tour and an album. My dad's dead and my brothers murdered him and suddenly I'm hot property. How fucked up is that?'

'Very.' He asked whether she'd seen her brothers since they were arrested. She said no, the lawyers had told her to steer clear. She'd managed to postpone her father's funeral but she expected to go alone.

For a moment Storey thought she was going to ask him to go with her, but the moment passed.

He said, 'You sound as if you're managing. Have they offered grief counselling?'

She sighed. 'Yes, but I'm not ready for it yet. I don't know how I feel about anything any more. I saw two people shot in front of me and I'm still having nightmares about it.'

'Sorry about that.'

'Not your fault—you did the right thing. As I suppose the video showed.'

'Didn't stop them questioning me for two days, did it?'

'But you're outside and my brothers are still inside. And those two Albanians are dead.'

'Perhaps I should come round,' Storey said, 'and we can talk in person.'

'No, I don't think so,' Geneva said. 'I don't need protecting any more. Even from myself. Thanks anyway. I'll see you around.'

Storey disconnected, then re-played the YouTube video of Geneva singing her song. He supposed he would never see Geneva Chance in person again.

But he thought he was going to hear the song a lot more in the months to come.

THE SONG OF GENEVA CHANCE

When the dust died down and I looked in your eyes
I saw you thinking 'bout all of your lies

The things you said and the things that you'd done
They kept me awake, kept me on the run

Daddy where did you go? Daddy where are you now?
I want to forgive you but I just don't know how.

You told me you cared and I trusted you so
But you left me alone with nowhere to go

A father to me, you went farther away
You went so far I had nothing to say

Daddy, where did you go? Daddy, where are you now?
I want to forgive you but I just don't know how.

Now I'm living alone and I'm living a lie
I sometimes wonder what it's like to just die

I feel like a woman but remember the girl
And those feelings I have keep me all in a whirl

Daddy where did you go? Daddy where are you now?
I want to forgive you but I just don't know how.

ACKNOWLEDGEMENTS

Thanks to Pete and Sheila Hendry for background information, and to Graham Evans for the joke.

Reviews mean a lot to authors so I'd be grateful if you could offer a few words on the site where you bought this book.

ALSO BY KEITH DIXON

The Sam Dyke Series

Altered Life
The Private Lie
The Hard Swim
The Bleak
The Strange Girl
The Secret Sharers
The Innocent Dead
The Second Guess (short story)

Paul Storey Crime Thrillers

Storey
One Punch

Standalone Novels

A French Darcy – a Romance
Actress – a Contemporary novel

Essays on Writing

The Idle Writer
Crime Writing Confidential

Blog

www.cwconfidential.blogspot.com

Webpage

http://www.keithdixonnovels.com

ABOUT THE AUTHOR

Learn more about Keith by following him on Twitter @keithyd6, by reading his blog at cwconfidential.blogspot.com or connect with him on Facebook at facebook.com/SamDykeInvestigations/ On his website you can download a couple of free books and find out more about the others: http://keithdixonnovels.com.

www.ingramcontent.com/pod-product-compliance
Lightning Source LLC
Chambersburg PA
CBHW032137190626
46814CB00005BA/1725